SOMETHING WAS DIFFERENT...

The closet was open. Hadn't I closed it? Was I imagining this? I tried to shake off the feeling of danger as I undressed and went into the bathroom.

I turned the shower on and stepped in. It felt good. I put my head under the nozzle and started to wash my hair. The glass doors steamed up. I turned toward them to get my hair conditioner off the ledge.

I saw a shadowy figure dart into the bathroom, then run out.

I screamed, threw open the door, grabbed a towel to wrap myself in, and ran into the living room. The glass door and screen were wide open. I rushed to the patio, looked both ways. No one.

Was someone going to hurt me, too?

Fly Away Home

SUSAN BERMAN

AVON BOOKS ◆ NEW YORK

FLY AWAY HOME is an original publication of Avon Books. This work has never before appeared in book form. This work is a novel. Any similarity to actual persons or events is purely coincidental.

AVON BOOKS
A division of
The Hearst Corporation
1350 Avenue of the Americas
New York, New York 10019

Copyright © 1996 by Susan Berman
Published by arrangement with the author
Library of Congress Catalog Card Number: 95-94724
ISBN: 0-380-78179-4

First Avon Books Printing: February 1996

AVON TRADEMARK REG. U.S. PAT. OFF. AND IN OTHER COUNTRIES, MARCA REGISTRADA, HECHO EN U.S.A.

Printed in the U.S.A.

RA 10 9 8 7 6 5 4 3 2 1

Acknowledgments

I wish to acknowledge my deep gratitude to Charlotte Sheedy, my outstanding and caring agent; to Carrie Feron, my remarkably insightful editor; and finally to Aviva Goode, for all her hard work while she was at the Charlotte Sheedy Agency.

I would like to thank my loving and loyal cousins Deni Marcus, Tom Padden, Raleigh Padveen, Fred and Vicki Shorr. I also wish to express my deep appreciation to Julie Baumgold Kosner, Jim Milio, David Milch, Dinah Harter, Susan Schreiber, Diana Ungerleider, and Doug Wolf for their invaluable support.

1

This is my first day as Ariane Richardson. My real name is Paula Jean, but that's too dull, mundane, like the place I'm from—Scappoose, Oregon. Changing my name is the first step in eradicating my past. It may be necessary that I become someone different, to carry out my plan. But I also want to forget most things in my life—as Paula Jean Richardson, anyway.

Some childhoods are sparkling and light; mine was dark. Gnarled, overgrown pine trees conspired to block out any sunlight from our dirty, little windows. Thick, ancient, dusty curtains finished the task, kept the place perpetually gloomy. Even the air was melancholy.

The eyelet tablecloth on our kitchen table was terribly thin. We were afraid to touch it for fear its threads would dissolve. We ate on old newspapers on top of it. And the house was eerily quiet; beyond quiet. It was deathly still.

Even today, at twenty-three years old, I think of our house when I smell anything musty, and drown in malaise. The odor of old things and rotting wood came up from the basement. No matter how hard we scrubbed the floors, we couldn't get the smell out.

A family is like a corkscrew; it twists like a spiral within you, silent and deep. You're born into a family, a tribe, a combination of genetics and personalities. You can leave it, but it never really leaves you. Like a corkscrew, which has no beginning and no end, the place where the family leaves off and you begin is impossible to say. You can't really pull away without leaving a scar.

As a child desperate for sunlight and escape, I ran into the backyard, climbed the big filbert tree; its branches were open and loving, its foliage was profuse and fluffy, a perfect hiding place. I would climb higher and higher in that protective tree until I reached the last steady branch. I would step on it carefully. It wasn't really strong enough to hold me after I had turned six.

In the airy treetops at last, I was bathed in bright light. Purify me, cleanse me, change everything about my life, I would beg the distant yellow fireball. Burn the past, scald the present, give me a chance for a different future. Destroy my fierce discontent.

I stayed there, enjoying the freedom of the limitless expanse of sky, until dark. Sometimes I was scared to climb down. My older sister, Dana, would climb up to rescue me. She was only two years older, but more like a mother than a sister. We never knew our father or if we even had the same one.

Our mother died when I was ten. She was sick all that time. I used to be afraid to go into her room, fearful that I would catch whatever bad thing she had. Dana told me it wasn't contagious, that she had lost her mind from the way men treated her.

She would stare vacantly at the wall for hours.

Sometimes, for no reason at all, she'd start to laugh, a tinkling laugh like a music box. Dana has the same laugh. Men love it.

Our mother stayed in bed most of the day, taking tranquilizers. One day when Dana and I went in to feed her dinner, she was dead. It took us about half an hour to realize it, since she didn't look that different. She must have taken too much medication, either by accident or on purpose, or she might have died of a heart attack. We never knew.

We called our aunt; she came over, took the body away. We removed the heavy gold curtains that always hung in our mother's room. I tried not to take a breath near them.

I thought I would feel better after she died. When she was alive, sadness permeated every room of our house. But even her death did not remove that paralyzing feeling of stillness. I lived in a whiteout of emotion.

I never felt very much except when I was with Dana; then everything was different. It was as if my veil of detachment was torn away. I saw things before unseen, sound was louder and sharper, smells seemed stronger and even my sense of touch was heightened.

By myself, I lived in a limited, shadowy, black-and-white world. Experiences, forms were vague, amorphous. With Dana, I lived in color, in a well-defined, exciting, expansive universe.

We were born in Scappoose, Oregon, a small mill town outside Portland. Some of our relatives looked after us after our mother died, but mostly it was just Dana and me living in a house without adults. When Dana was eighteen, she left home. Scappoose is somewhere you move away from, she always said. She moved to Portland; two years later I followed.

Dana has pearl-white porcelain skin, black hair and blue eyes as round as quarters. I don't look like her, though I have the same coloring. On me it's less vibrant, as if I were a fainter imprint. Her complexion is creamy and clear; people said it was from all the rain in Portland.

The rain also makes rose petals velvety soft, which is why our rose gardens are famous world-wide. Visitors to Portland find the rain refreshing, cleansing. I find it gloomy, depressing. I yearn for bright sun to illuminate my surroundings. So once again I'm following Dana.

"Good afternoon, ladies and gentlemen. We're starting our descent into Los Angeles International Airport. Please make sure your seat belts are fastened."

The plane was descending. We were in L.A. already! The smog was shrouding the windows, blocking out the view. I couldn't really see the city yet, but I was getting nervous. I knew that I must stick to my plan, steer a straight course. I must not get involved in any situations, any intrigue, that could distract me, especially relationships with men.

I have what they call in self-help books "boundary problems." Once I fall in love with a man, I cannot tell where I end and he begins. This problem started when I was a child. Since I felt nothing, I wanted to merge with Dana; that way she could feel for me. I imagined that we were one person connected by dots, like those in the "Connect-A-Dot" books. I was safe being part of Dana. She loved me, she told me what to do, and I didn't have to think or feel for myself, Paula Jean. Or rather, Ariane.

As Ariane, I plan to be very careful about men. I cannot allow myself to fall in love. Once I start an affair, I lose my will, do whatever my lover tells me to do. This wouldn't be a problem for me if my lovers were as kind and loving as Dana was. But they weren't at all like Dana. They made me do things, terrible things, things I would rather forget.

If only I *could* forget! Why do bad memories stick around forever, while beautiful ones fade so quickly? I always have to be reminded of good memories. I might hear a childhood song, remember Dana singing it to me. I see a lavender rose, then remember that they grew gloriously wild in our school yard. These images should be embedded in my mind always, but I need reminders.

But bad memories, they are ready to strike at any moment, set off by any trigger. That's why I have to avoid men, because any relationship will end up being a bad memory that will torment me night and day.

Like my affair with Steve. I had no idea that he used drugs. He never used them around me, or maybe he just hadn't used them when we first met. After about three months, his personality seemed to change without warning. He became abusive in every way. He said such hurtful things to me that I cried.

But I was so submerged in him I couldn't leave. One night he came to pick me up; his eyes were gleaming unnaturally. He wanted to go to a foreign movie I had never heard of—it was about a man killing his girlfriend. During the movie Steve turned to me and said, "She wanted to die, she

wanted him to kill her." I just looked at him. I
thought he was kidding; after all, he couldn't be
crazy. He was going to Reed College in Portland.
When we got back to his apartment and started to
make love, he knotted my hands with a scarf.

"What are you doing?" I asked.

"You'll like it," he said. Once my hands were
tied, he kissed me, then started to choke me. I
started to gag.

"Steve, Steve, stop!" I screamed.

"Get out of my head," he yelled. "You're trying
to see inside my head. This is what you've always
wanted—you're dating me so I would kill you," he
said, continuing to choke me. I believed him, because I was him. I stopped struggling. If he told me
I wanted to die, he must be right. Then, abruptly,
he climbed off me, untied my hands.

"Get out of here, it's the meth," he said.

"What?" I asked, struggling for breath.

"It's the crystal meth, so just get out of here," he
said as he threw me my clothes. I put them on, still
not wanting to leave. I couldn't leave. I couldn't
get out of him.

"Get out, save yourself!" he yelled, opening the
door, shoving me out into the hallway. I ran home,
sobbing all the way. I told Dana the story, ending
with, "He didn't even love me enough to kill me."
I had ceased to exist as an independent person; any
connection with him, even a violent one, was better
than none. That's when Dana decided I needed
help. And someday I'm going to get it. But for now,
I just need to avoid men. And I will.

"Is this your first trip to L.A.?" the man beside
me asked. I had been trying not to notice him ever
since I saw him at the Portland airport. When I

realized we were both boarding the flight, I made sure not to stand near him in line. I hung back to the last call, avoiding him. As I searched for my seat number, I was astonished to discover that he was my seat partner. I hoped there might be some mistake. I double-checked my number: there was no mistake.

He was a dark man, always my weakness. Some women like men who look completely different from them, but I always like men who have black hair like I do. There are a lot of blond men in Portland, but they're not my type.

My seat partner had brown eyes, not blue like mine, but still he would do; he would do just fine, if I dared. But I didn't dare. I couldn't let myself. He had on a well-tailored suit, a silk shirt and smelled of Eternity. He looked vital, completely alive. I am always attracted to athletic, vigorous men, because I am a little dreamy myself.

I knew I had to resist him, just hoped I had the strength. He smiled at me when I sat down. I gave him a quick, dismissive look, not inviting acquaintance. He got the hint, opened his newspaper. For most of the flight I pretended to be asleep.

"I said, is this your first trip to L.A.?" he asked again. I thought he had gotten the hint, but I was wrong. Many people mistake my tentative manner, thinking instead that I have not heard them.

"Yes, yes, it is," I said in what I hoped was a brusque manner. I glanced furtively at his left hand. No wedding ring; luck was going against me.

"I'm Hank Thackeray," he said expectantly.

"Ariane Richardson," I murmured in reply. When Dana and I had discovered our birth certificates as teenagers, we were disappointed to see that Richardson was our mother's maiden name. We had always hoped that a tall dark stranger named Mr. Richardson would arrive in Scappoose one day, claim to be our father. He never had.

Hank Thackeray leaned past me to look out the window. I could feel myself start to dissolve. It was all I could do not to throw myself on his chest and disappear into the smell of Eternity. His hands were thick, square and strong, with shiny black hair on the backs of his fingers. I wondered if his olive skin was natural or if it was an L.A. tan.

"Just visiting?" he inquired, relaxing back into his seat.

"No, I'm moving here," I answered, trying to make my reply sound final, as if I didn't want to engage in any more conversation.

"You're moving here? You may be the only person in the world moving to L.A. Everybody else is moving away," he said, laughing.

"They are?" I asked, surprised.

"Between earthquakes, fires and gangs, it isn't the irresistible place it used to be. I can think of a lot better places to move to," he said. I'm sure he wasn't referring to Scappoose. I turned toward the window as I felt the plane descend.

"What kind of work do you do?" he persisted. I've always suspected that men like me for my dreamy quality, a quality that I despise. It seems to them they could sleep with me without my noticing.

"I hope I'll be able to get a job at Madison's, folding clothes or something, anything," I said. It had to be at Madison's but he didn't know that. Now I was sure he would lose interest. Los Angeles was filled with fascinating career women, beautiful women in the entertainment business, actresses.

"I like Madison's—they have that piano. Practically all the New York stores are now open in L.A. Barney's opened in '94," he said. He had the most sparkling teeth I had ever seen, sunbeams that broke through the smog from the window, bounced off them.

"Need a ride from the airport?" he asked. Now he was getting dangerous. I had to pull back before it was too late, had to discourage him. I couldn't resist much longer. If he knew me, he wouldn't want me anyway, because I would just collapse and melt on him.

"No. I'm taking the shuttle."

"You'd take the shuttle over a ride in my Lexus?" he asked, smiling.

The plane bounced down. Safe at last. We both inhaled as it bumped to a halt. As soon as it stopped, he jumped out of his seat and retrieved his trench coat and briefcase from the overhead rack. He was ready for action.

I hung back, slow, cautious as usual, making sure the plane was fully stopped before I reached for my coat, my cosmetics case. I was relieved; the conversation was over.

As we filed down the aisle, he turned toward me. His body was so close I yearned for the comfort of it. It was like a magnet pulling me toward it.

"How about I give you a ride home and we go for a drink? I live in the Marina, and the water is beautiful in the afternoon," he said.

Had anything ever sounded so tempting? If only he knew how much I wanted to take him up on his invitation, if just for the one evening of warmth

and connection. But I couldn't trust myself. I might
not be able to get myself back from him, to disengage. I wanted to embrace the intimate danger, but
I resisted.

"I can't, I just can't," I blurted out. My voice
sounded panicky and strained. He looked surprised, then turned around; a woman on the edge
was not what he wanted. I resisted an impulse to
apologize, ask if the offer was still good. In just a
few seconds he would be off the plane, and the
temptation would be gone.

My feet floated off the ramp onto the floor of the
airport. He went in one direction, I went in the opposite direction. I sat down for a minute. My knees
were shaking and I had to compose myself. I stared
at the floor; when enough time had passed, I went
to the baggage claim area.

There were my two navy blue canvas bags. I
grabbed them, made my way to the shuttle. I
climbed in, handed the driver the voucher. The
shuttle seemed to take forever, more and more people crowding into it, before it finally got on the
freeway. I looked out the windows at the sunbaked
road and I felt a sense of excitement.

But that feeling was quickly tempered by fear,
rooted in the knowledge that I had a frightening
task ahead of me. A task I could not shirk.

It would be comforting to be anonymous here. I
had thought I would be anonymous when I moved
to Portland, but I was wrong. I could never really
escape Scappoose. People asked where you were
from, and somebody always knew somebody from
Scappoose, somebody who knew our family. Most
of my uncles and cousins were drunks. No one had

ever distinguished himself. I was tired of the stain of the past.

Now that I was in L.A., I didn't even plan to tell people I was from Portland. I'd just say, "A small town in the Pacific Northwest." My region was trendy these days—plaid shirts and coffee beans were everywhere. The Pacific Northwest made people think wholesome; think forests; think lumberjacks; think Seattle, alternative music, latte.

I tried to look at L.A. as it zoomed by, but all I could see was the freeway. I scanned the faces of the people seated around me, wondering if they were Los Angeles natives or if they were tourists. The shuttle stopped several times, letting people off at fancy hotels.

I had rented an apartment in a certain building in West Hollywood. I was afraid there wouldn't be a rental available, but I had been lucky. The shuttle pulled up in front of a small hotel, down the street from the apartment building.

I got out. It was cooler than I thought it would be in L.A. A huge silver touring bus pulled up and musicians got out, carrying their instruments, suitcases. I looked up at a very blue sky. It reflected a sheen off all the shiny parked cars.

I took a step to cross the street, when all of a sudden a dirty white hearse with a sign that said GRAVE LINE TOURS drew up, cut me off. I jumped back onto the curb. A driver with a chauffeur's cap got out, opened the doors of the hearse. Five people with cameras piled out onto the street before an old, faded Spanish duplex. "That's the place where Sal Mineo was murdered, right there," the driver said. The people began taking pictures.

Suddenly the street went dark. A large cloud appeared in the sky, gray, angry. Was it a prophecy? The shadows of the musicians' instruments falling on the sidewalk seemed grotesque. The turbulent sky threatened to pour rain. I shivered as I tried to step off the curb.

A feeling of foreboding came over me. I remembered why I was in L.A. I was on a mission. It might turn out to be a matter of life and death. Jeopardy was everywhere.

I felt a tight knot in my stomach. Anxiety settled on the back of my neck; it was palpable, like needle pricks. For a moment I was frozen in panic. Would I be able to accomplish my agenda?

I looked at the gray, low-rise apartment building that might hold the answer. I was in such terror that I couldn't move. A step in that direction was a step toward the truth. What if the truth were too awful to imagine?

I had come this far, I had to go on. Weak, insignificant Paula Jean was gone forever. I was now Ariane. I took a deep breath, stepped off the curb, crossed the street.

The bright lobby was cheery, the floor a pink-and-gray-swirled marble. A winding staircase in the middle led to the floor above. The rails of the stairway were gleaming brass. A gay couple in workout clothes walked in. They stopped at the front desk. A man in a uniform with "Carlos" on a name tag smiled at them.

"Mail here, Carlos?" the taller man asked.

"It's here, Mr. Black," Carlos replied. The men walked to the mailboxes on one part of the wall. Carlos turned his attention to me. I put my suitcases down, looked around. Did these walls hold a secret? Was this building the beginning or the end of my search? How could Dana afford to live in such an expensive, luxurious place?

"May I help you?" Carlos inquired.

"Yes. I'm Ariane Richardson, the new tenant in three-nineteen. I believe the owner of the unit left me the keys?"

"Ah, yes. Mr Louis told us you would be arriving," Carlos said as he handed me an envelope.

"There is also a key to the common areas. We have a pool, two Jacuzzis in the back and a sauna in the underground garage, first level. The gym is in the East Club, near the pool. And there's a tennis court in that area. You'll also find a mailbox key."

"Thank you."

"The elevator is right there—just take it to the third floor," he added. I resisted an impulse to ask Carlos if he knew anything. But I couldn't trust him. I couldn't trust anyone.

I smiled at a woman who got out of the elevator. I had to make a good impression on everyone, since one of these people might be able to help me. The elevator doors closed. I was surrounded by reflections of myself in the mirrored interior.

A well-dressed woman of medium stature stared back at me. My clothes telegraphed efficiency. I stayed away from anything seductive or overly feminine, not wanting to compound my man problem. Better they shouldn't notice me; it wouldn't lead to anything good.

My shiny, straight black hair hung to my shoulders; I had bangs. My blue eyes didn't seem outstanding. They blended into my face. I had on just a little makeup, some blush, lip gloss.

I wore a black silk ankle-length dress, medium heels. I carried a tan raincoat. Forgettable? I hoped so. I needed the cover of ordinariness. I could have been any one of a million women arriving in a new place to find a new life.

But I was Ariane, and I had only one thing to do. Nothing could dissuade me, throw me off my mark. I stared at my face. Did I have the strength? The fiber? The tenacity? The courage? No great determination or outstanding look of character stared back at me from the mirrors. I had the desire to carry out my terrifying task. That strength might not be evident to the world, but it was definitely there.

The elevator door opened. I stepped out, heard sounds all around me. Were the halls whispering commands, or had I imagined it? Then they abruptly ceased. For a moment I felt that horrible stillness from my childhood. I seemed to separate from my body, watch myself from overhead. My feet felt immobile, filled with lead. I was the observer, when I had to be the participant. I took a deep breath, mobilized every bit of energy I had, to walk down the hall.

This was the very floor. I couldn't believe my good luck in being able to rent an apartment on the same floor. I resisted a compulsion to run right to the other apartment, 326. I went toward 319 instead. Everything in due time, under the cloak of secrecy. I had to be careful, very careful, until I knew who was friend, who was foe.

Apartment 319 was just as the rental agent had described it over the phone. It was a spacious one-bedroom with a bath and a half. The owner had furnished it minimally. I was renting it furnished. I had saved up enough money to keep it for three months on a month-to-month lease. Mr. Louis had even left linens.

I threw my bags down. There might not be a moment to lose. I pulled the wood shutters over the bedroom window just for extra security, then turned the lights out.

I rushed into the living room, turned the lights out there. I drew the wood shutters all the way across the living room wall that was a sliding glass door. Then I carefully opened one wooden slat.

I could see apartment 326. It was diagonal to my own. There was a large garden on the floor below in the common area. There were two green lounge chairs with an umbrella between them on the patio of the apartment. On either side of them was a tall, thin cactus.

The glass door was open a couple of inches. The screen was closed, perhaps locked. The only way to get in was to climb around the inside of the balcony. There were five apartments between 319 and 327. They all had glass doors through which I would be visible. The floor I was on was only one story above the ground, so if I fell I would probably not be hurt, but I could be discovered.

I'd have to wait until the middle of the night to make my treacherous journey. It was frustrating to wait even a minute, not to mention hours. But there was no other way. I opened the phone book, made arrangements for a rental car. I called Madison's, found out their job application procedures.

Every moment counts, there wasn't any time to lose. I quickly opened the packet that Carlos had handed me, took out keys labeled "Common Area" and "Mailbox."

I went out into the hallway. Should I walk past

326? Why not, since who could fault me? It was my first day here. If questioned, I could say that I was looking for the elevator. There had to be two ways to get to both of the elevators. I could even be looking for the stairs.

From the outside, it looked as if there were about a hundred units in the six-story building, but it appeared that no one was home. Most people probably worked, although some, no doubt, worked at home. The hallway was deserted.

I turned the corner and beheld 326. It had the same white French double doors as my unit. My heart started beating quickly. I felt my adrenaline surge. The lights from the low stucco ceiling seemed to get stifling hot; the walls were beginning to close in on me.

What had happened behind those doors? I noticed that there was a tiny peephole in the door; what if someone inside was looking at me? I didn't want to tip anyone off. I moved to the side, away from the peephole.

There were stains on the gray, thin carpet in front of the door. I looked up and down the hallway. There were stains all over, maybe mildew. Maybe this was the original carpet from years ago.

But weren't the stains in front of the door darker? They were browner than the rest of the stains. Could they be blood? I didn't want to jump to conclusions. I didn't trust my reality testing. I had been questioning this for the past two months. Relax, calm down, I told myself. I needed more pieces of the puzzle.

"Can I help you?" a woman asked, opening her door, startling me. I didn't realize I was standing with my back to her door. She had one of those low, cigarette-whiskey voices. She looked as if she had just gotten up. She wore a duster over some black silk pajamas.

"No, I, uh, was just looking for the elevator to get the mail. I just moved in . . . down the hall," I stammered.

"Oh, I was hoping you were Pink Dot."

"Pink Dot?"

"The place you order food from. I just ordered a bunch of stuff from them. Work ran late last night. I'm starved. Well, I guess you're not," she said as she slammed her door.

Should I have introduced myself? Should I have made friends with her to find out if she knew anything? No, too soon; first I had to get into the apartment. I followed the hallway to the passenger elevator near my unit.

I pushed the button for the first floor. It seemed forever before the gold doors opened. Maybe I was on a time delay from anxiety. Sometimes when I became extremely upset, time seemed to slip by or else go incredibly slowly.

There was another man in uniform now behind the desk. His name tag said "Roberto." A tall Asian man dressed in an expensive purple linen shirt and white trousers walked in. He was graceful.

"I got a campaign. Nestea, regional," he said excitedly to the man behind the desk. He raised both his fists in the air in jubilation.

"Way to go, Johnny," Roberto said. Johnny smiled, bounded up the spiral staircase two steps at a time. I walked over to the mailbox, opened number 319. Was there any chance that my key opened all the mailboxes? Not likely. Still, I couldn't resist an impulse to try my key in number 326.

I turned quickly toward the desk. The men were engaged in a conversation. They couldn't see what I was doing anyway. I opened my mailbox, took out a letter from the building management. Then I quickly tried to stick my key in 326; no luck. A tall woman in a nurse's uniform came up to the mailboxes. I quickly put my key down. I don't think she saw.

I opened my letter from the management; it was a standard greeting, a copy of the rules and regulations. I felt let down.

In my imagination, the solution to what was troubling me would have miraculously been included in the envelope. An explanation that would have said all my worst fears, all my nightmares, were just products of my imagination, that it was going to be all right.

But my intuition told me it wasn't going to be all right. I had to reserve judgment until I knew for sure. Two women walked through the lobby in bathing attire, going out for an afternoon swim. I looked through the glass windows. The marine layer had quickly burned off.

I followed the women through a door, down some steps, then into the pool area. Several people were tanning by the pool. A few people looked up with mild interest as I walked by. Did they know anything? Did they know who I was? Was someone waiting for me?

Last week I had received a message in the mail. Had one of these people sent it? No one seemed to be watching me. Would someone come forward? When? How would the person know me?

I felt as if I were walking between live wires. Any moment I might get a shock, an unpleasant shock. I walked toward the East Club. The tennis court was deserted.

The East Club was air-conditioned, refreshing, and the first room was a meeting room, empty. The second room was a small, executive-suite gym with about twenty machines. A man was running on a treadmill as he watched MTV. A sophisticated woman, her blond hair in a ponytail, was working out on an arm machine with a trainer.

If only I knew these people well enough to ferret out the information I needed. But how could I approach them? They would think I was insane. What proof did I have yet? What did I really have, except that message, my suspicions? And what if no foul play were involved, what if it was the plan we had discussed?

An attractive dark-haired man walked into the gym and smiled briefly at me. I felt an instant attraction, so I avoided eye contact, avoided his smile. I left the gym quickly.

I stopped at the front desk.

"I see that a parking place goes with my unit, number ninety in the lower garage."

"That's right," Carlos said.

"So the numbers don't correspond to the units?"

"No, we assign whatever is available. Why, is there a problem with your space?"

"It's fine. I was just curious."

That meant there was no way I could know which parking place went with 326. I would just have to check for Dana's car.

The rental car pulled up outside the building, I walked out, got in, and checked the Thomas Guide for directions. I drove to the Westside Pavilion, off Pico, where Madison's was located.

On my way to Personnel, I passed the cosmetics department. It was here that I might learn something. I walked past a woman demonstrating a new perfume on two teenage girls. I looked quickly at all the glistening counters of cosmetics and then I found it—the La Prairie section.

There were two women working the counter, both beautiful, perfect makeup, thin as a bone. The blonde was applying makeup to an older woman; she was dusting powder on her face with a big black brush. The other woman, her long brown hair in a ponytail at the nape of her neck, was spooning what looked like caviar into a royal blue jar. Upon closer inspection, I saw it was labeled a face product.

The blond woman must have caught sight of me, because she strained trying to see me. I quickly walked the other way, toward the escalator to go down to Customer Service.

I walked into Personnel, filled out an application. A Mrs. Buchanan began to interview me.

"Have you worked here a long time?" I asked her.

"Three years. Why?"

"No reason," I said. Three years—she might know something. She might have heard something, but it was too soon to ask her.

I resisted the urge to start shouting, "Tell me the truth! Someone here in L.A. knows what happened. Tell me now, before it's too late!" Ariane had to learn patience.

Mrs. Buchanan said she would call me when the head of the department could interview me. On my way out I circled the La Prairie counter again. I toyed with the idea of buying cosmetics as a way of getting information. But it might seem strange if I got the job in a week, then tried to make friends with the same women.

Better not chance it. I left, drove home. Suddenly I was beyond exhaustion, worried, confused. I walked into my apartment, collapsed on the bed.

I was almost asleep when I remembered to unpack my alarm, set it for midnight. That was the witching hour.

✲ 2 ✲

I fell into a deep sleep, began to dream the dream I had often. I was a child, dressed in a white lace dress, climbing the steps to our attic. I had been told, repeatedly, not to enter the attic. I quietly opened the door.

It had the same stillness as our house. There were cobwebs in the corners, yellowed magazines on the floor. I saw a couple of old steamer trunks locked with brass locks. I pretended I was a detective, looking for answers about my life.

I picked up all the pieces of paper on the floor, ancient receipts, old lists. I'd read them, try to imagine if my mother had put these things here, or if not, then who?

In my dream, the deep quiet was suddenly broken by noises in the far corner of the attic. I walked across it to a little room, opened the door. My mother was there, in bed with a man.

"Get out," she yelled.

I woke up trembling, looked around. Where was I? Los Angeles. I shook the sleep out of my head. Just a few minutes later the alarm went off.

It was time. I threw on black jeans, a black sweater, black tennis shoes with soles that gripped. I looked through the kitchenware the owner had

22

left, found a serrated knife. I put it in a small black backpack along with a flashlight. That was all I needed.

I walked into the living room, opened the glass door, then the screen door. I looked outside; the three apartments that separated me from 326 were dark. Either the occupants were asleep or they weren't home yet. The courtyard one floor down was deserted; there were small lights illuminating the palm trees.

The only sound was an occasional faint car horn from Sunset Boulevard, a block away. I stepped out onto my patio, threw my leg over the white railing in the corner. For an instant I straddled the thin slab of concrete that separated my patio from the one next door; then I jumped onto the patio of the adjoining unit.

The wood shutter was pulled all the way across the sliding glass door, so it was dark. The difficult part would be navigating this next stretch. There was a two-foot hollow area between this unit and the one to the right. It was connected by a narrow concrete ledge.

I threw my foot onto the ledge, stepped onto it. It was narrower than it looked. I quickly crouched on my hands and knees, decided to crawl across it, rather than walk it. Just as I was near the next unit, I heard a sound from the courtyard.

I looked down and saw someone from the security staff walking by, checking. He shone his flashlight all around. Had he heard me? Or was he just making sure no one was here? He continued on toward the pool. I crawled across the rest of the ledge, vaulted onto the next unit's patio. The glass door of this one was slightly open. I tiptoed toward the end of the patio.

Just as I was almost there, a dog started barking. It ran to the screen door. I could see it was a Chihuahua. It barked like crazy. I froze, hoping it would give up.

"Moses, stop barking. It's just the guard," said a sleepy voice from the living room. I could see the dim outlines of a foldout couch. Moses didn't stop; he became more agitated. I quickly swung my leg onto the next ledge, crawled across it. The barking stopped. I was no longer a direct threat to the dog's territory.

The next three units provided no problem. Finally I was there. I crouched near the door to 326. I could barely see into the living room. It was furnished with some old wood furniture, a stereo, a TV. I tried the screen door, but it was locked. I took out the kitchen knife, quietly plunged it in, cut the screen door around the lock.

I stuck my hand in, cutting my finger on the torn screen. I jerked my hand back, wiped the blood off. Then I put my hand back through the jagged hole, unlocked the door.

Soundlessly I opened it, walked into the living room, closing the door behind me. It took me a few seconds to acclimate my eyes to the darkness. This apartment seemed to have the same layout as mine. It was probably a one-bedroom. I was standing in the living room, which flowed into the small kitchen. There was the same half bath near the French double doors.

I walked over to the desk; there was dust on everything. A fern in the corner was sickly, desperate for water. I looked at the phone machine. It said there were twenty messages waiting to be re-trieved.

I went into the kitchen, which had no signs of recent occupancy. A coffeemaker was on the counter, clean. I opened the refrigerator; it was half full. I took out a milk carton whose expiration date was eight weeks previous. It smelled rotten. I opened a fruit-and-vegetable bin—moldy aspara-gus, lettuce.

What to do first? What to think? Was it the plan we had often talked about? Or had something sin-ister happened?

Maybe I should listen to the messages—there might be a clue. I closed the sliding glass door, locked it. As if locking it could keep me safe from what I might find out.

I shone my flashlight on the phone machine to see the message button. I pressed it. The machine made an eerie whine as it prepared to tell me what it had.

"Hi, it's me. I'm worried about you. Please call me, okay?" I recognized my own voice on the tape. I sounded as fearful as I had felt that day. I hunched over the phone machine, waiting to hear the next message.

All of a sudden a finger pushed down the stop button. I jumped back, screamed.

"Who are you and just what do you think you're doing?" a tall, dark man asked me.

I struggled to find my voice. My heart was now beating so loudly I was sure he could hear it.

"Isn't this . . . Dana Richardson's apartment?"

"Yes, it is. Who are you?"

Who was *he*? He was about thirty-five years old, strikingly good-looking, with dark, straight hair combed back, cut just below his ears. He had eyes like periwinkle-blue clearie marbles. He stood over six feet, maybe six-two, in white silk boxer shorts, nothing else.

I had to think fast. Should I admit my identity or make a run for it?

He grabbed me, shook me by the shoulders.

"Who are you?"

"Ariane Richardson. I'm Dana's younger sister," I said.

"Her only sister's name is Paula Jean. Now, who are you and what have you done with her?" he yelled at me.

"I am her sister. I changed my name from Paula Jean to Ariane," I said as I broke away from him. He stopped, stunned.

"You're Paula Jean?"

"I was. Now I'm Ariane. Dana changed her name, too; she was born Thelma Ann. Who are you?"

He took a deep breath, suddenly became aware of being naked, except for the boxers.

"Just a minute, let me get my robe," he said as he ducked back into the bedroom. I took a deep breath. Who was he, and what was he doing in Dana's apartment? What was his robe doing in Dana's apartment, and most importantly, where was Dana?

She had moved into this building two years ago, and we had been in constant contact until recently. I hadn't heard from her in two months. But maybe nothing was amiss. When we were younger, we used to talk about reinventing ourselves totally, not just name changes.

Dana always said if she had the opportunity, she

would just disappear. She talked about hoping to
meet a man who would take her to Europe, where
she could reappear as someone new. Living in Italy
was her favorite fantasy.

She bought a book on Florence, read it continu-
ally. She knew the names of the museums, where
the various famous statues were, even the names
of some of the hotels. Somehow she thought it
would be easier to disappear in Florence. She
looked young for her age, thought she could blend
in with all the art students there.

Whenever she spoke of this fantasy, I begged her
to take me with her. She said she would bring me
into her new life as soon as she had one. She said
that I was the only person from the past whom she
wanted anything to do with.

I knew exactly what she meant. When all you
have been, all you have known, is embarrassing,
becoming a different person sounds like the solution. The most I could do was change my first name
and move to L.A. And that was only to find Dana.

She said that if the opportunity to disappear pre-
sented itself, she would just grab it, no warning, no
good-byes. Then she was thinking more and more
of going to Europe. I begged her to take me. She
said she would call me on that next Wednesday.
Wednesday never came.

Then last week I received, not a phone call, but
an urgent letter from her. It said, "Paula Jean, come
to L.A. at once. I need you. Love, Dana."

What was going on? She never told me much
about her life in L.A. I know she had dozens of
boyfriends, many of them lovers, but the only
name she had mentioned recently was that of Mark
Farrington, a man she dated for a while. They both

worked at Madison's, that's why I had to get a job
there.

I know she had lived in this apartment, worked
in the La Prairie cosmetics section of the store. I
know she did people's makeup at night to earn extra money. I know she frequented a bar at a hotel
where she met many Europeans.

That may seem like a lot, but that's all I know.
Until that day two months ago, when she didn't
call me back. Never had she not called me back. I
continued calling, still got no answer. I called the
store. They said she had quit. They couldn't tell me
anything else.

Yet her phone continued working. I called, left
messages repeatedly. She didn't have it discon-
nected. Her electricity was working.

"What are you doing here?" the man asked,
walking back into the living room. He was dressed
in jeans and a T-shirt, barefoot. He moved with
grace, seemed comfortable in his body. I tried not
to notice any of that.

"I'm looking for Dana. Why are you in her apartment?"

"I'm her boyfriend, Tom Crandall," he said as he
stuck out his hand. I shook it coldly.

"Listen, I'm sorry I overreacted—sit down,
please." He pointed to the couch. He was telling
me I could sit down, in my own sister's apartment.
I sat down. He sat down, too. I could feel his body
heat, but then, I was very sensitive to men. It felt
like he was invading my body space, but maybe
the space between us was appropriate. What was
he, her boyfriend? One of many?

"What are you doing here?" I asked.

"I've been very concerned since she disappeared."

"Do you live here with her?" I asked.

"No, I rent a house in Brentwood. It's twenty minutes from here, in west L.A.," he said.

"But what are you doing here now?"

"I've been staying here the last few days, hoping that someone or something would turn up, help me find her. I filed a missing-persons report with the police. I didn't know how to contact you, or anyone else in her family."

"Do you know anyone else she knows?" I asked.

"No, not really," he said. "She just seems to have disappeared into thin air." He sounded very upset.

"When did you last see her?"

"Monday night, eight weeks ago. We went out to dinner, then caught a movie at the Beverly Center near here. I dropped her off after that, around eleven P.M. I watched her walk in past the security staff, then I drove home. I called her the next night, got no answer.

"That wasn't unusual—she was out more than she was in. I left a message, figured she'd call me at my office the next day. She didn't," he said.

"Was that unusual?"

"Yes, because we had tickets for the Music Center that weekend. I needed to arrange the time I was picking her up. So I called her at work—I hardly ever did that—and they said she had quit." Wearily he put his hand over his eyes.

"Had she talked about quitting?"

"No, not at all. She loved it there, she was even up for a promotion. People were always telling her to quit and become a model. But she liked the se-

curity of the job. She talked about becoming a
makeup artist for films someday."

"Do you think she would have just ... disappeared ... I mean, on purpose?" I asked.

He looked as if the idea were completely foreign.
Obviously she had never revealed that fantasy to
him.

"Why would she do that? What would be the
point?" he asked, looking baffled.

"I don't know. I was just trying to think of some
reasonable explanation."

"You mean, like if she was in legal trouble or
had gotten into something criminal? I can't imagine
Dana doing that," he said adamantly.

"Well, what do you think happened?"

"I've been trying not to think the worst. Los Angeles is a dangerous city—carjackings, rapes, murders, gang shootings. I'm afraid something may
have happened to her. Her car is in its stall, she
didn't give notice on her apartment, she didn't tell
anyone she was leaving. If nothing happened to
her, it just doesn't make sense." He was getting
more emotional.

"At this point I'm almost losing hope that we'll
find her," he said, his voice breaking.

He jumped up, went over to a decanter of whis-
key, poured himself a drink.

"Sorry. It's just that I'm so worried and I've been
so isolated in my concern. We had only been dating
about three months, but I was ready to get serious," he said, looking down at his empty glass. He
sighed, walked over to the couch, sat down. I in-
stinctively moved my legs in the opposite direction
from him.

He and Dana must have looked like movie stars

together. I felt such a strong attraction to him, my neediness problem compounded by the emotion of the situation. I felt that horrible magnetized force again, trying to draw my body into his. I didn't trust myself to stay in the same room with him, but I had to find out what else he knew. I got up, walked over to the phone machine.

"You're welcome to do that, but I already did," he said.

"Have you checked through her things, papers, checkbook?" I asked.

"Yes, what I could find. There wasn't much. She made a cash withdrawal of all of her savings the day she disappeared, or the day I think she disappeared—that was on that Tuesday. She hasn't written any checks since then; at least that's what the bank told me."

"Why would the bank tell you? Isn't that confidential?"

"It usually is, but I'm a financial advisor. I know a lot of bankers. I was able to find out."

"But if something happened to her, why did she quit her job?" I asked.

He shook his head, depressed. "It doesn't make sense, I know," he said. "The front desk said she took her paper in Tuesday morning—they always leave it in front of her door. That morning she called Madison's and quit, just like that."

"Are they sure it was Dana who called?"

"Yes. Her supervisor took the call, said she was absolutely sure it was Dana."

"And nothing's missing here?"

"Her purse and her wallet, but she would have had those with her. I seem to remember that she had a little jewelry. I didn't find it, but I wasn't that thorough."

"What type of purse was it?"

"I don't know what all her purses looked like. She usually carried a beige straw bag; that's missing. And her wallet isn't in any of the other purses," he said.

I took a deep breath. Dana was efficient. If she'd left voluntarily, she might not have told Tom Crandall, but she would have given up her apartment, taken her things. She certainly wouldn't have left her car. She would have sold it.

Tom got up. "Look, I guess you're next of kin, or whatever they call it. I've been sleeping here these past few nights, just hoping I would discover something, or that someone would call, or that maybe she would call for her messages. I think I'll go. Will you be staying in her apartment?" he asked.

"No. I rented my own apartment here."

"That was efficient," he said amiably. "Well, I'm going to head home. Maybe you'll be able to catch something I missed. I'll get my things." He walked toward the bedroom.

A few minutes later he came out carrying an overnight case. He reached into his pocket, handed me a key.

"Here's her door key. A few months ago there were a series of burglaries in the building. They thought it was an inside job. The front desk told her not to leave her key down there. She left one at my house.

"Well, good-bye, Paula Jean—I mean Ariane. Give me a call. Two heads are better than one," he said, scribbling down his phone number. "I'm willing to do anything to find her."

"Fine. I'll call you," I said from across the room. I couldn't wait for him to leave so I could start searching.

"Okay, bye," he said as he opened the door.

As soon as he had left, I missed him. I hated myself for it, but I had a longing, a yearning to call him back. It was my boundary problem again. I felt anxious. For that brief period of time when he had been here, I had felt validated in his presence.

How sick was I? Did I desire my sister's boyfriend? It was so wrong! Rational explanations didn't help my dependency problem. I experienced a compulsion to run down the hall after him.

I got up, paced around, tried to imagine the space between Tom Crandall and me as a strip of elastic getting longer. I imagined it getting so long that it was stretched very thin, until finally it snapped. This technique worked for me. The connection was broken; I felt better. I shook my head to rid myself of any images of him.

Dana was missing, that was the priority: my precious Dana was missing. I had to get to work.

I looked for the small footstool that had been in our home in Scappoose. It was walnut-colored with a needlepoint top. No one would give it a second look; that was how our grandmother had designed it. It had always been in our family.

I turned it upside down. It looked just like the underside of a footstool, but I knew how to get into the hiding place. I pressed the left corner of the false bottom and it fell out. I removed the panel, took out Dana's jewelry.

There was her gold watch with the rubies, which

had been our grandmother's and was our one heirloom. There were her silver bracelets, which she loved, and two matching silver pendants. The emerald-and-diamond ring that had been a present from a former boyfriend wasn't there, nor were the crystals she always wore around her neck. But she might have been wearing those when she disappeared.

If she had been abducted as part of a burglary, the robbers wouldn't have known about this hiding place. So this didn't prove she wasn't kidnapped, but it did prove that she hadn't disappeared voluntarily. She never would have left her jewelry behind.

I started to stick the jewelry back into the hiding place when I felt paper inside. I looked in, saw an envelope, pulled it out. It said, "Paula Jean."

I tore it open. The message was in Dana's handwriting, but in a scrawl; she must have been in a hurry. It said, "Paula Jean, If you find this, it's Mark . . ."

I froze. The next sixty seconds seemed to be an hour as the horrible message sank in. It was so awful that for a moment I forgot everything. It was an instant of amnesia. I looked around the apartment, couldn't imagine where I was or what I was doing there. Then that sense of unreality passed.

I had a brief feeling of euphoria: Dana hadn't gone to Europe without telling me. She would never just leave, worrying me to death! To death? What was wrong with me?

Dana could be dead! My Dana could be dead. I started to cry. This was no joke. She was always shrewd; she knew that I was the only one who knew about our hiding place for jewelry.

It hadn't been a random act of violence. She had known her enemy. And it had to be her former boyfriend Mark Farrington.

I sat down on the couch. Who would want to harm my beautiful Dana? Why? I felt a numbing sense of loss, and a piece of me died with the thought that I might never see her again.

They say every person bonds to one person more than to any other. Dana was my person. I could never be as close to a lover, a husband or even a child, although I didn't know that for sure. I lived to see Dana every morning when we were together, to hear her news since she had moved to L.A.

But wait! There was a chance she was alive, kidnapped, being held against her will somewhere. She was missing, someone might want her dead, but she might not be dead. It was a slim hope, but I was desperate.

I put the jewelry back in the footstool, put the note in my purse. I'd take that to the police in the morning. What else could I find here?

I played the messages on the phone machine. They were from Tom Crandall, a Karina and me, all asking her to call us as soon as possible. There was one other message, from the West Hollywood Sheriff's Station, saying Tom Crandall had filed a missing-persons report and asking her to contact them if she got the message.

I started to look through the drawers in her desk. There were just ordinary supplies; she didn't have a computer or any high-tech stuff. I found a schedule book, opened it eagerly. It was just a work schedule, with a few notations about when to pay bills. She had circled the date of my birthday. That made me incredibly sad.

I went into her bedroom and looked through her closet. She had bought a lot of clothes since she left Portland. Most of them were from Madison's, since she probably got a discount. The clothes seemed to be very expensive—leather jackets, designer dresses, even a fur coat. I wondered how much of a discount she got. Maybe some of the wardrobe was gifts, she dated so many men.

I looked all over for the beige straw purse, couldn't find it. That must have been the one she had with her when she disappeared.

Her bathroom was like a cosmetics counter, displaying every conceivable cosmetic and perfume. There were foundations, powders, blush-ons, eye liners, mascaras, over fifty lipsticks. It would take Dana an hour to put on her makeup. Then she always looked as if she were hardly wearing any.

I looked at her bed. She had black silk sheets on it. Her pillow still had the indentation of Tom Crandall's head. I shook it out until it was smooth. I pulled up her bed, made it. I didn't know why.

I tried to remember detective movies I had seen. Where else should I look? Phone bills. I had seen a movie where a clue was found in a phone bill. I went back to the desk, found the past two years' worth of phone bills. The only long-distance calls she had made were to me.

Her car—I should search her car. She must have a spare set of car keys. I ransacked the apartment, couldn't find one.

I found a copy of her rental agreement listing her parking space; it was number 37 in the lower garage. When Dana lived in Portland, she always had a Hide-A-Key under her red Hyundai, so it was probably still there.

It was now six in the morning and early-morning sounds were audible from the apartments. I found Dana's car. I noticed security cameras around— would someone see me breaking into her car? Dana's car was open. Of course it was, because she hadn't planned on going anywhere.

The Hide-A-Key was there. I looked through the glove compartment, the trunk, but there was nothing of interest. I locked the car, went back upstairs to Dana's apartment.

I walked around the place again, willing the walls to tell me what they knew. Dana, Dana, Dana. I'll find you, just hang on. And God forbid you're dead—I could never accept that—I'll make your murderer pay. If someone has stolen you from me, I'll punish them.

I closed Dana's torn screen, locked her door. I went back to my apartment, showered, changed. I called the rental car agency, asked them to pick up their car.

I went down to the garage, got into Dana's car. My head was spinning, so much had happened since I got off the plane yesterday afternoon. I had hoped against hope that she had been away on an exotic vacation.

Now my darkest fears had been confirmed. This was something that happened to other people, not to me, ordinary Paula Jean Richardson. What skills or tools did I have to find Dana if the police could not? The only thing I had was desperate motivation. I just couldn't imagine living without Dana. I didn't want to.

I started the car. I saw a gas receipt on the console from about two months ago; it had her signature on it. So she'd been alive then. The gas tank was almost full. Had she disappeared the very next day? Tom Crandall had said she'd picked up her newspaper on Tuesday. That would have been the day after she'd got her gas tank filled. That was the last day that I knew she was alive.

I drove into the parking lot of the West Hollywood Sheriff's Station. The officer in charge of the missing-persons reports was polite but overworked. He drank from a bottle of Snapple.

"They use us as social workers in a lot of these apartments in West Hollywood. We're always in your building, lots of tenant disputes. We never have a spare moment, but don't worry, I'll keep working on your sister's case," he told me.

"When did Tom Crandall file the missing-persons report?" I asked.

He looked through a bunch of papers. "Seven weeks ago. He said she had been missing a week by then. I asked him why he hadn't reported it immediately, but he explained that they weren't living together, that he didn't always know her plans."

"I found a note that Dana wrote me. It was hidden in a place that only I knew," I said, pulling out the scrawled message.

The officer looked at it. "Who's Mark?" he asked.

"I don't know for sure, but she did date a Mark Farrington, who works at Madison's in west L.A."

"Can I keep this?" he asked.

I said okay, although parting with it was wrenching. My last note from Dana.

"Have you checked the morgue for any Jane Does? No body has been found with her ID on it or that matches her description, but you can never tell. If somebody's been beaten, then killed, they can be unrecognizable. And you should call all the hospitals, check for amnesia victims."

I nodded, feeling worse. A phone call came in for him; he had to attend to another case. He had a million things on his mind, while I had only one: Where was Dana? I left.

I sat in Dana's car, started to panic. I had to pull it together. I had to be strong, Dana was depending on me.

I started to drive home.

⚔ 3 ⚔

I walked back into the building and the man at the front desk stopped me.

"Miss Richardson, someone dropped off an envelope for you," he said, handing it to me. I ripped it open.

The note said, "Ariane, call me. I'll be home tonight." A phone number followed. It was signed, "Tom Crandall." What was this about? Had he remembered something? I decided to call later, as he was probably still at his office.

I checked Dana's phone machine: nothing. I talked to Peter Ruggio, the building manager, showed him the missing-persons report, asked him who had been on duty on that Tuesday. He said it was Julio, that he would be in tomorrow. The manager gave me a passkey to Dana's mailbox.

I rushed downstairs, opened it. There was a month's worth of bills, nothing else. I went back to my apartment and finally unpacked. Whom had Dana rented her apartment from? When had she last paid? I had to find out. I called the front desk, got the name, called, no answer.

I called Madison's. They asked me to come in for the department interview.

One success. I had worked in stock at Nordstrom's in Portland, so I knew I could do the work. The department head said they had an opening. The interview went smoothly; she said she'd call me in a few days.

Now that I knew Dana was definitely missing, I couldn't wait a few days. I walked to the La Prairie counter. The young woman with the long ponytail was idle. She was rearranging a display.

"Hi, can I help you?" she asked.

"Maybe. Do you know Dana Richardson?"

"Dana doesn't work here anymore. Are you in our files?"

"No. I'm not here to buy anything, I'm Dana's sister, Ariane."

"Oh, I didn't realize Dana had a sister," she said coldly.

"Yes." I paused. She didn't say anything.

"What's your name?" I asked.

"Tracy," she said.

"Were you friends?"

"Well, we were friendly, not really friends. I told the police officer everything I knew, which wasn't much."

"Did the officer interview everyone she knew?"

"I don't really know. Look, I've got to make a phone call. Is there anything else?"

"What are the names of the other women she worked with?" I asked.

She spun around, went to a back counter, came back with a list that she handed to me.

"Here are the names of the employees. You can call them."

"Was she especially close to any of them?"

"Karina, the girl from Finland. She used to go out with her, and she'll be on in about an hour."

"Fine," I said, putting the list in my purse. "Tracy, do you have any idea what happened to her? Did she ever say anything?"

"Why would I have any idea?" she asked defensively.

"I just meant that you could have heard something."

"All I know is that she had the nerve to quit with no notice. I had to come in and work that Tuesday. She just up and left."

"But I think something happened to her. I don't think she quit on purpose."

"I don't think anything happened to her. Something better came along, and she bailed out. She knew a million guys. I think she just found a meal ticket and jammed."

All of a sudden Tracy's attention focused on something in back of me. She looked nervous. I turned around, saw a fast-moving, redheaded man approaching. He was dressed in an elegant navy blue suit. He was about action—alert, quick.

"Tracy," he began in a staccato voice.

"Wait, come back here," she said quickly. He gave me a cold look. The two of them walked toward another counter. I could see them, but I couldn't hear them. Tracy whispered in his ear as he looked straight at me. Then he nodded, gave me another frosty glance, left.

A tall blond woman went behind the counter.

"I'm in early. I have some orders to check," she said to Tracy.

"Karina, that's Dana's sister," Tracy said, pointing to me. Karina smiled at me.

"I'm Ariane Richardson, Dana's younger sister—from Portland, Oregon," I said.

"Have you found her? The policeman said she was missing! I can't believe this country. What happened to her?"

"I don't know. I'm trying to find out. Do you have a few minutes to talk?"

"Of course," Karina said as she walked out from behind the counter.

"Let's go to the ladies' room. Follow me," she said, walking down an aisle, swerving to avoid customers.

Once we got to the ladies' room, she sat down on the couch, motioned for me to sit next to her. I sat down. She lit a cigarette.

"Do you think she's dead?" she asked me.

I shuddered, I hated to hear my fears voiced out loud.

"I don't know what to think. Was there anyone she was afraid of?"

"Not that I know. Men, they really liked her. We used to, how you say, hang out together all the time. It was after she and Mark broke up. You know Mark Farrington?"

"Not well, but I know she used to date him."

"It was last year, when I first came to work here. They were dating, but—" She winked at me. "Dana always had a . . . like a . . . layaway plan. Backup men, in case. Anyway, she and Mark got into some terrible fight." Karina inhaled a drag.

"What was the fight about?"

"I don't know—she never told me. But they hated each other. After that, we used to go to a couple of bars all the time. We met a lot of guys. She liked guys from Europe."

"Did you meet Tom Crandall?"

"No. Who is this Tom Crandall?"

"He said he was her boyfriend recently."

Karina laughed. "She had so many boyfriends."

"Do you think she just would have called up and quit, with no notice?" I asked.

"No. I was surprised. I was off that week. When I came back, they told me that she had quit. I was shocked. She didn't even call me."

Karina glanced at her watch, jumped up quickly.

"I'd better get back. I hope she will be all right, Ariane. Will you call me?" she asked as she walked toward the door.

"Yes. Thank you, Karina."

I went back to Personnel, asked for Mark Farrington. I had to talk to him. I had to! Maybe I would just know the truth once I set eyes on him. The receptionist pointed to a group of offices.

"If he's back there, he'll be at the first desk. But I don't know if he's in town," she said.

I walked into the offices. The first desk was occupied by a thin, ethereal-looking man, twenty-five years old. He looked boyish, in a preppy sweater and chinos, nothing like Dana's usual type. She usually went for a more manly type. How could she have had a terrible argument with this gentle-looking man?

I approached his desk. He looked up.

"Can I help you?" he asked.

"Are you Mark Farrington?"

"No. I'm just using his desk to make a call. He was around here this morning. Just a minute, let me see if he's here," he said as he turned around to survey the office.

At that moment the man who had talked to Tracy walked in.

"There he is, that's Mark," said the boyish man.

That was Mark Farrington!

"Mark, this lady is looking for you," the man at the first desk said. Farrington regarded me with hostility.

"I'm Ariane, Dana's—" I began.

"I know who you are. What do you want?" he asked gruffly.

"Could, could I talk to you privately?" I asked. He looked like nothing would make him more miserable. He pointed to a back office; we walked toward it.

He rushed ahead of me into the office. He waited for me to walk in, then closed the door behind me. The room was empty except for the two of us. As he glared at me, I started to tremble.

"Just what do you want?" he asked me.

"I'm afraid something has happened to Dana. I just wondered if you had any ideas, or if she said anything to you."

"I haven't dated Dana for six months. I've hardly seen her, except occasionally at work. She probably met some guy and took off with him," he said angrily.

"It doesn't look like she left voluntarily, she left too much stuff behind. The police have listed her as missing, and there's an investigation going on," I said.

He walked up to within an inch of me, looked down so that he was staring me in the eye. I wanted to run, but I didn't flinch.

"I talked to the cop. I don't know anything and I don't want to. Your time is now up," he said, turning me around, roughly pushing me.

"It was not a pleasure meeting you. I hope we don't meet again. Now I've got to go—someone just paged me," he said, pulling a pager out of his belt, checking a number, then pushing me through the door. He slammed it after me.

I started shaking with both fear and anger. Why did he hate Dana so much? What had the argument been about? Did he have her now? Had he killed her?

People always said Dana was cold, aloof. If they knew what our childhood was like, they would see why she was aloof; she just didn't want to feel much anymore. I thought about the sadness and hopelessness of our mother. How much emptiness and shame could you feel?

If Farrington had only known how kind and tender Dana was when I was young. She fixed my meals, washed and ironed my clothes, from the time she was six. It had probably exhausted her emotionally, caring for me. She might not have had the energy left to care about others. But I never saw her as cold and aloof.

I walked out into the parking lot thinking about Dana. Wait! Was that her getting into a Toyota? No, just a woman with hair like hers. I wanted to see her so badly, to touch her, to have her brush my hair, like when I was a little girl. If I could have just one moment with her, to find out what had happened!

I drove back, thinking I saw her in every store and cafe along the way.

I walked back into my apartment. I went into the bedroom. Something seemed different. The closet was open—hadn't I closed it? I tried to concentrate. I remembered unpacking, then putting my suitcase in the closet, pulling the mirrored, sliding closet door all the way across the wall.

Was I imagining this? Why would anyone look in my closet? I tried to shake away the feeling of danger as I undressed, went into the bathroom.

I turned the shower on, stepped into it. I put my head under the faucet, it felt good. I started to wash my hair. The glass doors steamed up. I turned toward them to get my hair conditioner off the ledge.

Suddenly I saw a shadowy figure dart into the bathroom, then run out. I screamed, threw open the door, rushed out, grabbing a towel to wrap myself in. I ran into the bedroom. Nothing. I ran into the living room. My glass door and screen were wide open. I rushed to the patio, looked both ways. No one.

I sat down, shaken. How could someone get into the building? Was this about Dana? It could have been the building burglar. I called down to the front desk; they sent security to check immediately.

Was someone going to hurt me, too? Was I in danger? I had never considered this, couldn't believe it. The only reason someone would want to harm me was to keep me from finding out what had happened to Dana.

I got dressed, went back to Dana's apartment. As soon as I walked in, that awful stillness came over me. Stillness can have a sound all its own. It's a light, windy type of sound that gets louder and louder, blocking out normal sounds. It has a feel; the very air gets leaden, heavy. It closes in on you like heavy fog.

I started to move around to defeat the feeling. If I couldn't defeat it, the next step would be panic. I walked it off. I called Dana's landlord. Her rent had not been paid for the past two months. She was never late with her rent. The owner would have noticed, but he had been on vacation.

I explained the situation. He said she had signed a new one-year lease. I told him I would call him next week.

She had just signed a lease, so there was no way she was planning on moving. I glanced around the apartment in desperation. Was there an answer here?

The phone rang. Who could it be? Was it Dana? Had she escaped? I waited.

"Hi, it's Dana," said the recorded voice. "Not here, leave a message. Wait for the beep. Bye."

Then, with no hesitation, a voice said, "Ariane, it's Tom Crandall. If you're there, will you pick up? I need to talk to you."

I grabbed the phone. "Tom?" I answered, with more warmth than I had intended. I was feeling shaky, Farrington's malevolence, Tracy's coldness, the intruder in my apartment. But most of all, I was beginning to feel my lethargic side take over. I just didn't think I'd find Dana alive.

"I was hoping you'd be there. I got home from work earlier than I thought. I remembered something. Are you free for dinner? We can get a bite and discuss it."

"All right. Where shall I meet you?"

"I'll pick you up at six, we'll go to a place on Melrose. Did you find anything?"

"No," I lied. It was too early to trust him.

"I've got to go, see you at six," he said.

I looked forward to six o'clock more than I wanted to. There was something comforting about Tom's take-charge personality. He must have been able to see into Dana's soul to love her so much after only three months. He had perceived her goodness.

The only people in the entire world who missed Dana were Tom Crandall and me. She didn't make close friends; no one was calling to find out where she was. She could be erased off the face of the earth; it would be like she had never existed, had never breathed the air, taken up space, had a life. The thought made me unbearably sad. Dana, Dana, you are worth more than that.

It was unjust. Hundreds of people should be missing Dana, looking for her. If she were dead, who would mourn her, remember her? Just Tom Crandall and me.

But wait, I was jumping to conclusions. I had to keep reminding myself that no one is dead until there is proof. They found people after years of incarceration; the world was a very strange and complicated place.

Should I call the relatives in Scappoose, tell them what had happened? Why? They had barely cared about us when we lived with them. The one first cousin I had liked, Beth, had died in a car crash.

· Would any of my friends care about Dana? The truth is, my relationship with Dana, even long distance, had been so involving that I had not made many good friends. After our mother had died, it seemed like Dana and I were the only two people in the world.

The thought of a world without Dana made everything appear meaningless. Suddenly it seemed like life itself had no definition, because I had always defined myself by her. I did things to please her, for her approval, to make her proud.

When I got into dangerous situations with men,

she rescued me. She made me see that the abuse was familiar, because of things our mother had done to us. Dana always said it wasn't our mother's fault, she was crazy, but no sane person had the right to be abusive. No crazy person had that right, either. But Dana felt that in our mother's case, there was an explanation.

My thoughts returned to Tom Crandall. A three-month love affair was not long, even by L.A. standards. And now she had been missing for a while. Many guys would already have found someone new. But he was still thinking about Dana, seemed obsessed with finding her.

I was going to tell him about the two notes from Dana. I breathed a sigh of relief, knowing I would have a confidant in this treacherous journey.

I dressed for dinner. I decided to wear a black cotton halter dress. I told myself I wanted to look really good in honor of Dana, because I was going out to dinner with her boyfriend. But I knew the truth.

There wasn't a woman alive who wouldn't be attracted to Tom, no matter what the circumstance. I didn't have to be ashamed of my attraction to him, just as long as I didn't act on it. And I wouldn't; he was my sister's boyfriend. All I was concerned with right now was finding her, or finding out what had happened to her. If Tom Crandall could help me, then so be it. If he couldn't, then I would do it myself.

My buzzer went off, indicating he was here. I walked out of my apartment, pressed the elevator button. It arrived immediately. I smiled at the two men in the elevator. I was going to start interviewing everyone in the building tomorrow, so I wanted to look friendly.

Tom waited in his car, a shiny black Jaguar. He wore a casual blue suit, a white silk shirt. He didn't look any more relaxed than when he had left early this morning; his brow was still furrowed. He would probably never be relaxed again until he found out what had happened to Dana.

He leaned over, unlocked my door. I got in.

"Hi," he said as he started the car, then pulled out of the driveway. "Melrose okay with you? Italian?" he asked.

"Anything is fine." I had no appetite, hadn't had one since Dana disappeared. None of my senses seemed to be working as well as they usually did.

He stared straight ahead, driving fast, talking at the same time.

"Did you find anything out at all?" he asked, a trace of desperation in his voice.

I decided to wait to tell him about the messages.

"The police know nothing. I talked to her friends and acquaintances at the store, but they said they didn't know anything, either."

He jammed on the brakes to make a stoplight.

"Madison's—that's what I wanted to tell you," he said, turning to look at me for the first time. His eyes had a laser intensity to them, major kilowatt energy.

"I remembered something that could be important," he continued. "It struck me as strange at the time, but Dana didn't want to talk about it. When she cut off, she could really cut off.

"I picked her up at the store one afternoon and as we walked out, she admired a Calvin Klein suit on a mannequin. I told her I would buy it for her and she laughed and said, 'Why should you spend your money on that? I can just talk to Mark. Take me to Hawaii for the weekend instead.'

"I asked her who Mark was, and she said she used to date a guy at the store named Mark Farrington. I took offense and asked her if she was still dating him. She said, 'No, that's not necessary anymore.' "

The traffic started up. He turned down Melrose.

"What happened then?" I asked.

"I took her to Hawaii, the Mauna Kea Hotel on the big island," he said.

"What was strange," he continued, "is that a couple weeks later she was wearing that suit when we went to a party."

"Why was it strange?"

"Well, she never could have afforded it on her salary. And why would Mark have bought it for her? And how could she have been sure that he would? I meant to ask her about all that, but she disappeared soon afterward.

"Dana never liked to be questioned; she didn't talk about the past. I had to respect her wishes, but I wish I'd pressed harder on this one point, in light of what's happened," he said.

He pulled up before La Cucina, an Italian bistro, and motioned for a valet to take the car. I got out, waited on the curb.

This was obviously a popular dinner spot. Laughter could be heard all the way to the curb. I could see the patrons through the glass window, most of whom looked to be in their twenties and thirties, well dressed, full of energy. The place was jumping. Tom led me inside.

I saw many couples standing around, some going into the bar in the connecting restaurant. There would probably be quite a wait. Tom walked up to the hostess, a dark-haired, vivacious woman with shiny red lipstick, whispered something in her ear. She smiled, led us immediately to a table in the back.

"Did you want a drink?" he asked, sitting down.

"No, I'm fine," I said.

He looked down at the table for a moment, then up at me.

"What are we going to do?" he asked.

"We're going to find Dana or the person that harmed her if she's . . ." My voice dropped. I could hardly utter the word, but I had to. "Dead."

"I can't accept that she's dead," he said. "I'm going to hire a private investigator. The police can't give Dana the attention she deserves."

"I'm certain that Mark Farrington is involved somehow, or that it was someone she knew," I said.

"I agree. She wasn't the victim of a mugger. She was street-smart, she'd been on her own a long time. That's one of the things I liked about her. She was centered, she seemed older than her twenty-five years."

"I know what you mean. She could always take care of herself," I said. And of me, too, I thought. There was a very long silence. Tom looked sad.

"How did you meet?" I asked.

"At Madison's. Just a chance meeting—you never expect to meet someone like that. My secretary had a birthday, I went to get her some perfume. I saw Dana across three counters. I walked over and smiled. She smiled back. That was it." He smiled a private smile, maybe remembering their first exchange.

"So you're from Portland, too, right? Where do you live now?" he asked.

"I still live there. Dana and I lived together until two years ago, when she moved down here." Hopefully, Scappoose had never been mentioned.

"Have you ever been to Portland?" I asked.

"No, I've never been to the Pacific Northwest. I moved out here from New York two years ago—business opportunity. How did you happen to come down yesterday? You got worried?"

The waiter gave us menus. "The specials tonight are—" he began.

Tom shook his head, cut him off with a wave of his hand.

"The regular menu is better," he said. The waiter nodded, left.

"Tom—can I call you that?" I asked.

"Of course. What else would you call me?" '

"Mr. Crandall? I don't know. I just felt I should ask you. Anyway, the truth is, Dana wrote to me and asked me to come."

He looked shocked. "She did? What did she say?"

"She asked me to come to L.A., said she needed me. I tried to call her a jillion times, but there was no answer."

The waiter returned. Tom looked annoyed at the interruption.

"I'll have the pasta primavera, Caesar salad to start. How about you?" he asked me.

"That sounds good. I'll take the same," I said. Then I realized I should have ordered something different, maintained my individuality.

"You're easy," he said, smiling.

But I don't want to be, I thought, even though I knew we weren't referring to the same thing.

The waiter scribbled the orders, left.

"There's more, Tom," I said. I discovered I liked saying his name.

"More?" he asked, looking even more surprised.

"The reason you couldn't find her jewelry was because she had a secret hiding place for it—the footstool in the living room. When I looked in it, I found a note she had written me."

"What did the note say?"

"It said, 'Paula Jean, it's Mark.' I think she was interrupted, that she would have gone on to say that her enemy was Mark Farrington."

"Mark?" he repeated. His face was a sickly shade of gray. "I'm sorry to be so upset, but this means she's definitely in trouble."

"I know. I had the same reaction."

"Why would he want to harm her?" Tom asked.

"I don't know. I just don't know why anyone would want to hurt Dana. She didn't go around with violent people, she wasn't attracted to that." Like I was, I thought sadly. But no more; I was changing that pattern.

"Did she meet any of your family or friends out here?"

"My family?" he said, distracted for a moment. "I don't have much family left. I'm an only child and my dad's dead. My mom lives back in New York. How about your and Dana's parents? She never mentioned them," he said.

"Oh, our parents are . . . dead," I said.

"I'm sorry," he said.

He took my hand.

"Ariane, I know how much you love her. We'll find her, or we'll find out what happened to her. I promise you that."

Was it my imagination, or did he hold my hand just a second too long?

Later that night, I tried to sleep, but thoughts of Tom kept me awake. Men always appeared in 3-D to me; everything else faded into the background. When Tom put the fork of pasta in his mouth, the motion was so seductive I had to shut my eyes. I longed for the image of his strong hands tearing the French bread in half.

His voice was so deep, so smooth, it pulled me in, comforted me, made my own voice seem high and weak in comparison. He moved in a languid way, full of confidence. My movements seemed jerky, unsure next to his. He seemed more; I felt less.

My spirits sank so low, it felt like a change in my biochemistry. I was disappointed in myself, that mere nearness to a man could provoke such upset in me. And this man was my beloved sister's boyfriend, my only comrade in my journey to find her alive.

How like Dana to have never told me about Tom. Because to her, he was just one of many men. She was searching not for merger, but for herself. Men were amusements to her, small enjoyments or maybe means to an end, but not an end in itself.

Dana could effortlessly get the men whom most

women could only fantasize about. Was it because there was a place in her that was unreachable? Could men fathom that? Did it make them feel safe from vulnerability? Or was it that she truly heard, responded to, only about one-third of what they said? I knew she was lost in her own thoughts, simply paid them no mind most of the time. She was remote.

But they always thought there was a pattern to her responses, that they were going to find the secret to her heart. Instead they found only intermittent reinforcement. Dating Dana had the allure of gambling, of playing the slot machines. You put a dollar in, you win or lose. Soon they became addicted to her. I don't think anyone ever dropped Dana, she just moved on, in as subtle a way as she had moved into their lives.

Only I truly knew her. I figured that when she finally found herself, she would find a man worthy of her trust to share her life with. Would Tom have been a candidate to be Dana's lifelong mate?

He obviously thought so. But what had she thought? Oh, Dana, Dana, would I ever find you? I turned over in my bed, drew my knees up to my chest in a comforting fetal position. Suddenly I realized. I missed Dana so much it hurt.

There it was, that brown butterfly birthmark on the inner side of my left ankle. Dana had an identical one in the same place. We used to compare them, searching for the tiniest difference, but there wasn't one. Our mother didn't have it—we examined both of her ankles endlessly. We fantasized that we had the same father, that we had gotten it from him.

I stared at the fluttery outlines of it in the moonlight. It was barely discernible, unless you knew it was there. We used to think that if we got tans—which we never did in Scappoose—it would be covered up forever, and possibly peel off.

It was such a fragile imprint. When I used to stare at Dana's, then look back at mine, it seemed more substantial. Maybe just knowing that she had the same birthmark made me feel stronger. Mine alone faded in value.

I had never envisioned going through life without Dana. The thought gave me a chill. She was my main connection. I refused to believe she was lost to me.

If finding her alive was a matter of will, then I could do it. I fell asleep, dreamed that Dana was in a burning house. I saw her at the window, calling for help; orange flames lapped at her arms, her hair. I jumped through the window, emerged into a billowing, smoky orange oven.

I searched for Dana, then saw her. Just as I touched her hand, she turned to wax, she melted into an orange-and-black pool of paraffin. I threw myself into the hot wax that had been her, just as I woke up.

The clock said eight. The sensation of my dream was so strong that I thought I smelled acrid smoke in my nostrils. The dream reinforced my feeling of urgency. I had to find Dana in time, if there was still time.

I got dressed to the strains of Peter Gabriel that blared from the apartment next door. Their speakers must be up against the other side of my living room wall.

I knocked on the glass door of the manager's office. He motioned me in. I asked him for the phone numbers of tenants around Dana's apartment. I wanted to call—maybe they saw something the day she disappeared.

"Of course," he said, then handed me a list with phone numbers.

"West Hollywood is such a safe area and it's a good part gay, so I can't imagine that she disappeared around here, like she was a rape victim or anything like that. It wouldn't make sense.

"When I took this job, I knew we had to retrofit all the pipes after the earthquake in January '94, and I knew we had to paint the garage and solve tenant squabbles, but I didn't expect a missing person. I just hope you find her," he said, shaking his head.

"I just hope I can find her . . . alive," I said, my voice shaking.

He got up, patted me on the back.

"Don't worry, maybe it's just a misunderstanding, maybe she just went away without telling anyone."

"Maybe," I said doubtfully, "but I don't think so. Thanks."

I went down to the front desk, called to order a phone.

"Do you have a work schedule of who was working the desk two months ago last Tuesday?" I asked the doorman, whose name tag said "William." A slight man walked in, carrying an instrument case. He was the second person I saw drink a Snapple. He had a cockatoo on his shoulder.

"How's the bird?" William asked the tenant.

"Fine, but some of the tenants have been complaining that he starts screaming about three P.M.

So I rented a studio in the hotel across the street, lots of musicians there. I take him with me, he likes it. Don't you, Cody?"

Cody screeched his approval, spreading his beautiful colored wings. He then nuzzled his owner, who walked toward the mailboxes.

William handed me a work list, smiled politely.

"Can I help you with anything?" he inquired with a Spanish accent.

"Yes. Do you know Dana Richardson?"

"Oh, yes, Miss Dana. She's very nice. Have the police found her?"

"No. I'm her sister."

"Miss Dana's sister? Very nice."

"Did you or any of the doormen notice anything strange?"

"Something strange?" He thought for a moment. "No, not me."

I scanned the list. A Julio had been on duty that Tuesday.

"Is Julio here?"

"No, ma'am. Julio come tomorrow."

"Okay, thanks," I said, then got in the elevator to go to Dana's apartment. A Spanish maid with a huge load of laundry was in the elevator.

"Quarters, do you have any quarters? I need for the machine," she said, offering me a dollar bill.

"Sorry, no purse," I replied, holding up my keys.

The door opened on the third floor. As I exited, a beautiful man and woman in their twenties entered. They both were six feet tall, with long brown, straight hair down their backs. They were slim, lovely, perfect in jeans and white T-shirts; they took your breath away. People didn't approach such perfection in Portland.

I opened Dana's door with a feeling of trepidation. Would anything unpleasant await me inside? Nothing seemed different.

Once again the silence threatened me. I quickly switched on the radio. It was on a news station that seemed to be giving an endless traffic report about every freeway. There seemed to be accidents and slow lanes everywhere, even though it was only 10 A.M. I switched around to a music station, found Seal.

The music didn't have its usual effect on me; it didn't raise my spirits. I tried to let it flow through me, to feel it tingling in my fingertips, but I couldn't. All my sensations were on hold.

I saw a framed picture on the desk that I hadn't seen before. I picked it up; it was one of the only pictures of Dana and me ever taken. Two tomboys, both in plaid shirts and jeans, scruffy, smiling.

Her hair was falling all over, but she had carefully parted mine down the middle of my head, braided it into two tight braids. We were sitting on the ground and she was holding a pine cone; I was looking up at her. I quickly put the picture down. I felt tears well up in my eyes.

I had to keep my energy up. I couldn't let the sadness overwhelm me. I got to work, calling all the neighbors.

"My name is Ariane Richardson. I'm Dana Richardson's sister. She lives in three-twenty-six. As you may know, Dana disappeared two months ago, on a Tuesday morning. I was wondering if you knew her, or knew anything that might relate to her disappearance. If you do, could you please call me at the following number . . . ?"

I dialed again. The name I called was Sara Fein.

She answered. She lived on the same side of the hall as Dana, a few units down.

"I knew Dana pretty well. We used to hang out together. Why don't you come down to my condo?" she said. I rushed down to meet her, someone who knew Dana "pretty well." I couldn't believe my luck.

Sara opened her door. She was a beautiful, dark-haired, small-boned woman in her early thirties. She had flawless olive skin, a few freckles. She was nervous, with a brilliant intensity about her; she took rapid, short puffs of a cigarette.

She welcomed me into her apartment, furnished with pine antiques, a big pink overstuffed couch, matching chair. Everything about her was energy and drive. She paced as she talked.

"Dana and I are friends. We met here by the pool and we used to hang out together," Sara said. "I'm a television producer and she used to come down to my office, have lunch with me on her day off. Sometimes we went shopping. She had a practicality to her, you know—target, goal."

Sara stubbed out her cigarette in a marble ashtray. "Want some coffee? I've got a few minutes before I meet my trainer in the gym."

"That would be great."

I followed her into the kitchen, which connected to the living room, just like in my unit. She opened the refrigerator, took out a bag of coffee, started to make it.

"Sara, what did you mean, target, goal?" I asked.

"You know. Whenever Dana wanted something, she went after it."

"Like what?"

"Anything. She grabbed first and worried about

the consequences later. She got her job at the mall the first day, and whenever she needed extra money she came down to the studio and just picked up makeup clients right and left.

"She'd go right up to the actresses on my show and tell them how she could do their makeup better. And, of course, since she was more beautiful than most of them, they all wanted to look like her.

"If there was a cute guy around, she'd go into her dance before she knew the full story. She figured she'd decide if she wanted him after he took the bait. And he always did."

Sara stopped talking for a moment, seemed lost in thought.

"I can't believe something happened to her. She was savvy, she knew her way around the block."

"I know," I said.

"If she'd been killed, wouldn't they have found her body? I know people disappear without a trace, but the chance of that seems so remote," Sara said.

"I think it may have something to do with one of her boyfriends, Mark. Did you meet him?" I asked.

"Only once, briefly. I've been going with a guy for a couple of years, so I'm hardly ever here on the weekends. Why do you think it had something to do with him?"

"People said they had a terrible argument when they broke up. I met him, he was rude to me, he kicked me out of his office."

"Really? I only met him for a few minutes, but he didn't seem like the rude type. They were going into her apartment. She saw me coming down the hall and called me over. I do remember that he seemed uncomfortable meeting me. I don't know why."

Her phone rang; she answered it.

"Hello? Yeah, I know it's bad. I'll be in soon, bye," she said, hanging up.

She poured my coffee, slid the cream and sugar over to me. I put some in.

"We've got some script problems on a pilot. I've got to go into the office. Take the mug of coffee with you. Look, I really feel bad about Dana. Call me if there's any news at all or any way I can help you."

I thanked her, carried my hot mug of coffee into the hall. The mug was shiny yellow and said "Golden Girls" in black letters. It must have been a show she used to work on.

As I started toward Dana's door, a thin, distinguished, white-haired man hailed me. He wore a white T-shirt that said "Pop Art."

"Are you Dana's sister?" he asked.

I nodded.

"I knew her, just got your message. Come on in," he said, holding open his door. He lived next door to Dana.

I walked into his apartment, which looked like a tropical garden. There were lush green plants everywhere, and beautiful paintings hung on the walls. Small, lit votive candles burned brightly on every coffee table. His patio doors were open; it looked like the Garden of Eden outside.

He had defeated the dry harshness of southern California all by himself. Brightly colored religious statuary fought for space with the plants and thick candles outside. I had wandered into an enchanted land.

"Go ahead, sit out there. I'll bring some tea out," he said. I sat down in a canvas chair near a white Madonna statue. He came out with tea in a brass teapot; it smelled exotic. He poured me a cup of the spicy brew. I put aside the mug of coffee.

"I'm Micky O'Hanlon. I own an art gallery down on La Cienega," he said.

"Your apartment is so charming," I said as two dogs came up to nuzzle my foot. One was a brown-haired mutt, the other a graceful black-and-white Border collie.

"Your dogs are very friendly," I said, petting them.

"Do you know PAWS?" That's the organization that gives away AIDS patients' dogs. I got these two there. The Border collie's owner died and the dog was depressed, so I took him.

"They're trying to make some rule about one pet per condo. But the previous manager allowed people to have two pets, as long as you put down a two-hundred-and-fifty-dollar deposit for each one," he said.

"Why do people object?"

"I don't know. There's a guy who complains about them all the time. He fills out complaint form after complaint form, and files them with the grievance committee. Who knows?" O'Hanlon waved the annoying thought away with a good-natured flip of his hand.

"I may have inadvertently heard something that could help you," he said in a soft voice.

"Something Dana told you?"

"No. Dana's living room and my bathroom share an air vent. Sometimes you overhear a conversation. The reason I remember it is because I always take my shower at about nine-thirty in the morning, after most everyone else. The water is only lukewarm at eight-thirty."

He lifted his teacup, took a sip. He had thin, pipe-cleaner, angular arms. My eyes were riveted to his face. What had he heard? I was ready to pull the words out of him.

"Anyway, she was usually long gone by the time I got up—she had to be at work early. This was on a Tuesday morning, the day I open at noon."

"Tuesday?" I said, my voice rising in excitement. "That's the day she disappeared."

"I'm sure it was Tuesday, about two months ago. I didn't realize she had disappeared that day until I heard someone talking about it weeks later.

"I was just stepping into the shower. I heard her yell, 'You'll never get away with it.' Then I heard a male voice shouting, but the words were indistinguishable. When I got out of the shower, it was quiet, about nine-forty-five A.M. Can you make any sense of this?"

"Yes," I said, imagining her telling Farrington that he wouldn't get away with killing her. I got up. I had to get busy.

I went back to Dana's apartment, called Madison's. The director of personnel told me that I hadn't gotten the job.

I wondered if Farrington had had anything to do with it. The idea wasn't inconceivable, because he had an important position there and someone might have alerted him to my application. I would have to figure out another way to get information about him.

I knew he wouldn't talk to me. Nor would Tracy, who was either his friend or his girlfriend. How about Karina? I called her. She said to meet her in the hotel down the street in an hour. It was her day off.

The hotel was set off the sidewalk by heavy green foliage. Two white stretch limos were parked outside. I walked into the lobby, asked for the bar. The hostess pointed to the left.

There were three attractive, young Asian women, dressed in short black dresses, seated with men in their forties. There were a few other young women with middle-aged men, and a couple of famous actresses from a television show. I sat down at a vacant table. Was this the hotel where Dana had met European men? Probably.

Karina walked in. She was so glamorous that I hardly recognized her. She was dressed in a white linen, low-cut sundress. Her blond hair was swept up in a twist; a gold locket dangled in her cleavage. She wore gold high-heeled mules, the kind with the little hourglass-shaped heels that I could never balance on.

"Hi, Ariane," she said as she sat down, delicately crossing her legs.

"Hi, Karina. Is this the place you used to come to with Dana?"

"Yes. It's easy to meet men here. Most of these women are floaters—that's what they call them in L.A. Women from other countries who float into men's lives here, hoping to get married and get a green card. They try to marry men with money. American women, they are so liberated, many men prefer European women."

She laughed. "But I don't want to get married yet. I just want to have a good time. I'm only twenty-five years old; I was raised on a farm in

Finland. I want to travel, see America, see all over," she said as the waiter appeared.

"Vodka tonic," she told him.

"Orange juice," I said. Karina gave the other patrons a cool, appraising eye.

"This is the new 'in' Hollywood bar," she said. "It really starts to get crazy around ten at night. Dana and I used to laugh so much here." Suddenly she fell silent.

When the waiter served our drinks, Karina asked me what I wanted her to do.

"I'm sure Mark Farrington is involved in Dana's disappearance, Karina. I didn't get the job at the store, so can you help me find out some information about him?"

"But I don't know him. I see him only at the store, and we are in different departments."

"Would Tracy help you?"

"God, no. She hates me."

"Why?"

"After Dana dumped Mark, he asked me out. I never went—there is something not right about him. But Tracy, she had a, how do you say, liking for him back then. Now they are going together."

"Look, I have an idea," I said. "I'll come to the store to buy some makeup. Maybe we can find something out, look around on your break, whatever. It's a start."

"Yes, anything we can do. I'd love to get to know you better. Come in around eleven, Friday morning."

"I'll be there."

* * *

I went back to my apartment to wait for the phone man. The phone man was a woman; she had cables and receivers coming out of every pocket on her overalls.

"Do you want Call Waiting or any of the extras? Your order ticket said just one outlet. That it?" she asked.

"No extras, just one outlet," I answered. She installed my phone quickly, humming the John Cougar Mellencamp song "I Was Born in a Small Town" while she worked. She said she had applied to the phone company three times before she got a chance to train for a job. She especially liked scaling the telephone poles. She finished her work, left.

I went over to Dana's condo to check her message machine. There was a call from the police. I called back, left my new phone number, went back to my apartment.

What else? What else? What other leads could I think of? Wait, Dana was compulsive about her hair. Though I didn't think she had left town willingly, if she had planned to leave town she would have had her hair done. I called Karina, who gave me the name of Dana's hairdresser.

The hair salon was at the Beverly Hilton Hotel. The hallway leading up to the salon was lined with framed pictures of Merv Griffin and various other celebrities.

The salon was clean, shiny, obviously doing great business. Wealthy, bejeweled hotel guests and other clients were having manicures, pedicures, haircuts.

I found Jeffrey at his station; he was a slender, handsome man with brown hair, a brown mustache. He was blow-drying the blond hair of an older woman. I introduced myself, and he was eager to help.

"I'm so worried about Dana, she's one of my favorite customers. Have they found anything?" he asked.

"No. I was wondering when you saw her last."

"I do her hair every three weeks—it grows fast. She has a regular standing appointment every third Wednesday, on her day off. She missed her last two appointments. She's never missed appointments before.

"She also had me buy her hair products at my beauty-supply house, I get a ten percent discount. She would have run out of shampoo and conditioner about four weeks ago," he said, finishing the blow-dry. The woman got up, admired her hair, hugged him, thanked him.

"Come where we can talk," Jeffrey said.

He led me to a little coffee room in the back of the salon. He closed the shutter doors.

"I've been so worried about Dana, like I said. She's more than a customer, she's a friend. I bought a little bungalow on Romaine Street in West Hollywood, and she came to my housewarming a couple of months ago." He sighed sadly. "I just hope she's all right."

"Jeffrey, did she talk to you about her dates?"

"All the time. She was so popular, so beautiful. And she consoled me when I broke up with my lover. She understood that I adored him, but I just wasn't in love with him."

"Did she talk to you about Mark Farrington?"

"Yes. He was really serious about her, but she

felt he wanted to control her. I think he was also involved in something shady."

"Shady?"

"She wouldn't tell me. It wasn't that she was shocked, it was that she wanted to use it to her advantage somehow."

"To her advantage?"

He looked embarrassed, took a drink of coffee.

"That sounds bad. I didn't mean it like that. I don't mean she was mercenary. From what she implied, she had discovered something he was doing. I think she worked the situation to her advantage," Jeffrey said.

"Did they fire her? They said she quit."

"No, they didn't fire her. She wanted to work at another store—that's what she told me."

"Did she mention Tom Crandall?" I asked.

"No. I know she was dating a new guy before she disappeared, but there was always a new guy on the horizon for her."

As I left, I glanced around at all the women getting their hair done. Why couldn't one of them be Dana? Why had this nightmare happened?

When I got home, my phone was ringing. It was the police. There was an unidentified Jane Doe at the morgue. Could I come down, check it out?

I put down the phone, frozen in horror. Was it Dana?

It couldn't be Dana. I felt her presence. I knew she was alive. Or maybe that was just what I was hoping. If she was dead I'd know it, wouldn't I? The dead woman could be anyone of average height and build, like Dana. I called the coroner, got directions. They said the body had been found with no identification.

Hadn't Tom told me that Dana's purse and wallet were missing? I felt cold all over. As I grabbed my purse, the phone rang. It was Tom; the police had called him, too. He wanted to go with me, said he'd pick me up in fifteen minutes.

If there was a God—or a Higher Power, as my friends in Portland who were in AA called it—was it too late to make a bargain with Him/Her? What could I promise in exchange for this woman not to be Dana? I would rather my own life be cut short than hers.

Dazed, but trying to hang onto hope, I walked down to the lobby. An attractive older woman, wearing a matching beige hat and trench coat in eighty-degree weather, was sitting in the lobby with two pet containers. She was talking to a doorman named Ricardo.

"These two cats are my favorites. They're strays,

they live out in the parking lot on the corner. I just had them spayed. I feed them every night," she said as I sat down in one of the big pink-checkered chairs.

"Do you like cats?" she asked me. I was so worried that I could hardly talk.

"I'm more of a dog person," I said. She lifted a calico cat out of one of the boxes, nuzzled it.

"Isn't Ginger a cutie?" she asked. I nodded, thought about the tiny black kitten Dana had had when she was small. She fed him milk from an eyedropper. She named him Dino, carried him everywhere with her in a belt pouch. Our mother let Dino out of the house one day, and he never came back. Dana searched for days, weeks, but never found him. She had cried every night for months.

The cat lady put Ginger back in her carrying case, picked up the other case. She walked out the door toward the parking lot to liberate her charges. A delivery man entered the mirrored lobby with a huge bouquet of long-stemmed red roses.

"These are for Anna White," he said as Ricardo signed for them. Anna White was the star of a sitcom I watched. I hadn't realized that celebrities lived here.

But of course Dana would pick an exciting building. Dana, Dana. She was always getting flowers from men when we lived in Portland. She liked getting flowers, hated getting plants. She said she didn't have a green thumb.

Dana had kept her bouquets forever, preserving them carefully. Once the flowers died, they stayed on their stems, the petals keeping their color. Her flowers never wilted or fell off their stems. I don't know what she did to them, but her bedroom had been filled with perfectly dried, delicate flowers. Someone had once said her bedroom looked like a funeral parlor. I shuddered at the memory of that description.

"Is anything wrong, Miss Richardson?" Ricardo asked. I managed a thin smile, shook my head. "No."

All of a sudden Tom ran up the front steps, taking them two at a time. He rushed into the lobby, tense, upset; whipped his black sunglasses off when he saw me.

"Thanks for waiting for me. I didn't want you to go down there alone. I want to go with you."

"I know it's not her, Tom. I just know it," I said, but without much conviction.

"I hope not," he said shakily as we left the building.

Even though I knew that someone else would suffer a grievous loss if the body was not Dana, I didn't care. Not only was Dana too valuable to die, I didn't know if I could survive her death.

I glanced at Tom, taut behind the steering wheel. No matter how much he loved her, he could not love her more than I did. I didn't honestly know if romantic love was as deep as family love, since it was so threatening and complicated for me.

It was hard for me to believe that romantic love could be simple and sustaining for anyone, but maybe it could. Maybe Tom and Dana had a special feeling between them.

"It could be any one of a million people," Tom said, also with a lack of conviction. I just looked at him. I couldn't even get up the energy to answer him. As we drove on, I felt like every bit of my lifeblood was being sucked out. Tom fell silent for the next few minutes.

I looked at the other cars zooming around us on the freeway. If only I could be in one of them, going to a different destination—home, job, errand, anything but the possible loss of Dana. I felt moisture in my eyes. I blinked quickly, and all the colors of the cars blended together.

Tom slowed down, got into the exit lane. I started to take deep breaths so that I would have strength. I stared at Tom; he looked as terrified as I was.

I gazed at the buildings we drove past. Would one of these turn out to confirm my worst fear? I shivered as I thought of Dana dead, her body covered by a sheet in a cold vault. She deserved a different fate. Maybe she was alive, smiling, clothed in a flannel nightgown somewhere on a big lacy comforter, and this was all a hideous mistake.

"It's supposed to be down here," Tom said softly as he searched for the address of the building. He finally nodded his head once, then drove into a tall parking structure. I began to feel weightless and numb, started to panic. Tom sensed my unease, put his hand on mine as he looked for a parking place.

I felt my strength evaporate. Where would I find the energy to get out of the car? I closed my eyes, trying to delay the inevitable. I felt the car glide into a parking space, heard the engine go off. I opened my eyes. Tom was staring at me, worried.

"Do you want me to go, you want to stay here?" he asked.

"No," I said. "I'll go, Tom, I just know it's not her. I can't lose Dana, she's all I have," I said, tearing up again.

"Let's go in," Tom said in a tight, grim voice.

I moved my paralyzed legs toward the door, turned the handle with my lifeless fingers.

"You look sick," he said as he slammed the door, switched on the car alarm.

"I'll be all right," I said.

Tom put a protective arm around me. "There's a coffee shop on the corner. Let me get you a quick cup of coffee. I need one."

I allowed him to lead me past dozens of brightly colored vending stalls. The smells of tacos and burritos, which usually made me hungry, now nauseated me.

"Let's just go to the coroner's office and skip the coffee," I pleaded.

"No, I need it to steady my nerves," Tom said as he pushed me into the coffee shop. We collapsed on two cheap green plastic stools. I wondered if every visitor to the coroner's office had to stop first at this coffee shop to find the courage to go on.

"Black coffee," Tom ordered.

"Senorita?" asked the counterman.

"Coffee with half and half," I said softly. The walls here were dirty, decorated with a few velvet paintings of matadors, bullfights. Three old men wearing white aprons and smoking cigarette stubs sat at one table. A heavyset, exhausted-looking woman in her early thirties, with five small children, walked in. They were dirty and scruffy, evidence of the family's struggle on all of them.

I used to pity women like this, raising children against incredible odds. But at this moment I would have changed places with her. I would have accepted the hardest, the most hopeless of lives if only I didn't have to face the next hour. Tom and I sat in wordless, scared silence.

Our coffees were put down in front of us. We reached for them simultaneously, brought the cups to our lips. Automatic movements that didn't take thought. Our eyes met.

"Tom, it just can't be her. There's a chance, isn't there?"

"I hope so," he replied hoarsely.

"Dana created her own life, she crafted it. I always pictured her getting everything she wanted, being able to succeed in every situation. I always wished she had more time for me than she did, but I figured when we were in our eighties we'd be together.

"Or that someday she'd get married, have children. I'd live with her family, help her raise them," I said, remembering all my fantasies of a future life with Dana.

"I . . . I . . ." Tom said as he put down his coffee. "I guess I thought we'd wind up getting married one day, not that I ever mentioned it to her. I didn't want to scare her away. I just know that I had never felt as alive as I did with her."

I put my head in my hands. "Let's not talk like this. We're assuming the body is hers, but remember, it could be anyone's. You said her purse and wallet were gone, too; that meant she would have them. But the body was found without identification."

"That's true. And the coroner's assistant said this woman hadn't been dead that long. Dana has been missing longer," Tom said.

"What you're saying is that if it was Dana's body, she would have been dead for weeks? Oh, I understand. That makes sense. Unless whoever took her kept her somewhere and recently killed her," I said, trembling at the thought.

Tom froze. "Oh, God, don't even say that. I can't even contemplate that Dana could have . . . suffered."

He jumped off the counter stool, plunked money down.

"The sooner we get in there, the sooner we'll find out it isn't her," he said with fake confidence. We walked out, started down the street.

Suddenly I heard a high-pitched tinkle of a laugh. I whirled around, half expecting to see Dana. But it was only a teenage girl whose voice had the same timbre as Dana's. Tom looked at me. I just shrugged. I couldn't speak. My words were buried somewhere deep in my chest, in fearful anticipation of the next few minutes.

We walked into the outer office of the morgue. It was cramped, grim, shoddy. There was an African-American family sobbing in the corner. I looked away, wondering if I was to suffer the same fate. Tom led me into a room. The secretary looked up.

"We're Ariane Richardson and Tom Crandall, and we have an appointment," Tom said.

"Yes, just a moment," she said, then picked up the phone.

"Mr. Crandall and Miss Richardson are here," she said into the phone.

"Fine," she said as she hung up.

"Mr. Romero will be right out. You can sit down over there."

Tom and I went over to the chairs and sat down. Everything was starting to move very slowly for me. A man came out a few seconds later, carrying a brown manila envelope.

"Miss Richardson, Mr. Crandall?" he asked us. We nodded.

"I'm Mr. Romero, the investigating officer. Please follow me."

He led us down a hall and into another room. It was even smaller, devoid of furniture. Detective Robert Martinez was waiting for them.

"Please sit down," Romero said, pointing to two chairs. I stared hard at the brown envelope, trying to see through the manila paper.

"Miss Richardson, if this is your sister, this may be very upsetting, do you understand?"

"Yes," I said.

"The victim's face is recognizable in these pictures. We don't know how long she's been dead, but it hasn't been that long. It's been unseasonably cold in L.A., so there's not as much decomposition as there usually would be," Romero said. "Do you want to look at the pictures in two different rooms or do you want to look at them together?"

"We'll look at them together," Tom said.

Romero handed Tom the envelope. Tom glanced down at it nervously, then opened it, slid a photo out so I could see it.

It was a photo of a woman's face. She was dirty, looked asleep.

"It's Dana," I screamed; then I started to sob.

Tom nodded. "It's her," he said, quickly averting his eyes. Detective Martinez gently took the photo and envelope from Tom's hands, laid the photo facedown on the desk. He handed me a box of Kleenex. Tom was crying, too. He put his arm around me; I cried on his shoulder.

"I'm sorry for your loss," Detective Martinez said to us. "We'll get a set of prints on her just to verify. The autopsy will take about three days to determine time of death. I can't discuss with you how she died, but it wasn't natural causes. We don't think she was killed at the site we found her; we think her body was dumped there."

"I want to go home—I want to get out of here," I said to Tom. We got up.

"Listen, would you both mind coming down to the West Hollywood Sheriff's Station at your convenience tomorrow?" Detective Martinez asked.

"I told them all I knew before," I said, sobbing, "and the police didn't seem that interested."

"I'm sorry. Yesterday this was a missing-persons case," Martinez said. "Now it's a homicide." I just stared at him.

The moment I found out Dana was dead, I became a different person. My safety net had been stolen; life was now a high-wire act without it. I was vulnerable, unprotected, in a way that I had never been. My standard of measurement and meaning had been Dana. Now she was gone.

The future seemed dull, uninteresting. I could think of no reason to even keep going until tomorrow. I couldn't fathom why the three men in the room were looking at me with alarm.

"Ariane, are you going to faint?" one of them asked. He was . . . ? Oh, yes, Dana's boyfriend, Tom.

"No, why?" I asked in a monotone.

"You'd better sit down," he said, shoving me into a chair.

"Maybe you should get some medication from your doctor," said the policeman. He was . . . ? Oh, right, Detective. What were they so upset about? Dana was dead; that's all there is to it—now nothing will ever matter again.

"She's green," Martinez said. "She looks like she's going into shock."

"I'm going to take her back to her apartment," Tom said as he helped me up. It was too much of an effort to say anything on the way to the car.

"Ariane, I've got some tranquilizers at home. Have you ever taken them?" he asked.

"Yes, Xanax," I responded. It seemed as if someone else were talking, my voice sounding disembodied, with no relation to my mind. I studied my hands; did everyone have ten fingers? There was something odd about my hands. It was as if I had never seen them before. I turned them over. All those lines and ridges in my palms were fascinating.

I had never noticed how fleshy the upper parts of my palms were before. I touched that fleshy part; it felt soft. I turned my palms down. I had never really looked at the joints in my fingers, but they seemed a little big.

I curled my fingers into a ball. I felt my fingernails cut into my palms. It was an odd sensation. I liked it. I opened my purse, took out my pointed steel nail file and stuck the point into my palm. Then I stabbed my palm, harder and harder, until blood spurted out.

"Ariane! What are you doing?" Tom said, grabbing the nail file from me. He stared at my hand.

"My God, what have you done?" he screamed. I looked at my bloody palm. Then everything faded into blackness. When I came to, I was in my bed. Tom sat reading in a chair. My hand had a gauze bandage on it.

"Tom . . ." I began. He rushed to my bed.

"Just take it easy. You've had a shock," he said.

"What happened? The last thing I remember is seeing the picture of . . . Dana . . . and now I'm here. What happened to my hand? Did I pass out?"

"Yes, it's all right. You passed out and scraped your hand. Do you feel better?"

Tears streamed down my cheeks. Oh, Dana, Dana, I'll never see you again. How can I ever feel better?

"I know," he said. He handed me a pill and a glass of water.

"Take this. I got it from a doctor—it'll make you feel better."

I swallowed it quickly, handed him back the glass. "None of this feels real," I said. He nodded his head in agreement.

"I don't know who . . . would do . . ." he said, his voice trailing off.

"Farrington. He did it," I said.

"Let's see what the police have to say." Tom looked away for a moment. Then he said, "Ariane, I hate to bring this up, but when they release Dana's body to us, do you want to bury her in Portland?"

"Bury her?" I never thought that someday I would bury Dana.

"I know, it's horrible," Tom said.

Portland? She hated Portland, it was too close to Scappoose. She wouldn't want to be brought back there.

"Let's bury her here," I said sadly.

"You know what she told me once? We were driving back from Malibu during a spectacular sunset. She threw her head back, gave that wonderful laugh and said, 'If I get hit by a car, cremate me and spread my ashes over the ocean, Tom.' "

"She said that?" I could imagine the freedom of the ocean thrilling Dana. Tom nodded.

"Then let's do that. Just you and me, Tom, on a beautiful, beautiful day."

"Okay," he said softly. "I'll call the mortuary and make the arrangements."

I had a crazy thought. I wanted to keep Dana's body, keep it with me always. But I knew that wasn't possible. If she were cremated, there would be no grave. Where would I go to mourn? Maybe I could keep some of her ashes. I'd ask about that.

Maybe I could just pretend that she was on an extended vacation. No, I thought sadly, I had to accept the awful truth. Dana was gone forever. I was very sleepy—was it the grief or the pill? I didn't know, but I soon drifted off.

In my nightmare, Dana was drowning in the ocean. I was walking on the shore when I saw her. I wasn't a strong swimmer, but I jumped into the current. I threw off my shoes and clothes, started swimming as fast as I could.

I was swimming against the current; the water was cold. It started to rain. Dana was being carried farther and farther out to sea by the churning waves. Her head bobbed up and down wildly.

She saw me as I got closer. Instead of waving me to her, she motioned me to go back. I barely heard her as she yelled, "Paula Jean, save yourself!"

The waves seemed as thick as steel. I desperately tried to break through them to get to Dana. They got higher and higher, and I couldn't see her any-more. A cold spigot of water splashed into my mouth. I gagged. It seemed for a moment that I would go under. I took small gulping breaths until I caught my breath.

I was going down. I was aware I could die, here in this blue ocean. I might have had the strength to swim back to shore, but I didn't know whether I would if I rescued Dana. Could I make it drag-ging her on my back, even if I could grab her?

It was not a choice for me. I knew I had to try to save Dana's life, even if it meant losing mine in the process. I took the deepest breath I could, threw myself under the waves and did a furious breast stroke underwater.

Finally I reached her. I grabbed her around the neck—then suddenly she disappeared! Had she slipped underwater? No. I looked around for her frantically, but she had evaporated into the air.

"Dana!" I screamed. "Dana, where are you?"

Suddenly someone was shaking me.

"Ariane, wake up, wake up," Tom said.

His voice seemed to come from a great distance. I tried to focus on it, bring it closer.

"Wake up. I've been calling you and calling you. I finally just came over, had the doorman let me in. We have to go see Martinez in an hour," Tom said.

Appointment with Martinez? Oh, my God, it was morning. I dragged myself back into the waking state, looked at the clock. Nine in the morning. I had slept more than twelve hours.

"Tom, I'm so sorry, I overslept. I'll get ready right away," I said as I got up, rushed shakily for the bathroom. I jumped into the shower. The water hurt me with its harshness. I felt as fragile as a silken spiderweb. In less than twenty-four hours, every single thing in my life had changed. Dana was dead. I was completely alone. The next fifty years seemed unbearable.

I got dressed in a hurry, and went back into the living room. Tom looked as bad as I felt. His eyes were red and swollen.

"Rough night?" I asked.

"The roughest," he answered.

"We have to keep going, if for no other reason than to remember Dana. If we don't, no one will," I said.

Tom nodded. We rode down to the police department almost in silence, each of us lost in depression.

As Tom was parking, I said, "I wonder if Martinez has questioned Farrington yet."

"He's probably waiting to find out what we know."

"I think with Dana's warning note, there won't be much doubt," I said.

Martinez was waiting for us. He asked to see me alone first. I went into a small room with him. He made me repeat everything I had told the officer in charge of missing persons.

"Please don't be insulted, Miss Richardson, but where were you when Dana disappeared?"

"Me? You suspect me? I'm her sister!"

"It's just a formality."

"I was in Portland, working," I said. He asked me for witnesses. I gave him my former landlady's phone number and that of my former boss.

"As to a possible motive for Farrington, jilted lover?" he asked me.

"I don't know, but I think it may have to do with

something she found out about him. A neighbor overheard her tell him that he wouldn't get away with it."

"That could pertain to anything," Martinez said. "Well, I think that's it for now. I'll call you after the autopsy results. All we have is suspicion where Farrington is concerned. There's also a serial killer loose in the Western states, and there are gangs. I have to look into everything. We'll question everyone she knew."

"Would anyone have seen anything, seen her being killed or being thrown out of a car?" I asked.

"We're sweeping the area right now, looking for anyone who could have."

"Thank you, Detective Martinez," I said. He asked me to send Tom in. I did. I tried to read a magazine while he was in there, but I couldn't concentrate. It seemed like Tom was in there for an hour. He finally came out and we left.

"Boy, he sure grilled me," Tom said when we got in the car.

"You?" I was surprised.

"Sure, boyfriend of the deceased, likely suspect. He's just doing his job. I gave them references, everything he asked for. I'm happy he's so thorough. He'll find Dana's murderer."

Tom suggested that we go to his house in Brentwood for a while.

"I was planning to buy that house if Dana and I wound up getting married. Now I'm thinking that I might as well go back to New York," he said.

And me? Should I go back to Portland? Should I stay here? Should I wander the earth aimlessly, remembering Dana? What did it matter now?

We rode in silence. We drove down Sunset Boulevard, cut over to San Vicente. I recalled that Dana had told me she spent time in this community on the Westside. There were small, elegant malls and shops on both sides of the boulevard, with expensive Mercedeses, Jaguars parked everywhere.

"Shall we get a cup of coffee?" Tom asked, pulling into a grocery-store parking lot before I replied. Why not?

We got out, walked into Starbucks. Everyone was drinking coffee, young, attractive people in workout clothes. Some were young mothers with children in strollers; some were couples in their twenties. All looked carefree, tan.

There was one exception, a young female death rocker. She had short, greasy black-and-green hair, a studded dog collar around her neck, several body piercings, and she wore a short black miniskirt revealing the well-developed calves of someone who worked out regularly. She held a copy of the book *The Mummy* while she checked the ingredients on the side of a bag of cookies.

I could just see Dana here, in all her vitality and beauty. Tom ordered a tall espresso and I ordered a short café au lait, remembering to be different from him. We went into a small room, sat down.

"Dana and I used to come here all the time," Tom said, his eyes misty. "She only liked hot coffee, even on the warmest days. She never ordered an ice blend. Occasionally she'd have a bran muffin, but no pastries—she was always dieting."

"She was always like that, even though she was always thin," I said, remembering all of Dana's crazy diets.

"You know, I dated a lot of women, but I never fell in love with anyone before her," Tom said.

"Were the women out here?"

"No. I grew up in New York, Manhattan. I've only been out here a couple years. Most of the girls I was involved with were from home. Many were the daughters of my dad's friends when I was in high school. My parents were pretty well off; my dad was a financier on Wall Street.

"Then there were the women I met at Harvard. All the women there were smart, strong women. My parents wanted me to marry Linda Haag—she's an attorney now. Her parents and my parents grew up together in Greenwich—in Connecticut." He paused for a moment or two. "I don't know why I'm telling you all this," he said.

"If you go back to New York, will it be soon?" I asked.

"They always say not to make big decisions when you've had a shock. I guess I should hold off a few months before I decide," he said.

"I'll stay here if Farrington goes on trial, just to make sure Dana gets justice," I said, seething with anger. What justice can there be for Dana now? She's dead.

"If you need money, anything, I can help you, Ariane," Tom said kindly.

We left, drove to his home. He pulled into his garage, parked. He lived in a beautiful ranch house on a street called Saltair. The inside decor was done in brown wood and warm colors. It looked like ski resorts I had seen in movies. Glass doors led to a large, enclosed outdoor Jacuzzi. Hot steam sizzled in the air above the water.

"I never cover the Jacuzzi. I like to see the steam, the condensation." Tom said. In the back of the yard was a smaller house, a guest house.

"Do people live back there?" I asked.

"No. In fact, it's locked up. The owner just put all his things in there before he left. He's using it for storage while I'm here." Tom looked around disconsolately, as if unsure what to do next.

His mood was somber. He walked over to the stereo, turned some music on. He sat down on a couch across from me and we just stared at each other, thick with depression. Silence wrapped around us.

"I don't seem to be feeling very social, so maybe I should just take you home, Ariane," he said finally.

"Okay," I agreed, but I didn't want to go.

❊6❊

"*I know Farrington* did it," I said, feeling as if I were in a tidal wave of horror as I got up to leave.

"They'll get him," Tom said. "And if they don't, I will. I've looked into the possibility of hiring my own private investigator." Before I knew what I was doing or had a chance to stop myself, I threw myself into Tom's arms.

"Oh, thank you, Tom, thank you so much," I said, sobbing. My grief was overwhelming. That he grieved for Dana, too, meant so much to me. Tom, surprised, put his arms around me in a fraternal way, gave me a quick hug. I pulled back.

"I'm sorry, Tom. It's just that I'm so upset. And I'm so grateful that you loved Dana, and that you'll help me find whoever did this horrible, horrible thing to her. I just don't know what I'd do if it weren't for you. I wouldn't know how to cope with all of this alone." I sank into a big couch.

I saw a framed photo of Dana on the coffee table. She was wearing one of her knockout black cocktail dresses, a single strand of pearls. I picked up the picture to look at it. Tom seemed uncomfortable; my hysterical neediness had thrown him. I hated myself.

"I didn't mean to collapse on you. It'll never happen again. This has all been so difficult to deal with, so unexpected," I said. "I feel like I'm at the bottom of a pit, clutching at straws to get out. And that this is a nightmare I won't wake up from, that there is no fairy-tale ending. Even if we catch the murderer, Dana will still be dead."

"No need to apologize," he said, brushing his hair back nervously. He was probably wondering how long he would be stuck with me. I was reflecting badly on Dana's memory. I was so ashamed, I just wanted to crawl into a hole where he couldn't see me.

"You can take me home now, please," I said. "We can scatter Dana's ashes together; then we don't have to see each other again. I don't mean to saddle you, Tom."

"Don't be foolish, Ariane, you didn't do anything bad. We're both upset. There's been a terrible tragedy here. We'll work together with Martinez to catch Dana's killer. Nothing can bring her back, but it's a mark of how wonderful she was that we both loved her so much."

Yes! What a beautiful thing to say. I felt comforted. It was a mark of Dana's worth that we were both so upset, especially that he was upset. I was her sister; of course I would love her. But Tom, Tom could probably have his choice of all the women in the world. And he had picked Dana. How special she was!

"Your house is so nice, Tom, so well put together," I told him, trying to lighten the mood.

"None of this is mine. I rented it from a television producer who's shooting a picture in Europe for a year. He's a bachelor and we have similar tastes. The best thing about it is that there's a fully equipped office over there," he said, pointing to a closed door off the living room.

"There's the latest high-tech computer, a fax, six phone lines—everything I need for my business," he said.

"I thought you had an office somewhere else."

"I do. I'm a consultant to Myers and Roberts, a financial management firm in Century City. But I also have my own clients. I invest for several people privately and I do it from here."

"So you're in . . . big business?" I asked, aware of how I must sound like a hick from a small town, just like I was. I didn't even have the proper vocabulary to talk to him. That was the thing about Dana. She was a quick study; she could talk to anybody about anything or, rather effortlessly, get people to talk about themselves.

"Big business?" Tom said, laughing. "As opposed to small business? Yeah, I guess so." He looked at his watch; it was a Rolex. He saw me looking at it.

"It was a gift from my dad, before he died. He gave it to me when I graduated from Harvard," he said.

"That's so nice. Did he inscribe it?"

"Just the usual, but I always wear it for luck. Look, I'd better run you back. I'll call you when I know about the cremation ceremony."

"Tom, would you see if they could save some of Dana's ashes for me, just scatter most of them?"

"Sure, I'll ask"

"And I have about a thousand dollars saved up I can give you, if it's more expensive than that . . ."

"Don't be silly, Ariane. I'm paying for it, so don't start an argument over it, okay?" he said forcefully.

I nodded. Someday I would make it up to him, however I could.

All that night I had dreams of Dana's cremation. Even though I knew she was no longer in her body, cremation seemed like a violation to me. I didn't want her beautiful flesh and hair burned. I wanted her here, alive, with me.

In my dream, Farrington walked into her bedroom while she was asleep. He lit a match to her hair and laughed as he watched it burn. He held a match to her fingernail; it exploded because it had nail polish on it. He lit her white cotton lace nightgown afire, watched while Dana burned to death. As she was dying, Dana woke up and screamed, "No! Paula Jean, save me!"

At that moment my alarm went off. I stayed in bed for the next three days, going out only to get food. I felt paralyzed. Finally Tom called. He said the cremation was the next day.

I woke up numb that morning. This was a day I had never anticipated, the day I would lay Dana to rest.

I thought I would be hysterical during the ceremony, but I was strangely calm. The boat was a big, clean white motorboat; the ocean was quiet.

Tom handed me the box of ashes as the boat motored out into the waves. The sun knew no mercy. It shone on my back with the same searing heat that I felt inside, an uncontainable fury. I wanted to kill Farrington with my own hands.

The boat captain did this regularly and offered to perform a ceremony. I said no. Neither Tom nor I wanted to speak. We just wanted to think our own private thoughts as we said our final goodbye to Dana. The boat stopped. It was time.

I took the box of ashes, gently tossed them into the Pacific Ocean. Each tiny ash was a piece of my heart breaking into a million splinters. I pictured each minuscule ash protected by a gold globe, floating to a watery, safe berth.

Tom just stared at some point in the distance. His hands gripped the side of the boat so hard that his knuckles were white. We couldn't even look at each other for fear we would break down. As Dana's ashes disappeared, I pledged my love to her, told her I would avenge her murder, no matter what.

Tom drove me home. We seemed connected to each other, but alienated from the rest of the city. He stopped in front of my building, handed me a small urn.

"The rest of . . . you know," he said. I took them, nodded.

"Martinez called about Dana's case. He said she was killed about five days ago. They don't know the exact time for sure," Tom said.

"He said they weren't allowed to discuss other aspects of the case with us. They're waiting for a few more test results; then they're going to question Farrington." I swallowed hard, Dana was a case now.

"Look," Tom said huskily, "I'm sorry I can't talk anymore now, Ariane. I'll call you tomorrow."

"Thanks for everything, Tom," I said as I got out.

That night I fell asleep clutching the urn.

"Come with me," Karina said as I approached her at the La Prairie counter in Madison's. This section of the store was packed with women buying cosmetics. I had called her when I learned that

Dana's death was definite. She was devastated. I asked her to help me find out what had happened. She agreed, as long as I didn't put her in danger. Danger was the least of my worries.

I followed her into the ladies' room again. She motioned me to follow her into the stall area. She bent down to check that we were alone.

"Something strange is going on with Farrington, Ariane. I've seen the same man come in three different times in the last two days and buy ten designer suits—Armani, Hugo Boss, Calvin Klein."

"The same man?"

"Yes. Each time he came to see Tracy first at my counter. They talked for a while. Then she called Mark, and the man went to the men's department. I followed him all three times. It happened twice on my lunch hour and once on my break. I saw him select the suits. He didn't even try them on, just grabbed them, handed them to Mark and paid."

"What could be going on?"

"I don't know, but I can't follow him anymore. I think Tracy is suspicious. He may be coming today. You need to stand somewhere so you can see me for the next hour, and I'll motion to you if it's him."

I found a counter across the aisle from La Prairie where I could see Karina but was partially obscured. I pretended to be buying perfume. I tried every scent, wasting time, until I had to buy something. I selected Trésor. I saw a tall blond man walk over to the counter, talk to Tracy. Was that him?

Finally I saw Karina give me the high sign. I grabbed my purchase, started following the tall blond man. He went into the men's department, glanced quickly at Farrington, who pretended not to know him. He approached a rack of expensive leather jackets, the ones with wire coils attached to guard against shoplifters. He looked through them quickly. I crouched behind a suit rack.

He walked over to Farrington, asked for help. Wait, wasn't Farrington a buyer or in management? He had an office in the back. Did he wait on people? I wasn't close enough to hear what they were talking about.

The man led Farrington to the rack of jackets. He pointed out eight. Farrington started to detach the jackets, glanced in my direction. I ducked. Had he seen me? I didn't think so. He went back to his task. I crept out of the area, upset that I couldn't hear what was going on.

I left the store quickly, without even acknowledging Karina, determined to pursue this lead, however shaky it was. I planned to call Karina tonight, somehow enlist her aid.

I steeled myself to make all the unpleasant calls when I got home, the calls that truly said Dana was dead. I called the owner of the apartment she rented, told him the sad news, said I'd move everything out.

The intercom went off. I figured they had rung the wrong apartment, and if I just waited a minute, the ringing would stop. But it persisted. I picked up the intercom. There was a Mr. Cassio in the lobby for me, would I come down?

Mr. Cassio? I searched my mind. Nothing. Who was he? As I rang for the elevator, Sara came rushing toward it. She was gaminlike in black leggings and an oversized black sweater.

"Oh, hi, it's Dana's sister, right?" she asked as

we got into the elevator. I searched for some proper way to tell her the bad news. There was none.

"Dana's dead. She was murdered," I said very quietly.

Sara jerked her head around to look at me, stunned.

"What? Oh, my God, I'm so sorry," she said, throwing her arms around me, hugging me. I started to cry.

"I am really so sorry. I just can't believe it," she said. The elevator door opened. She stopped herself from rushing out, obviously late for a meeting.

"Do they know who . . . ?" she asked.

"No." I shook my head.

"I'm so sorry," she said again, then gave a panicked look at her watch. "I'll be home late tonight, after the read-through. Should I stop by?"

"That would be great," I said.

"It might be very late, around one A.M."

"That's fine. I'm too upset to sleep."

"See you then," she said, looking crestfallen.

I walked up to the front desk and stood beside a new potted plant with big pink flowers.

"There's a Mr. Cassio to see me."

"He's sitting over there," Ricardo said, pointing to a short, middle-aged man in a big chair. The man looked like he was down on his luck. His suit was shiny with wear; the heels on his scruffy shoes were worn way down; wisps of silver hair hung down on his collar, which was covered with dandruff.

"Mr. Cassio?" I asked.

"Miss Richardson?" he said as he stood up. I smelled liquor on his breath.

"Yes. Have we met?"

"No. I'm the private investigator hired by Tom Crandall. Can we go somewhere to talk?" he asked, slurring his words.

"Let's go to my apartment," I said, leading him to the elevator. Should I ask for identification? But Tom had said that he was hiring a private investigator, so this had to be him—who else could he be?

"Please sit down. Would you like some coffee?" I offered when we entered my apartment.

"Do you have anything to drink?" he asked as he sat down.

"No, I don't."

"Oh, well, let's get down to business, anyway. Now, could I see that letter you found?"

"I gave that to the police. Tom knows that. Have you talked to them?"

"No, I have a call in to Detective Martinez," he said. Then he opened his briefcase, took out a notebook and pen.

"Now, what day did you arrive in Los Angeles?"

"Me? Why?"

"Well, it's a standard question. I ask it of all the suspects."

For a moment I couldn't breathe. What was he saying? Was he saying that he suspected me of killing Dana? I couldn't believe it.

"Are you saying you suspect me of killing my own sister?"

"Everyone is a suspect, Miss Richardson."

"That's preposterous. I loved Dana. Didn't Tom tell you that? I'm trying to find her killer, too."

"Mr. Crandall hired me to find Dana Richardson's murderer. I can't rule out anyone."

I was furious. How dare he!

"Mr. Cassio, I think you'd better leave."

"I think you're overreacting. This is all part of the process."

"I don't think so. You have just insinuated that I may have killed my own sister. Now please leave!" I shouted at him. He got up slowly, shook his head, walked out the door. I slammed it after him, rushed to the phone, dialed Tom's number. It was busy.

Before I could think twice about it, I left the apartment in a fury, jumped into Dana's car, headed for Tom's house. I was in such a state that I was on automatic pilot, driving down Sunset Boulevard at eighty miles an hour. How could Tom suspect me? Didn't he know how much I loved Dana? I had come here to find her, to save her. He knew about the note accusing Farrington. What was going on? I skidded to a stop in front of his house, ran up the front walk. I pounded on the door, leaned on the doorbell.

"I'm coming," Tom yelled. He opened the door, stared at me in surprise.

"Ariane? What's wrong?"

"How could you? How could you hire someone to investigate me? How could you suspect me of killing my own sister? Are you crazy?" I yelled at him from the door.

"Whoa! Hold on, what are you talking about?"

It was then that I saw her. She was a tall, very pale blonde, the kind who had to wear makeup, carefully applied, to bring out her features. She was wearing a tight black skirt, a wraparound black blouse that showed a lot of skin. She looked athletic; she probably rode her bicycle around town for fun.

Who was she? Was she Tom's new girlfriend? Had his heartbreak over Dana been bogus? Was I about to find out he was a total fraud? He realized that I had seen her, and he looked uncomfortable. She came to the door, looked at me curiously, then smiled at Tom.

"Ariane, come on in," he said. "This is Lori Wells. Lori, this is Ariane Richardson, Dana's sister." He opened the screen door, let me in.

"How do you do?" Lori said.

"Hi," I said. Tom owed me no explanation, but I wanted to hear one. I glanced into the kitchen. They had finished eating together; there were take-out bags from somewhere called Chin-Chin.

"Want something to eat? It's Chinese," he said.

"No," I said, sitting down in a black leather chair.

"Well, I was just leaving," Lori said in an efficient tone. She looked at Tom expectantly. He didn't say anything.

"So I guess I'll drop over Saturday. Would that be convenient?" she asked him.

"Saturday? I think that's too soon. Could you make it Monday?"

"Saturday's too soon?" she asked with a hint of displeasure. "Fine. Monday, around two," she said as she grabbed her purse. She turned just before she walked out, gave Tom a big smile.

"Bye, Tom," she said, then, as an afterthought, "Bye, Ariane."

"Good-bye," I said quietly.

He slammed the door after she left, turned to me. "Now, what is wrong with you, Ariane?" he asked.

So much was going on in my head, I couldn't think straight. I could hardly think anyway, I was so bowed with grief for Dana, but now I was on sensory overload.

"The private detective you hired, he practically accused me of murdering Dana!"

"What? Is he a moron? I can't believe that. I gave him a list of everyone who knew Dana, and I explained that you were as anxious as I to find her killer. He's really barking up the wrong tree."

"Then you didn't actually suspect . . . ?" I asked.

He came over to the chair next to me, sat down and took my hands in his.

"Of course not. How could you even think that for a minute? Maybe this guy's no good—he was a referral. Maybe I made a bad decision." He shook his head. "So much has happened so quickly, and I'm in the middle of a big business deal. A friend had used Cassio on a divorce case."

"He was drunk, Tom."

"He was drunk? I'm so sorry. I only met him once, briefly, to give him the retainer. We did most of our talking over the phone. I'll get someone else next week, after he comes back with a report. I know how overworked the police are here in L.A.—riots, earthquakes, muggings, gangs. I'm afraid they won't devote enough time to Dana."

"There must be somebody better than him."

"I'll check it out. But, Ariane, don't think for one second that I suspect you of anything but loving Dana as much as I do," he said. Then he looked down, sadly added, "Did."

Without meaning to, I stared out the window as Lori got into her car, a gold BMW, and drove away. I must have had a skeptical expression, because Tom looked uncomfortable again.

"I invested some money for Lori," he said, "mutual funds, as a favor. Now she wants to cash out. She's an old friend from New York."

"Is she interested in you?" I asked. Maybe I should have just asked if they were already a couple.

"Lori? No, we had a relationship years ago, but it's been over for a decade. Look, I have to get my car washed. Want to come?"

Was he telling the truth?

He grabbed his keys. I couldn't detach quite so quickly.

"Sure, I'll come," I said. I needed the comfort of him for a little longer. We walked into the garage, got into his car. He slipped a tape into his tape deck. It was an oldie, one of my favorites. "Ooo Child" blared from the speaker.

He turned into San Vicente. It had huge knotted trees in the island separating the two lanes. We stopped as traffic slowed down. A group of people walked across an intersection. A guy wearing a baseball cap, talking to a woman, hit the hood of Tom's car with his open palm, startling me. Maybe it was to emphasize his point. Tom hardly noticed. The cars started moving again.

"See that restaurant, Mezzaluna, on the corner?" Tom said. "That's where Nicole Brown Simpson and her children had dinner the night she was murdered. Ronald Goldman, her friend, was a waiter there. Dana was fascinated by that case."

Dana had been fascinated by famous murders; then she herself had been murdered. How could murder happen in such a bright, sunny city? Didn't murder hang in the shadows, happen in the dark, transpire in foggy old cities like London? I looked down.

"I'm sorry, Ariane. I guess I shouldn't talk about Dana," Tom said.

"No," I fairly shouted. "We have to keep talking about her, to keep her alive."

He turned down a wide street, then finally off to the right. I saw a sign for a car wash.

"There are so many car washes out here," I said as we got out. Tom gave his order to the attendant.

"This place has TVs. One is usually tuned to CNN," he said. We went in to pay. He handed the woman at the cash register a credit card.

"What are you doing later? Can I take you to dinner?"

"I'd like to, but I have to pack up Dana's things and clear out her apartment," I answered quickly.

"What are you going to do with her stuff?"

"I don't know. I gave up my apartment back in Portland. I guess I'll store everything."

"Let me store it in my house until you decide what you're going to do. I have rooms I don't even use over there. I'll send a moving service to pack it all up."

"Are you sure?"

"I'll be sure if you go out to dinner with me tonight, so I can make up for Cassio's insensitivity."

"Can we make it tomorrow night?"

Tom nodded, then we watched CNN in silence. Finally Tom scanned the dozens of cars being wiped down. He found his car, led me to it. We got in, headed back to his house. I told him what I had observed at Madison's.

"I don't know what's going on, but he's making money somehow—illegally," Tom said.

"I'm going there tomorrow to get to the bottom of it."

"Ariane, please don't do this. We have the police, the private investigator."

"I don't trust anyone else to find out the truth."

"I just don't want anything to happen to you," he said.

Was it just because I was Dana's sister? I didn't dare think that there might be something developing between Tom and me. It was an uncomfortable thought. This was Dana's boyfriend; it felt like incest.

I didn't know what it would be, but whatever it was, it would be wrong. I just wished I weren't so attracted to him. Was it because he loved Dana, or was it separate from that relationship?

"Penny for your thoughts?" he asked. I didn't have a ready answer.

"You must be very tired. You've been through a lot, Ariane. Just take what you want from Dana's apartment and I'll send the movers tomorrow, okay?" he said kindly. He pulled into his garage, got out, opened my door.

"I guess I'm fading. I'm sorry," I said. He walked me to my car.

"Dinner tomorrow night—don't forget."

"I'll call you when I get back from the Westside Pavilion," I said. I drove home, trying to push away my thoughts of Tom. He was only being protective because of Dana, and that was all I should want. Nothing he said was promissory, nor should it be. I started to turn into my garage when I saw her.

It was her hair that I recognized first, that thick blond hair tied back with a twist. Then I recognized the car, the gold BMW. Lori Wells was parked across the street from my building. I didn't pull in.

I circled the block before she saw me. What was she doing here?

I had two choices. I could just drive away, avoid her. Or I could ask her what she wanted. Had she been in the building asking for me? I decided to confront her. I pulled up behind her car, walked up to her window.

"Lori?" I said. She blanched, surprised to see me.

"Were you looking for me?" I asked her.

"No, no, it's a . . . coincidence. You're Tom's friend Ariane, aren't you?" she said, not very convincingly.

"Yes. When I spotted you, I thought maybe . . ."

"Oh, right," she said, laughing nervously. "No, I had a meeting at the hotel there, across the street. I was just leaving. Hope to see you again sometime." She quickly started her engine, then sped away.

Was it just in L.A. that everything seemed so confusing? My head swirled with the recent events. I went up to Dana's apartment, looked through her things again. I found no new clues to her killer's identity.

I was glad that everything would be stored at Tom's. I could look at her clothes, hold them whenever I wanted. Wearily, I went back to my apartment, put on my flannel nightgown. I had just turned out the light when there was a knock on the door. I dragged myself out of bed, opened the door. It was Sara.

"Hi. Remember I told you I would drop over after work?"

"Sure," I said, trying to keep my eyes open. "Come on in."

"I wouldn't have come, Ariane, except I remembered something that might be important to Dana's murder," she said.

7

I woke up fast. I ushered Sara inside. Even exhausted, she had a delicate beauty, as if she had been a Russian ballerina in another life. There was something dark, smoky, fragile about her. She lit a cigarette, inhaled deeply.

"It's been a hard week. We've got three pilots to shoot."

"What do you do again?"

"I'm vice president of a television production company. We do half-hour programs; this is our busy season. I'm going crazy, I love my boss, but the hours are insane.

"This is a horrible question to ask," she continued, "but do they know who killed Dana? How it happened?"

"No. At least if they do, they won't discuss it with me," I said, sitting down. "I don't think it was random violence. I think it was her old boyfriend Mark Farrington. She wrote me a note asking me to come down here, saying she was in danger."

Sara nodded, folding her legs under her on the couch. She took up very little space, but had a big presence. She was silent, deep in concentration. Suddenly she jumped up.

"That's it. The note!" she said.

107

"What about it?"

"When she introduced Mark to me, she seemed nervous. As I was walking away, I heard her say to him, 'But she'll know it isn't my handwriting unless I write it.' I remember thinking that sounded odd. Why would anyone else write something as if Dana had authored it?"

"I thought it must be her excuse for not going to work, or an attempt to circumvent some bureaucratic rule. But if she was referring to the note you got from her, it makes sense."

"How could you recall something like that?"

"Oh, I read dozens of scripts a week, it's part of my job. And I have a good ear for dialogue. If something jars me, I remember it."

"But this had to be almost a year ago."

"Oh, no, it was about eight weeks ago," she said.

"You saw her with Mark Farrington around eight weeks ago?"

"Yes."

"Are you sure?"

"I'm positive. We had just gotten a pickup on the show I produce. It's been on five years already, and I was thrilled with the pickup. I was coming from the celebration party. That was the night I ran into her." She glanced at my clock.

"It's later than late. I've got to try to get some shut-eye. If I think of anything else, I'll call you," she said, walking toward the door.

"Have you ever met Tom Crandall?" I asked.

"Tom? No, I haven't."

"Thank you, Sara," I said as she left.

Eight weeks ago! Dana had been with Farrington eight weeks ago! What had he been doing here? Was it the note to me that they'd been discussing?

Had she refused to write it, and had he threatened to forge her words? Or did all this have a totally different meaning?

The answer was with Farrington and I had to find it. All night I tried to sleep, but I couldn't. The woman next door had to be multi-orgasmic. We shared an air vent; mine was in the bathroom; she was exulting, groaning all night. I kept going to the bathroom, brushing my teeth, doing anything to make the small hours of the morning go quicker. Finally, at dawn, I fell asleep for a couple of hours.

My eyes had been open for fifteen minutes while I waited for the red numbers on the digital clock to read 8 A.M. That was the time Detective Martinez got to work. At 8:01 A.M. I dialed his number. He was already in a meeting; he'd call back.

I tried not to think of the movers packing up Dana's things; it was merely a formality. The finality had come before. Maybe I was still in shock. I felt detached from Dana's death, but at the same time I felt the heavy weight of grief. It was an effort to move, to do anything, but I wasn't crying.

Maybe I was all cried out, but could I be? I got dressed, mindlessly, thinking about Tom. Did he care about me, beyond my connection to Dana, which was also my connection to him? Maybe I just felt close to him because of his mourning for Dana. I hoped that was it.

The phone rang. It was Karina.

"Ariane, don't come to the store today. Tracy got fired yesterday. She was my supervisor, so I took a sick day. I found out all about Farrington. Come to my place—here's the address." She gave me directions to a house on Benedict Canyon in Beverly Hills.

It was just a couple of miles down on Sunset, so I found it immediately. She lived in the guest house behind a huge mansion that looked like a new French stone castle. There were three large homes in a row, almost identical, newly built. The three lawns were similarly landscaped, and a shiny new foreign car stood in each driveway.

Karina was waiting in front by the gate as I drove in.

"Welcome to Teheran," she said when I got out of the car. "I'm a live-in nanny to an Iranian family. These people have so much money, you can't believe it—they're buying Beverly Hills. My boss, Amir, bought the house on the left for his brother and the house on the right for his son."

Karina led me inside the main house.

"Don't worry, they're on vacation, always visiting relatives. They let me have a day job because the wife is always home. It's just important I'm here at night for the kids, in case they go out, which they hardly ever do. And I watch the house when they travel, which is always."

We walked toward the back of the house, then went out by the pool. Near the pool was a white guest house.

"Come in here," she said, welcoming me into the frilly white living room. Charles Aznavour was singing in the background.

"Do you want any tea? I have herbal," she said.

"No, thanks. I just want to know what's going on." I sat down in a big overstuffed white chair. It was as soft as a bed, with thick, comforting arms. I sighed. Everything had been so harsh lately that for a moment I thought I was sitting on a cloud.

Karina went over to a white porcelain sink,

threw cold water on her face, patted it with astringent. She was in a pink jogging outfit, must have come back from running. She wiped her face, sat down.

"Yesterday, in the middle of the morning," Karina said, "Tracy was called to the head supervisor's office. When she finally came back, she was, how do you say, white. She was shaking.

"She told me she had been fired. She said they had accused her of helping Farrington with a scam at the store. He had various friends come in with phony credit cards. He would write up large orders, ship them to a fictional address—a series of post office boxes he rented. Then he sold the clothes to a fence.

"In the beginning, she said he did it very seldom, but he got greedy. He had a way of falsifying the orders so that no one knew he made the sale. Then he mailed them out himself from the mail room.

Dana must have found out about his scheme and threatened to bust him. Was that why he had killed her? Was that enough reason to kill someone?

"Where's Farrington now? At the store?" I asked.

"He didn't come in yesterday."

"Do you think Tracy would talk to me?"

"I wouldn't bet on it, Ariane, she hated Dana, but I'll write down her address for you." And she did.

I stood up to leave. "Karina, you don't think Tracy might have killed Dana, do you?"

"No, she's not the type. Jealous and catty, yes. But murder? No. But I know she has a gun for protection, so be careful."

"I will," I said.

Back in the car, I got out the Thomas map that the rent-a-car people had given me, found North Hollywood. I decided to drive straight over the canyon to the valley. There was a line of cars miles long in front of me, and it went slowly.

I found the address without any trouble. It was a run-down area; the apartments looked old and affordable on a salesgirl's salary. If this was where an average Madison's employee lived, I wondered how Dana could have afforded her apartment. Maybe Dana's boyfriends had helped her.

I parked on the street, went up to the outside mailboxes. Karina had told me Tracy lived in number 654. I knew she probably wouldn't let me in, so I had to think of a convincing story.

I rang the bell. Tracy called down, "Yes?"

"Registered letter for Tracy Owens," I said.

"Can you just leave it in my box?" she asked.

"No, you have to sign for it."

"Fine. I'll buzz you up."

I rushed into the elevator, pressed her floor number before she could discover my identity. How could I get her to let me in her apartment? The elevator door opened; I got out.

It was a dusty outside hallway. Luckily, across from Tracy's apartment a Latino woman was sweeping her porch. There would be a witness in case anything happened. My mind was racing, trying to quickly come up with something seductive enough to Tracy to make her talk to me. Suddenly it came to me. I knocked firmly on her front door, as firmly as I imagined a mail carrier would knock.

"Just a minute," came a muffled reply. It sounded as if she was crying. She opened the door.

"You!" she screamed.

"Tracy, wait, I think you're in danger. I've got to talk to you."

"What?!"

"Just let me talk to you for a minute—it's about Mark."

"What do you know about Mark?" she asked, starting to cry.

"Please, just let me come in. I'll tell you everything." The Latina was staring at us with curiosity. Tracy hesitantly opened the door wider, let me in.

"What do you want?" she yelled at me. Her makeup was smeared from crying; she wore a dark green silk nightgown, a matching robe. She sat down on the couch, picked up a faded teddy bear whose eyes were missing. She clutched it to her as she glared at me.

"You know something about Mark?" she asked hopefully.

"No—I mean yes, in a manner of speaking," I said, rattled. This was not the scene I had expected. I didn't think I'd find her so broken.

"Have you heard from him?" I asked.

"No, I haven't heard from him," she said, bursting into tears.

"Calm down," I said. I couldn't believe that I was in the position of comforting her.

"How can I calm down? He left me high and dry. He took my savings and now I might go to prison."

"What?"

"That's right. He said they weren't wise to us yet, but that it was only a matter of time. He asked me to give him the two thousand dollars I had saved up so he could buy us plane tickets to Spain.

He had put all the money we made in a bank in Madrid, and we were always going to go there. He told me to pack—said he'd pick me up later, take me to the airport.

"Only he never came. So I went into work the next day and I got busted. The police said he purchased a ticket to Madrid, one-way. He never even called me." She tossed her ancient teddy bear at the wall in anger.

"You mean you were planning to . . . marry him?"

"He told me we would get married," she said. "I mean, I always liked him even when he was with Dana. He was so dashing, so decisive, so different from the guys I met down in San Diego, where I'm from.

"I never thought I'd get a shot at him, Dana being so beautiful and everything. I guess he originally came on to me because he needed an accomplice, but it grew into more than that. He told me I was the only woman he ever truly loved," Tracy said.

The phone rang, and she answered it.

"Oh, hi, Mr. Margolin. No, I'm fine. Yeah, two o'clock is okay. I'll be there. Thanks." She hung up.

"I had to get a public defender since I have no bread and no job. I'm totally fucked," she said. "And you know the worst thing?

"If Mark called me right now and said he was sorry and that he wanted me to join him, I'd forgive everything." Tracy started to cry again.

"I think Mark is the one who murdered Dana," I told her. She sat up straight, stopped crying.

"What? What are you talking about?"

"Mark is her killer. You could be his next victim, Tracy. I'm not kidding."

"No way. Mark's a con man, but he's no murderer. He's not crazy, he's just larcenous. He wouldn't have any reason to kill Dana. They broke up over six months ago, they barely even spoke, he had no feelings for her."

"I think she found out."

"Found out what?"

"About the rip-off scheme. She threatened to turn him in."

"I hardly think so."

"Why?"

"Because the entire scheme was Dana's idea."

"It was what? Dana's idea?" I asked, gasping. Was she telling the truth? This threw such a spin on things that I couldn't even grasp the ramifications.

"She thought of the whole thing, she figured it out, she told Mark what to do. She said she worked the same ruse in Portland with a friend."

It could be true. Dana had saved up the money to go to L.A. pretty fast; she had always seemed to have more money than anyone else. As usual, I had assumed she'd got it from boyfriends.

"She used to hang out at some hotel," Tracy said. "She found guys willing to come in and act like customers with the phony credit cards she gave them. After they broke up, she wouldn't do it anymore, but she still got a cut of the action. Mark paid to keep her quiet, since we never knew what she would do."

"Why did they break up?"

"Dana met somebody else. It wasn't like Mark had a broken heart or anything. She figured the store would eventually find out about the scam, so she was already out looking for another gig, I think at I. Magnin's, when she disappeared."

"Did she and Mark still hang out together at all?"

"No way. They hated the sight of each other."

"But someone saw them together eight weeks ago," I said.

Tracy's face puckered in anger. "Then he was a two-timing son of a bitch."

I was silent. I knew Dana had been no angel, but the arrogance of her crime shocked me. She had always been a shoplifter. If she spotted some item of clothing that she couldn't afford, she saw no reason not to simply boost it. In our early days with our mom, she even stole food so we could eat.

I was just surprised at the risk she'd been willing to take for money, now that it wasn't about survival. But had she been at risk? Maybe she had rigged it so that if they were caught, Mark would shoulder all the blame.

This information did not make me love her any less or feel my loss of her less intensely. I loved Dana for who she was to me, not for who she was to the world. I valued her for the way she treated me, not how she treated the world. It did not make the fact that some thief had brutally stolen fifty years from her any easier to live with.

"Were you often in Mark's house?" I asked.

"All the time."

"So there's no way he could have kept Dana out of sight if he had kidnapped her?"

"Kidnapped her? That's the last thing he would have done. There's no way he wanted to even see her. Look, he didn't kill her, and he's not going to kill me. I've got a lot to do before I see the lawyer. Could you go now?" she said. I stood up, dazed.

"You're barking up the wrong tree," Tracy said. "Mark didn't care enough about her to kill her."

I left quickly, rushed outside, threw up on the curb. Too much everything. Suddenly I felt overwhelmed, boxed in. It was sizzling hot; the smog hung in the sky in a brown-and-pink clump. For as far as I could see, there were ticky-tack apartments and yellow brush taking over green grass. As much as I disliked Portland, I longed for the sight of a sturdy, fresh-smelling tree, the cleansing rain.

I rested against the hood of my car. When I felt less dizzy, I got in, started to drive. Somehow I got stuck on the freeway. I meant to take the canyon, but I missed the turn. It wasn't rush hour, yet the freeway was packed.

I had heard someone say that all day in L.A. is now rush hour on the freeways. It made my boxed-in feeling much worse, I wasn't only boxed in by an acrid sky, I was pinched between two cars—a dusty Range Rover and an old Mustang. It was as if each car were a rung on a ladder, a very long ladder, each rung separated by only about two feet. This serpentine row of metal moved at two miles an hour. I finally got off the freeway.

I had some free time. I drove all over the Westside and Beverly Hills, stopping the car whenever I saw a HELP WANTED sign. I had to find employment immediately. I was running out of money quickly and I couldn't leave without finding Dana's killer. Finally I ran out of steam. Should I tell Detective Martinez what I had learned? Would it reflect badly on Dana's memory? But could it help find her killer? I drove to the West Hollywood Sheriff's Station, asked for him.

"What is it, Miss Richardson?" he inquired, striding into the office.

I quickly told him what I had learned about Dana and Mark from Tracy, but I omitted Tracy's involvement in the store theft. Detective Martinez took notes.

"The only motive I can think of is an argument about money. But why would he keep her somewhere before killing her or having her killed?" I asked.

"I'm sorry," he said, "I can't discuss aspects of our investigation with you. We have our best detectives working on this and I'll stay in touch, Miss Richardson. We're trying to find Farrington in Spain."

"Are there some murders that are just never solved?" I asked, depressed.

"We're going to solve this one," he assured me. "Our detectives are working around the clock. And we never give up. There's one case that happened ten years ago," he continued. "A woman and her two-year-old son were stabbed to death in Venice. I saw the crime scene. The murderer stabbed the little boy in his jammies. I'll never forget how terrible it was. I know who did it, but I don't have hard evidence. I've been working on this ever since, trying to trap him—he won't get away."

I didn't feel any better. Dana was dead, but her murderer was alive, breathing the air and taking in the complex sights and sounds of life.

"Can we be in touch every day?" I asked hopefully.

"We'll call you just as soon as we have something to report. And, Miss Richardson, please don't do any of your own sleuthing. There's a killer out there, and someone who kills once can kill again."

"Okay, thank you, Detective," I said as I got up. It seemed like every other desk had victims of muggings and carjackings looking through books of mug shots. Snippets of their conversations hung in the air.

The information I had been told felt like an endless tangle of yarn snarled in a huge ball. There was no beginning, no end. No one could find a loose thread to straighten it all out.

I noticed the West Hollywood city hall nearby, walked over to inquire about parking permits. The clerk said that if I lived in West Hollywood, I could park on the street in designated areas for just five dollars a year. I filled out the paperwork, gave them a check.

"Anytime you have a party, just come down and get free party parking passes. They're good for twenty-four hours," he said, holding up a handful. "People are always giving parties in West Hollywood."

I thanked him. I couldn't imagine ever going to another party, ever feeling carefree abandon or a desire for fun. Dana could not go to parties, Dana could not have fun. Her existence had been extinguished. I felt as if my flesh had been ripped off. The outrage also made me feel that my hair was on fire, my eyes stung.

I drove home, feeling as if my body had no form. I was one with the smog, foul-smelling, lumpy, heavy, spread all over the place. I pulled up to the apartment building, saw three police cars in the driveway. Had they discovered something, were they looking for me?

There were several people in the lobby with the cops; everyone looked upset. I rushed over to the desk, but no one noticed me. Maybe this was about something else.

"What's going on?" I asked the doorman.

"One of the unit owners, he took a baseball bat to the board of directors. They have him in the police car now," he said.

Ruggio saw me, came over.

"What a day," he said, with the air of a diplomat used to working in crisis situations.

"What happened?" I asked.

"There were problems with the old board of directors. We had an election and elected new ones. We had to fire the old manager. He was never here and there was money missing.

"Moss was a friend of the old manager. He just went bonkers and showed up at the board meeting an hour ago with a baseball bat, started swinging. He called everybody 'fags,' grabbed one member by the tie, tried to choke him, yelling at him because he had asked for an audit of last year's records." Ruggio sighed, then added, "It's all under control now."

"You don't seem that upset," I said.

"Running a hundred-and-twenty-unit condo building in West Hollywood is easy for me. Last year I did a hotel in Beirut," he said, shaking his head. He walked off to comfort an upset couple.

I was disappointed that the police weren't here about Dana. I rode up in the elevator with the

Asian model, Johnny. He was dressed in a stylish gray suit on a very hot day.

"I heard about your sister. I'm so sorry," he said.

"Thanks," I mumbled. What to say?

"I'm from a very close family—we're Filipino. I have two brothers and a sister, and I couldn't stand it if something happened to one of them. Were there just the two of you?" he asked.

"Yes," I said, although I thought it was more like one. We were both Dana, living for her.

"I just came from a fashion show and I've got to get out of these clothes, but if I can do anything to help, let me know. I'm in three-forty-five," he said as we got off the elevator.

What could anybody do? Just help me find her killer. On my way to my apartment I ran into Dana's neighbor Micky. He was with not two but three dogs. He had acquired a shelty.

"Hi," he said with exuberance, his tall, lean form leaning forward in greeting, like an exclamation point.

He bent down, petted the gleaming brown shelty.

"This is Dunaway, named after Faye. He wouldn't get off Sunset Boulevard, either, where I found him. He might have wandered down from the Hollywood Hills.

"Good news," he said. "I found out that the West Hollywood City Council says the building can't kick me out for having two dogs because it has been a two-dog building." Then he put a big hand on my shoulder.

"Enough small talk. I heard about Dana, and I'm terribly sorry. I know there isn't anything I can say to make you feel better. I've lost so many friends to AIDS in the last ten years. Every loss is so terribly hard. I'd be happy to cook you dinner, if you need a friend," he said kindly.

"Thank you, Micky," I said, petting all three dogs before he left. Maybe I would get a dog—not that it would replace Dana; that wasn't what it was about. An animal would just be something to love.

I felt alone. Dana had been that point in the geometric circle that you stick your compass on. Everything radiated out from her. Things were halved and quartered according to Dana. She was the beginning and ending emotional reference point for me.

I let myself into my apartment, drained of all feeling. I could never get a dog—that was a ridiculous fantasy. I had nothing left to give. I didn't have an ounce of love left for a pet. Dana's death had depleted me of all that.

I checked my machine—nothing. I went over to Dana's apartment to check hers. I opened the door, then I remembered. Tom had sent the movers. The apartment was completely empty. It felt forlorn. One asparagus fern, struggling for life in an old clay flower pot, was left. Someone must have given it to Dana; she hated plants, and hers always died.

I grabbed it. We could struggle for life together in the ensuing days. Just as the little fern needed light and water to live, I needed Dana. She was my connection, my nutrients, my life-giving fluid all rolled into one.

My world was Dana, when she had been alive. Now I had no world. I was drifting with no anchor. I went back into my apartment, put the flower pot on a stool near the sliding glass door. I poured some bottled water into the soil around the fern, giving it every chance to thrive.

Fatigue gripped me. I lay down on the bed. The phone rang. It was Tom.

"Ariane, I have to see you right now! Whatever you do, don't talk to Lori Wells if she comes to your building. Do you understand me?"

8

Lori Wells? What did Lori Wells want with me? It had to be important if Tom was coming over now. It was only 4 P.M.; he wasn't supposed to pick me up for dinner until later. Was it that urgent?

I looked in my closet, took out a white Fruit of the Loom T-shirt and a black knit jumper. I was so dispirited over today's revelations, I didn't have the energy to wedge my feet into fashionable shoes. I pulled out my old, black high-tops and put them on. I lay down for a few minutes, still exhausted.

Twenty minutes later the intercom buzzed. Was it Tom or Lori Wells? I noticed the intercom had a television screen, technology so you could see your visitor, but the building literature said it wouldn't be operating for a year. If only it were already working.

Should I pick up? I didn't want to miss Tom, but I didn't want to see Lori Wells. The intercom buzzed again, insistently. I picked it up.

"Miss Richardson? A Mr. Crandall here to see you."

"I'll be right down."

Lori Wells must still be in love with Tom. She had probably mistaken me for a competitor and was coming over to scare me off. Maybe she had secretly hated Dana and was happy to hear she was dead. What if Farrington hadn't done it? Could Lori Wells have had anything to do with Dana's death?

Well, she needn't worry about romantic rivalry. I could never get a prize like Tom Crandall, even if I weren't Dana's sister. He deserved the best, like Dana. Even though he thought he had picked Dana, I'm certain she'd seen him across the aisle and sent some special telepathic message in her smile. Once a man had met her, he was hers.

The elevator door opened. Tom rushed over to me, relieved.

"She hasn't been here?" he asked. I started to answer, then broke off. Over his shoulder I saw Lori stride in. She recognized Tom's back and stopped. I pointed to her, and Tom whipped around.

"Lori, we have to talk," he said sternly. She nodded mutely.

"I'll be right back," he said to me. He took Lori's arm, pushed her out the front door. Was I mistaken, or did she give Tom a smirk of triumph as they went through the door, as if she had been the victor in some mysterious battle? He steered her off to the side, out of my sight.

The lady who lived across from Dana's former apartment walked in. She was in her forties, lumpy, wearing shorts and a tennis visor. She was hanging onto the arm of a small man with a gray beard and short, curly gray hair.

She did a double take when she saw me.

"Didn't I see you in the hall recently?" she asked.

"Yes. You thought I was Pink Dot."

"You live here?" she asked.

"Yes. I'm Dana Richardson's sister," I said. Her face clouded over.

"I heard about what happened to her. It's all over the building. I didn't know her that well, but I'm sorry. Oh, by the way, I'm Rhonda, and this is my boyfriend, Rolf. He's a writer."

"Ariane Richardson," I said, and shook their hands.

"What do you write?" I inquired.

"I teach botanists how to write, out at Cal State. But I'm also a director," Rolf said.

"We produce dinner theater together," Rhonda added. I nodded, there was an awkward silence, then they walked toward the stairs.

"I'm sorry again about your sister," Rhonda said.

"The reason I seem so cheery is that I'm on forty milligrams of Prozac," she added. "Nothing can touch me. But I really am sorry," she said, emitting a high-pitched giggle. If she were thinner, she could have been a two-martini, madcap heiress in a thirties movie.

I sat down at a glass table. There were several copies of a free magazine on Beverly Hills. The glossy cover showed a color photograph of a newscaster, his wife and their blended families. I looked through it to see if there were any free grocery coupons but there weren't. Instead there were ads for expensive cars, furs, jewelry and restaurants. All the women looked like Zsa Zsa Gabor.

Through the front windows I saw Tom walk Lori to her car. He didn't open her door for her. She did it herself after nodding once at him. I couldn't see his face, but from his posture he looked angry:

hands in his pockets, legs spread apart, back rigid. He walked back up the driveway.

"I'm sorry," he said when he walked in to the building. "I think you were right. Lori wants to rekindle the relationship. She came here to ask you if we were together. I always seem to get involved with obsessive women. That's why Dana was so different." He was embarrassed.

"Look," he continued, "it's early, so let's drive to the beach and walk around. Then we can go to my favorite dive, a little place on Pacific Coast Highway. You game?"

"Sure," I said, thinking that one place was just as good as another, now that Dana was gone. It was all the same. It was all meaningless. I told him about Farrington fleeing the country. The news seemed to depress him further.

It was sunset. The Santa Monica beach was deserted except for a few large Hispanic families, spread out on blankets and under umbrellas, who weren't going home until the last bit of sunlight had disappeared. Tom pointed to a weathered brown pier in the distance.

"Let's walk to the pier. Give me your shoes," he said, taking his off. I unlaced my high-tops. How had he known that I didn't have the strength to carry those light canvas shoes? He tied the shoe-laces together and threw one shoe over his shoulder. Then he took my hand. I jerked it back, surprised.

"Sorry." He looked at me closely. "You just look so tired, I thought you could use some help," he said.

What to do? If I withheld my hand, that might convey that holding his could mean something to me. Then again, if I gave it to him, I might never be able to get it back. Touch was deadly to me where a man was concerned; that was the first of my desperate attachment.

"Right, sure," I said, putting my hand in his, feeling my face flush. He didn't see; he was already walking toward the pier, half dragging me behind. My hand felt so secure in his, there were no mingled fingers, just his big hand covering my small one.

We walked toward the pier, soldiers of sadness. No one else had experienced what we had recently. Tom led me out to the end of the pier. I stared into the ocean, hoping for the peace that looking at the endless water used to bring me. I felt none. I was aware of a slight breeze tousling my hair for a moment; then I didn't feel it. Tom stepped close to me, cutting off the breeze.

"How was your day?" he finally said.

"Confusing," I replied quietly. I told him of my conversations with Tracy and Detective Martinez. I omitted Dana's culpability in the thefts, because I didn't want to poison his memory of her. I knew Detective Martinez might tell Tom about her part in the scam, but I couldn't bear to.

"So Tracy doesn't expect to hear from Farrington?"

"No. And what if he didn't do it?" I asked.

Tom took a quick step backward in surprise. He looked dubious, then mystified.

"But if he didn't do it, who did?" he asked.

I shrugged, all of a sudden exhausted again. Lori Wells? Someone else? But why would anyone kidnap Dana and keep her for two months? I sighed.

"I don't know," I said, taking my hand back, sitting down on the edge of the pier. He sat down near me, but instead of dangling his feet over the edge like I did, he crossed his legs, put his chin in his hands.

I wanted to ask him about Lori Wells, but I didn't have the nerve. If it had nothing to do with Dana, then it was none of my business. I glanced at him quickly, wondering if he would be receptive to such a question. Probably not.

"Are you going to stay in L.A.?" he asked me.

"I have to, I owe it to Dana. I'll stay until they catch her killer."

"What will you do?"

"I've got to get a job somewhere. I noticed a sign in the window of Ferrara's Italian restaurant in Beverly Hills, for a cashier. And there was also a sign in Super Crown on Wilshire in Santa Monica. So I picked up those two applications."

"Can you use a computer?"

"The minimum."

"How about a calculator?"

"I could certainly try if they teach me."

"What jobs have you had?"

"The usual. At sixteen I was working at Mc-Donald's, usually fast-food places; then the last two years at Nordstrom's, folding clothes."

"How much is your rent, Ariane?"

"Eleven hundred a month."

"Do you want to stay there?"

"It doesn't matter, but it would be good only because people knew Dana there. I might be able to find something out."

"You won't be able to earn enough to live there with those jobs. Didn't you know how expensive it is here when you came from Portland?"

"I had enough saved up for the first and last month's rent, and I thought, I hoped, I'd find Dana . . . alive, and then go home."

"Why don't I loan you the money for your rent?" Tom suggested. I hadn't expected such an offer. I couldn't take it—it would just encourage my dependency. I'd start to imagine Tom as my protector, start to fantasize that he had a romantic interest in me.

"Really," he continued, "it's not much money for me. I'd be doing it for Dana."

"Thanks so much, Tom, but that's okay. I'll be able to get something."

"Well, look, I have an idea. I need an assistant a couple days a week—light typing, filing, phone— at my home office when I'm in Century City. Maybe you could do that until you get hired, or work part-time or something. If you need the money."

"Well, maybe until I get something, if you really need someone, if this isn't a job created just for me."

"No, I'd already called an employment agency a few days ago. Then with all this . . ." He shook his head. "I forgot to follow up."

I didn't really know how to respond. It might be too tantalizing to be with Tom daily. I might start having inappropriate feelings and imagine them to be reciprocal. On the other hand, I would be with someone with whom I could endlessly discuss Dana, a singular opportunity.

Tom stood up and grabbed my hand, pulling me up.

"You think about it and let me know," he said, steering me back down the pier. A seagull flew overhead, soaring into the dusky sky. It looked so free, so light. I knew I would never feel like that again. I was now weighted down by a painful reality; my loss was like a heavy rock around my neck.

"Penny for your thoughts?" Tom asked.

Should I tell him my private thoughts? Before I could censor myself, my words came out in a torrent.

"Oh, Tom, I never want to forget Dana, even for a moment. But I wonder how long a person who feels as bad as I do can keep getting up in the morning," I said, starting to tremble.

"I don't know," I went on. "I mean, when do you just give up? I know I'll hang on until we catch Dana's killer, but I wonder, what then?" My voice trailed off quietly.

Tom looked down into my face. The fading golden sun shone on him like a natural spotlight.

"I feel the same way, Ariane. Maybe you'll discover something else to live for," he said, not moving away. I looked up at him, then looked away quickly, stepping backward.

"Maybe," I said.

"Let's get some dinner," Tom said, heading for his car.

We were silent as he drove. I closed my eyes, breathed in the ocean air. It startled me—I actually smelled it. It was as if my nostrils had been numb for the past few days.

I opened my eyes, too aware that Tom was a few inches away from me. I imagined that Dana must have fallen in love with him immediately. But then, maybe not. Dana never fell that hard. I would have, if I were dating him.

"Here it is," Tom said as he turned off Pacific
Coast Highway. We drove into a parking lot in
front of a Mexican-style cantina whose roof was
decorated with bright Christmas lights. Before I
could release my seat belt, Tom got out and opened
my door for me. He had a fluidity to his movement
that made him almost glide when he walked. He
was graceful for such a big man.

"Thanks," I said, getting out.

"It's kind of funky, almost like a bar in Tijuana.
No, not that bad—maybe a little restaurant in Ma-
zatlán."

"I've never been to Mexico," I said.

"Oh, right," he said as we walked toward the
restaurant. "It lifts my spirits," he continued, "the
silliness of the place. We could use a little of that,
Ariane. Maybe the festivity will help us relax."

Inside The Anchor, it looked like an all-night college party. Sunburned people of all ages were
laughing, eating and drinking. Funky artifacts, beer
labels, inner tubes, colorful lights hung from the
corrugated aluminum roof. T-shirts with the name
of the place were for sale. There was a huge sign
urging patrons to select a designated driver if they
were too tipsy to drive home safely themselves.

The din of laughter and merriment was loud, the
place smelled of Mexican beer. The long rows of
tables had glass tops, under which were stuck
thousands of business cards and messages for the
world to read. The cantina had a wild, uninhibited,
casual feel that, until the recent events, I probably
would have enjoyed.

Tom led me into a line of customers that formed
behind glass cases of salad and fish dishes. There

were two huge blackboards listing the specials of the day.

"Decide what you want and then tell the cashier," he said.

Food choices are bewildering in the midst of a depression. I decided to stick with roast chicken and fried potatoes.

"I'll have the shrimp scampi and a Heineken's," Tom said.

The pretty, blond, tanned cashier turned to me. "What would you like?" she asked with a smile.

"Roast chicken and fried potatoes, please."

"That'll be twenty-four dollars and six cents," she said.

Tom pulled out cash, paid her. Then he led me to a vacant booth overlooking Pacific Coast Highway, from which the whoosh of cars was audible. Beyond the highway was the ocean, just starting to fog in. We sat down.

"This place is so hang loose, it's almost like not being in L.A.," he said. As he drank his beer, I started to eat my chicken and then I looked up. Tom was staring at me. I met his gaze, expecting him to look away, but he didn't. What did it mean? Finally I dropped my eyes in embarrassment. He continued to stare at me.

"You know, I just realized that I feel better when you're around. I don't know if it's because you remind me of Dana, or just because you're who you are, but I do," he said.

I felt a suffusion of warmth and hope! If only I could find another person whom I could entrust my happiness to, like I had with Dana!

Could it be true? Could it be Tom? Did he mean what he'd said in a romantic way?

I felt nervous, wondering if he would go on. Apparently not. He dug into his shrimp scampi with relish. I tried to smile. He took a bite, swallowed it, then put his fork down.

"Yes, that's it, I do feel better when you're around. I just realized it. There's something about you, Ariane, that I'm attracted to. But I feel guilty saying that. Don't hate me," he said, choking up, quickly looking out at the sea.

Everything seemed hyper-real for a moment. Colors were very bright; all noises were amplified; I felt the heat from his body even though he was across the table. Tom seemed larger than anyone else in the place. I wanted to speak, but I was afraid I could not control the modulation of my voice. I remained silent.

He looked down at his plate, then up at me. His eyes seemed to magnetize and hold me, and for a moment I felt I was completely under his control. I hoped he couldn't see the effect he was having on me. Suddenly he reached over, took my hand.

"Do you feel any of this, Ariane? Please be truthful. I need to know. Am I crazy, or is there some sort of mutual attraction?"

I was scared silent. There was such an attraction—if he only knew! But what could he see in me, the younger, lesser, much less interesting sister of Dana? And was it fair to Dana's memory?

"Ariane, did you hear me?" he asked.

"Yes," I whispered. "I—I—don't know what to say, Tom . . ."

"Of course. I understand," he said, visibly disappointed. I started to panic. Dana had always told me you never get a second chance. Should I seize the moment?

This is a man I could never even have hoped to meet, if it hadn't been for the special circumstances that brought us together. What if his attraction to me was only because I reminded him of Dana? But that wasn't so terrible. In fact, it was a compliment!

All my life I had been looking for someone besides Dana to give myself to. I knew that someday she would move on, get married, and then I would be alone. None of that had happened because she hadn't had the chance. But the end result was the same, I was alone.

Wouldn't Dana want me to be under the protection of the man she had loved? (If she had loved him, but how could she not have?) If she'd loved him, wouldn't she want him to be happy? And I could make him happy, I knew that. I would devote myself to him, minute by minute, hour by hour, if he were mine.

So much had happened in the past ten days, I needed time to think. I felt I was falling down a well, going faster and faster, trying to stop but not being able to catch onto anything.

I felt a loss of gravity even though I knew I was grounded, sitting in a wooden booth in a Malibu restaurant. Then I felt like I was in the middle of some powerful centrifugal force. I took a deep breath, got my bearings. Luckily, Tom was staring at the ocean, hadn't noticed my discomfort. He finally turned toward me.

"I think I've lost my enthusiasm for L.A. It seemed like such a grand idea to move out here from New York, try something new, create new opportunities," he said.

"Now it feels like the city is in a shroud of death. People seem threatening somehow; the possibility of finding joy here seems remote. Maybe I'll go back to New York, or try some place completely new, once this is all over. Los Angeles is ruined for me." He drank some of his beer.

"I feel the same way," I said, relieved and disappointed that we were on a safer subject matter. "It sounds silly, but I planned to reinvent myself here as Ariane. I was going to say I was from somewhere in the Pacific Northwest, not Portland, not the little town we were actually from, Scappoose. Did Dana ever mention it?"

"No, she said she was from Portland."

"I thought so. I never dreamed I'd want to go back there, but now I kind of do. That's where we were raised, so maybe I can live the rest of my life with memories, looking at the schoolhouse we went to, the corner drugstore we hung out at, to keep reassuring myself that Dana existed."

"Have you ever been anywhere else?" he asked.

"No. When I came to L.A., it was the first time I'd ever flown. Dana and I had some big dreams about going to Europe. It sounded so exciting when she read to me from her travel books.

"We pictured ourselves watching the changing of the Guard in London, hanging out at cafes in Paris, taking gondola rides in Venice. Now I could never do any of that—it would take too much energy to even make the plane reservations."

"It all seems flat now, no more limitless possibilities, right?" Tom asked.

"Right," I said.

He was contemplative for a moment. "How about going somewhere this weekend, a driving trip?" he suggested. "Big Sur, Santa Barbara, Las Vegas—anywhere you want to go would be fine.

It would take our minds off things—at least for a while.

"Just as friends, two rooms, I'd have the pleasure of your company," he added.

It was so tempting, a whole weekend with Tom! But could I trust myself to remain just friends? I had no self-control when it came to men, almost any man, this one for sure. I'd melt on him the first night, scare him away, shame Dana's memory.

In my imagination, I saw my body outlined in white, hollow inside, fitting into his hollow, bigger, white-outlined body, eclipsed by it, no longer responsible for my own movement. When he moved his arm, mine followed suit. When he took a step forward, so did I.

Even more important, in this daydream all my feelings were dependent on his. I was truly part of a whole, freed from the horrible responsibility of making my own happiness. If he was happy, I was happy. If he laughed, so did I. I had ceased to exist as Ariane; I was now part of Tom. What a relief.

"What do you say?" he asked, jerking me back to reality. I prayed he wasn't a mind reader. Did every woman long for true, complete union, or were my needs to merge excessive?

Whom could I ask? What woman would be honest enough to reveal her true desires? Karina? Sara? I tried to focus on our conversation.

"Big Sur?" I mumbled.

"I think you'd love it. I always stay at a beautiful old log-cabin lodge; it's been there forever. It's not luxurious, but it has atmosphere. The hiking around Big Sur is wonderful, and the views of the ocean are breathtaking."

"Is it far?"

"Several hours, but we could drive up the coast highway—you wouldn't be bored for a moment."

"That sounds . . . exciting. I've never been anywhere like that."

"If I could take the time off, we could even go on to San Francisco. Or we could go to Santa Barbara, hang out by the beach, walk around, see a movie," he said. I was silent.

"I just really need to get away. I usually go off alone, but because of . . . everything that's happened, I don't really want to be alone. I could be, but it wouldn't be my first choice. What do you say, Ariane?"

"If I'm not working, I'd like to. I . . . probably won't be working by this weekend. I'm going to start applying at places tomorrow," I said, not really sure if I had said yes.

Maybe getting away would help me, give me a fresh perspective.

But I knew myself. I wanted to go away with Tom because I was attracted to him, because I was filled with a palpable desire for him. I thirsted for him like a dying man in the desert thirsts for water, like a starving man hungers for food.

Wasn't that what life was about? Connection, communion, togetherness, love. But was it about all those things with your dead sister's boyfriend? I was filled with beanbags, so off kilter that if they tipped over, so would I. I wondered if I looked as jangled as I felt. Was my sense of unease evident?

"Ariane," Tom said, "do you think we have a destiny from the day we're born?"

"I don't know. Do you mean, is our life all laid out, so that we can have no influence on it?"

"No, not the individual events, not the specifics,

just how we'll end up, our ultimate fate."

"You mean, was it Dana's fate to die young?"

"Right, or is it our fate to wind up ... however we do?"

"I don't know. I guess I like to think you can change your destiny." Maybe I wouldn't have to turn myself over to him, body and soul.

"Then it's not destiny."

"You're right. Maybe I don't believe in destiny. Do you believe you fell in love with Dana because of destiny?"

"I do. And now she's gone." He looked down sadly. "I believe destiny is everything, Ariane."

9

We finished dinner, walked out to the car. Somehow Tom seemed larger and I felt smaller than when we had walked in. I kept reminding myself that we were going on the weekend trip as "friends."

Tom was preoccupied on the ride home; he didn't notice the constant traffic jams. Night had fallen, and the sky was clear, dark. He drove around one deep curve on Sunset so fast that his wheels skidded. He looked from one side of the boulevard to the other.

"That's Dead Man's Curve. Have you ever heard of it?" Tom asked.

"No," I said. The name gave me a chill. "Why do they call it that?"

"A lot of people have died making the turn— they flip over. I think a couple of famous singers crashed their motorcycles there, among others. Maybe Jan and Dean. It always gives me a thrill to drive it."

"Why?"

"I'm a risk taker in my business, in the stock market. Risk gets my adrenaline flowing," he said. "Maybe I should have been a race-car driver or an Olympic skier. I love the rush of downhill skiing.

140

I wish life could be lived just for the highs."

"That's how Dana felt," I said. "She only wanted to live in exciting times. She tried to block everything else out." He seemed to be going too fast again, or maybe I was just nervous. The speedometer went up to eighty.

"Tom, aren't we going a little fast?"

"Oh, sorry, I didn't mean to scare you, Ariane," he said, slowing down. "Guess I was just blowing off steam. I feel like I've been in a pressure cooker. I have a tendency to speed, always have to watch it."

He pulled up before my building. "So I'll pick you up Friday. Let me know if you hear from the police. I'm going to try to get in touch with that PI I hired. I haven't been able to reach him. You okay?" he asked.

"Sure," I said. I smiled at him, then got out of the car and entered the building. I was lost in thoughts of what might soon be as I approached the elevator. A well-dressed older couple got in behind me.

The woman had obviously been a beauty in her youth, and she still had a charming, sweet smile. She had brown, curly hair; was wearing a white silk, off-the-shoulder blouse and a black silk skirt. Shoes and purse matched. Her handsome husband wore a black tux; he had a thick shock of silver hair.

"Aren't you . . . Dana's sister?" she asked.

"Yes," I said.

"We're terribly sorry. I'm Esther, this is Bill. We didn't know her well, but she was always very polite."

"Thank you."

"Bill's a pianist—he plays at dances, concerts. Will you come up for tea one day? He'll play for you. Apartment five-oh-six," she said.

The elevator door opened and I got out. "Thanks, I will," I said.

A good-looking Hispanic man dressed in tennis whites passed me in the hall. He had the smile of a debonair greeter at a restaurant.

"Hi, darling," he said in a free-spirited, chivalrous way as he passed, swinging his racket. I wished I knew him. I just wanted to hang out with someone, to not be alone. He continued down the hall.

I didn't want to go to bed yet. It was too early. I took a chance, knocked on Sara's door.

"Who's there?" she asked.

"Ariane."

"Coming," she said, then opened the door. She was in a black body stocking and a blue-flowered dress. She held a script in her hand.

"Hi, you have a few minutes?" I asked.

"Sure, how you doing?" She waved me in, slammed the door.

"Okay, I guess. But it's hard," I said, sinking down on her low green couch.

"I can't imagine what you're going through," she said, sitting on the floor cross-legged, inhaling quick puffs of her cigarette. A tape played, describing "The Tower of Song" in the background.

"Who's that?"

"Leonard Cohen, my favorite," she said. I liked it; the mournful lament fit my mood.

Sara scooted near me, looked up at me. "Have they questioned Farrington?" she asked.

"No," I said.

"I remember that time I met him," she said. "I thought he was really good-looking. I was attracted to him. So I figured something must be wrong with him."

"Why, Sara?"

"Because I'm kind of a freak magnet. Freaks like me, weirdos adore me. I never find out until it's too late. Guys who like me are practically certifiable—not my boyfriend now, but usually."

I hadn't noticed I was silent until she spoke again.

"You're deep in thought, aren't you?" she asked.

"Yeah, I guess I am. My head has been spinning ever since I got off the plane. So much has happened, everything seems speeded up in L.A."

"This place seems slow to me," she said. "I was raised in the Village, in Manhattan. But I picked the television industry, which moves at a breakneck speed, and the constant hysteria reminds me of home."

"Sara, do you believe in destiny?" I asked her.

"Destiny?" she said, laughing. I was embarrassed.

"I guess it does sound strange. It's kind of upsetting, but I think I'm beginning to get involved with Dana's last boyfriend, Tom. He asked me if I believed in destiny. Do you think it's wrong to go out with him?"

"One of Dana's lovers?"

"Yes. He seemed to love her very much. This has never happened before. In all our teenage years, Dana and I never dated the same guy, even years apart. That's why this is so odd."

"That you could be attracted to someone Dana was attracted to?"

"No, that he could be attracted to me. Dana was so much prettier, so much smarter. I could never hold a candle to her."

"I don't think that's true. Dana was fantastic, but so are you. You've both got that wholesome Oregon look, that healthy vibrancy."

"We always hated that. My idol is Bette Davis, in all those old movies. I wish I smoked. I'd like to be small and smoky like you," I said. Sara laughed. I smiled; it felt good to smile. Her phone rang, she grabbed it.

"Hello? Oh, hi, babe. Right. I'll be ready in half an hour. Bye," she said, hanging up.

"The BF—boyfriend. Gotta get ready." She jumped up, throwing the script down.

"I'm glad you stopped by, Ariane. And really, I am so sorry about Dana. If I can do anything, please let me know. We'll go out for lunch next week, okay?"

"That would be great," I said. I went back to my apartment. I opened the door slowly. I didn't know what I was anticipating, but my nerves were on edge. I turned the lights on, everything was fine. But there was that horrible stillness.

I felt let down. I realized that I was a reactive person, alive when I was with others, but hollow and empty alone. Life had never been as full of feeling as when I'd been with Dana. I felt there was the potential for the same excitement with Tom.

It was as if I needed a certain type of fuel to ignite my life force. Without it, I was a Fourth of July sparkler that wouldn't light up, that wouldn't do what it was meant to do.

How to defeat the stillness? Who else could I visit? The clock said 8 P.M. I was restless, uneasy.

It was probably too late to knock on any other doors. I wished I could call Tom; hearing his voice would revitalize me. But I couldn't. None of the usual pastimes quieted my echoes of terror. Music, television, reading—none of those filled me up.

Karina. I quickly dialed her number. No answer. Was she across the street at the hotel bar? Perhaps, but I didn't want to go over there. Was there anyone else? Tracy? No, I couldn't call her. The walls seemed to close in on me, and I began to think I could smell that musty odor from Scappoose.

I decided to go for a walk in the neighborhood, it looked safe enough. At least I would be surrounded by people. I went down to the front desk.

"Which way would I walk for shops or restaurants or whatever?" I asked Ricardo, the man on the desk tonight.

"Go down this way"—he pointed to the right— "then left at the corner, then right on the main street, La Cienega. If you walk a few blocks you'll see the malls—the Beverly Center, very big, very fancy. The other, the Beverly Connection, is across the street, very nice."

"Thanks," I said, then headed out the door toward Holloway. Many dog-walkers were walking their pets. I counted two wirehaired fox terriers, two schnauzers, a miniature Doberman pinscher, a King Charles spaniel and a boxer before I reached the corner. Someone was singing opera from a nearby window as I negotiated the crosswalk. She was having trouble with the high notes.

Every parked car looked occupied. But when I looked closer, I realized they were empty. People had put T-shirts on the drivers' seats, and red clubs were attached to the steering wheels to prevent car theft.

The Beverly Center was a tall gray mall with its parking structure on the top floors. A brightly colored escalator ran along one side of the building. I walked in and wandered through some department stores, expensive boutiques. I tried on fancy sunglasses in one store.

Because I was alone, I began to feel self-conscious. I took the elevator up a floor, went toward the cinema. There were several movies playing.

The crowd waiting to get tickets was composed of families, European tourists, groups of friends, I was relieved to see, not just twosomes. I picked a suspense film, bought a ticket, went in. The screening room was small and narrow and made me anxious. I was hoping for one of those huge, old-fashioned movie theaters. This was precise and minimalist. Once again I felt I was on display.

The lights went down. I tried to concentrate on the movie, but I couldn't keep my mind on the story. All my thoughts were of Dana, of Tom. Every time the movie heroine was in danger, I thought of Dana, wishing I had been there to protect her from harm. In every romantic scene I pictured myself as the heroine with Tom as my love interest.

It was obvious I had wasted my money; I couldn't enjoy a film. Halfway through, I got up and left. I hadn't managed to escape from my problems in any way tonight, but at least I had killed some time.

I joined the crowd waiting for the glass elevator that went down on the outside of the building.

When it finally came, we all crowded in. Being shoved to the back of the elevator between two people in Levi's jackets was the closest I had come to connection that night.

It felt good to be sandwiched between two sets of shoulders. I closed my eyes, enjoyed it. The elevator door opened, and some of the crowd lurched forward; the rest of us stayed inside.

The door closed again and we began our descent. I was close to the glass now, so I looked down. Right beneath me, walking on the sidewalk, were a man and a woman. There was something familiar about them as they strolled arm in arm. I looked closer—it was Tom and Lori Wells!

What was going on? I had assumed Tom had gone home after he dropped me off. Hadn't he just seen Lori Wells? Was their relationship romantic after all? I watched them until they disappeared from sight into the crowd. The elevator door opened, and I made sure I went out the exit in the opposite direction from them. I was too afraid to follow them—what would I say if I discovered Tom had lied to me?

I walked home, feeling disoriented. Nothing was as it seemed. I tried to shut down, to shut out all thought and feeling. I achieved a partial numbness by the time I reached my apartment building. I felt more alone than I had earlier today. I had invested heavily in the idea of Tom as my lover. Now that seemed like a foolish dream. There was no mistaking what I had seen.

I walked slowly up the driveway, unable to muster the energy for speed, because speed implied hope. How could I even have thought about romance when I had just lost Dana?

Of course Tom could never be interested in me.
I couldn't hold his interest long-term anyway. He
could do so much better than someone like me.
People are more vulnerable when they've had a
loss. He'd probably been drawn to me in a moment
of weakness. Better not to be a one-day, one-night
or one-weekend stand anyway, if I was just going
to get dumped.

I dragged myself into the building, happy for the
assistance of the elevator. I couldn't have walked
up even one flight of stairs. Depression flattened
me. No matter what else is going on in my life, if
I have a romantic fantasy, I can survive. Without
one I am anxious, hopeless.

If I am infatuated with someone, I can appear
perfectly attuned to my surroundings and whom-
ever I am talking to, while secretly thinking about
the object of my desire. Nothing else seems to matter; it's all background to my thoughts of men.

I don't know if my hormones are out of whack,
or if my thought processes are askew, or if I'm en-
tirely normal and all women think like this. I had
never confessed this minute-by-minute, daily obsession to anyone, except to Dana.

I went into my apartment, sat in the dark, mo-
rose, for an hour. Tears trickled out of my eyes. I
didn't want to feel this way anymore, to be used
this way, I wanted to be strong. The phone rang
and I picked it up. Tom!

"Have you been home all evening?" he asked
me.

"Yes," I lied.

"So have I," he lied, too.

"I just wanted you to know," he said, "that I
made a reservation at the Big Sur Inn for Friday

night. That's the place I told you about. Be sure to pack a sweater, because the coast is cold at night."

"That sounds great," I said, wondering why he wanted to take me away for the weekend if he was involved with Lori Wells. Or was he? Why had he lied? What else had he lied about? Anything?

"I'll pick you up at noon on Friday—let's get an early start." Then he added, "Oh, and, Ariane?"

"Yes?"

"I'm really looking forward to it," he said.

I sank onto my bed fully clothed. It was too much to figure out. What did it matter anyway? Dana was dead. We were not going to be wives, mothers or European expatriates together. I would probably be none of those on my own. Men found me very resistible. At least before when they dumped me, I had Dana for backup.

I suddenly realized how scary my situation was now. If I got involved in a relationship and got dumped, thrown away like trash, there would be no Dana to prop me up, to make me believe in tomorrows. How would I find the strength in myself to survive?

I tossed and turned, trying to get comfortable. Eventually I tried my last-ditch "get to sleep" trick. I stretched flat out on my back and put my arms over my head on my pillow. I focused all my energy on balancing my weight equally on the bed. I tried to feel the sensation of floating, feeling as if I were suspended in midair.

Then I pretended I was being rocked to sleep in a giant hammock of air, gently, very gently caressed by a slight breeze. I had no connections to the world, nothing dragging me down, no weighty feelings. I was light-headed, free.

I began to drift into sleep. Sometime later I began to dream. I dreamed I was a tiny white baby bird nesting in that big pine tree in back of our house in Scappoose. I had just broken out of my shell a few hours before, and I was still wet and cold. My mother was nowhere to be seen; she was probably out foraging for food. My brothers and sisters were still in their shells, but one was beginning to pick at its shell.

I took my first steps. I was shaky, almost fell. By using great concentration, I was able to climb out of the nest and fall onto a big branch. I saw something fluttering at the end of the branch, a delicate black-and-yellow butterfly. It was so pretty, I wanted to get closer.

I staggered out to the end of the branch just as it started to fly away. I stretched out my wing to touch it, lost my balance and began to fall. Down, down I spiraled, over and over, the ground coming up fast. I was going to die almost as soon as I had been born.

I so regretted my foolishness. Why had I tottered to the end of the branch? My curiosity was going to kill me. It was all going to be over just as it was beginning.

I felt radiations of heat from the ground. I curled quickly into a ball, hugged my wings to my sides, hoping death would not be too painful. Then all of a sudden a huge white, lacy gossamer wing enveloped me like a cradle, swooping me out of danger.

I uncurled in amazement, peeking at the creature with the glorious wing from under my own scrawny wing. I could hardly stare into its face, it shone with such radiance. And then I realized it was Dana: she was a beautiful angel.

She carried me carefully in her wings as she flew me back up to my tree.

"Don't take any more chances," she said in a high-pitched, melodious voice while she placed me in my nest.

She brushed some dirt off my feathers, said, "I love you, Paula Jean," then flew up into the sky. I watched her until she became a tiny white speck. I shuddered, now that she was gone. While she had been with me, I had felt a sense of union and peace.

The alarm went off. Maybe I'd been dreaming for a second, maybe all night. I woke up, called Detective Martinez to see if there was any news of Farrington. Martinez was out.

I got dressed, drove into Beverly Hills. I had observed the cashier in Ferrara's when I saw the HELP WANTED sign. She wore black and white, so I dressed the same way. I asked for the manager; someone pointed me toward a harried woman rushing around. I smiled, handed her my application.

"Great. I'll read it over and call you Monday," she said. I thanked her, started to walk back to the car. As I turned a corner, I saw Tracy get out of her car, go into a store a few yards away. I rushed ahead and entered the crowded shop behind her.

I saw her buy something at a counter. As I walked toward her, I looked around. The place was a travel agency. I quickly ducked to the back, out of sight.

I strained to hear where she was going, but there was too much noise. It took her quite a while to complete her purchase. I knew that she wouldn't welcome my questions. I wondered if the travel

agent would tell me her destination after she left.
Probably not.

Finally Tracy finished, pocketed her ticket and
turned to leave. Just before she reached the door,
she stopped at a rack of travel brochures. She
reached for one, put it in her purse. I quickly mem-
orized the placement of the slot. It was third from
the left, fourth from the top. I buried my face in a
magazine until she left. Then I ran over to the rack,
grabbed a pamphlet out of the same slot. It was a
brochure on Spain!

Spain. She was going to join Farrington. Had her
distress been an act? Had they planned Dana's
murder together? I rushed out to a pay phone,
called Detective Martinez, but he was still away
from the office.

What to do? I called information. Karina was
listed. I dialed the number. She picked up, said I
could come over.

I drove to her guest house. The family was home;
children and a golden retriever played by the pool.
She let me in. I quickly told her what I had just
found out.

"Can you go visit Tracy? Would she tell you anything?"

"Visit Tracy? But she doesn't like me. Now that
she was fired, she would never talk to me," Karina
said.

"Look, my sister was murdered. We have to do
something. If Detective Martinez doesn't check it
out, will you please go with me Monday to see
Tracy—if she hasn't left and Detective Martinez
hasn't reached her? It's for Dana, Karina."

"Yes, all right, I will come with you," she said.
"By the way, yesterday a PI came to me, said he

was hired by Tom Crandall. Maybe it is because I do not speak English so perfectly, but he seemed very crazy, very stupid."

"I know. I met him, too. I think Tom is going to get someone else," I said.

"Magnum, he was a smart PI on the TV. There must be a smarter detective person," she said.

"You're right," I agreed, told her I'd call her on Monday. I got home, Detective Martinez had called. I returned his call, told him about Tracy. He said he would look into it.

"Will you be around this weekend?" he asked.

"No, I'll be out of town."

"Where will you be?"

"I'm going away for the weekend with . . . Tom Crandall," I said, feeling embarrassed. I didn't know why I felt funny telling him. I owed the detective no explanation.

"You're going away with Tom Crandall? Socially?" he asked. I felt flustered.

"Well, not really socially, not like that. We just both really need to get away. All of this has been. . . . hard."

"I wouldn't get too involved with any of your sister's friends until we solve this murder, Miss Richardson. Remember, she could have been killed by someone she knew, and it might not have been Farrington."

I was outraged that he suspected Tom, but I remembered what Tom had said. Then again, how much did I know about him? What about Lori?

"Thank you for the advice," I said.

"Call me when you get back."

"I will."

I sat down, pulled out an old photo album I had

brought with me. I had thought that Dana would enjoy it when we were reunited. Now that would never happen. I turned page after page. I had pasted every photo ever taken of Dana and me in it.

I looked at the pictures of our mother. We really didn't look much like her, yet we looked alike. We always thought of this as evidence that we had the same father. After our mother died, we quizzed our relatives, hoping maybe someone would know the truth. No one did.

I put on my Lanz nightgown, which made me feel secure, like when I was a little girl. Dana and I favored the navy blue Lanz nightgowns. As I was pulling it down, my eyes fell on that butterfly birthmark.

How Dana and I used to compare our birthmarks. We measured them, traced them, reproduced them, always happy that they were identical. Now Dana's delicate birthmark was just ashes like the rest of her.

I was so sad that I was almost afraid to be alone. I hoped I could last till tomorrow. If I could feel again, maybe I could feel with Tom—if he was all he seemed. That was the only hope there was now.

❧ 10 ❧

I opened my eyes to the sound of an old Stevie Nicks song coming in through the air vent. I chose to keep the bedroom dark like a cave, the one window completely covered so I couldn't tell if the sun was up yet. I turned over, put the digital clock facedown. It was already nine o'clock. Another day that Dana couldn't have, another day that I was stuck with.

I didn't dare hope that my romantic fantasy of Tom would come true. When he'd said he was attracted to me, it was probably a passing fancy. He was vulnerable, confused, in the midst of a crisis. Maybe he liked both Lori and me. Did he really know what he was feeling and saying?

Besides, what good could ever happen to me now? I used to think that Dana was born lucky. If I stayed close to her, I thought I could share her luck. Now it was apparent that neither of us had good luck, that Dana had had the worst luck of all.

I got dressed, hoping I could bring Tom some comfort, if that was what he wanted. Yes, I could bring happiness to Tom, who loved Dana; that would be my reason to live, no matter what he thought of me, even if he was still involved with Lori.

There was no way he could have been responsible for Dana's murder. I was becoming paranoid from stress. I would devote myself to Tom. I was in service to Dana rather than to myself. It was the least I could do, for her memory.

Tom was probably dreading the weekend. After all, I was not Dana, not even a good substitute. Alone, he could remember their private times together. My presence might not comfort Tom; instead it might remind him that Dana was impossible to replace.

I packed a small overnight case. The thought did cross my mind that I should pack a decent nightgown and robe, but I pushed it away. I threw my Lanz nightgown in, sure the weekend would be one just as "friends."

I took the elevator down to the lobby. There were new white orchids in a big black glass vase. The postman was putting mail in the mailboxes, and tenants gathered around, waiting for him to finish. I noticed that attractive older couple, the pianist and his wife, holding hands while they waited for the mail. It was sweet; they had probably spent most of their lives together. Was that type of commitment and continuity a relic of past generations, or was it still possible?

Tom pulled up. I grabbed my bag, walked out to the car. He jumped out, threw the bag in the trunk.

"Ready for adventure?" he asked as we drove down the driveway.

"I guess. I haven't really had many adventures," I said. I used to think that great adventures happened in that attic of ours in Scappoose, that attic where I would see my mother with men. But I was not allowed up there, so I imagined most of my great adventures. The only hopes I had for real ones were with Dana.

"I'm going to take you for lunch in Santa Barbara," Tom said. "It's a little detour on the way to Big Sur, but I want you to see it. There's a beautiful old hotel there, recently modernized, where we'll eat. I've had some meetings there."

I liked Tom's decisiveness. He was never vague or unsure of what to do. He was like Dana. He could visualize a plan and execute it. I could plan to do something, then spend the whole day lost in a daydream.

He reached over, handing me my shoulder-harness seat belt. When he pulled it down, I felt the warmth of his arm graze my shoulder.

"I don't want you falling out," he said protectively as he pulled onto the freeway. "I've never seen so many bad drivers as in L.A. Every person I know that gets rear-ended, gets rear-ended by someone without insurance. You see people driving with doors and fenders literally hanging off their cars."

Tom was the leader on the freeway, moving at a steady clip. If he encountered a slower car, he swiftly passed it. I leaned back in my seat, happy to cede to him control of my life for the weekend.

"How did your job search go?"

"I turned in my applications, they said they'd call."

"Well, once Farrington is returned, it could take several months before he goes to trial. You'll be here for quite a while. If those jobs don't work out, I really meant what I said about doing temp work for me. At least till you find your niche."

"That would be great."

"I almost had to go into financial planning—that's what my father did. I still think of him when I work, even though he's dead."

"How long ago did he pass away?"

"A year ago."

"Oh, I didn't know it was that recent. I'm sorry," I said. Tom had an odd look on his face, not sorrow, not grief. Was it anger? Was he angry that his father had died, left him?

"Do you miss him? I bet you were close."

"Actually, we never got along that well. I got in some trouble when I was young that my dad never really forgave me for. He was a real straight arrow, or at least that's what everyone thought—that's what he wanted them to think."

"You mean he wasn't?"

"I don't know," Tom said, shrugging. "He was so sanctimonious, so righteous. He couldn't have been as perfect as he pretended to be."

"What kind of trouble did you get into?" I asked.

"Kid stuff," he said, looking embarrassed.

"What?" I asked.

"Oh," he said, looking sheepish, "I worked at this popular restaurant called The Wharf."

"The Wharf? There's a restaurant in Seattle called The Wharf. My friends used to take vacations in Seattle and eat there."

"Really?" he said, surprised. "Well, this one is in New York, kind of a yuppie lunch place on the East Side. A lot of places have names of locations that aren't in Manhattan. There's Jackson Hole for hamburgers, and a bunch of restaurants named after places in France."

"There's probably a million Wharves," I said.

"At least a hundred," he said, smiling.

"So what did you do wrong there?"

"Just got involved with a group of older, bad kids. They were stealing from the restaurant, forging credit cards. It had been going on for a while."

"Forging credit cards?"

"When someone ordered food to go, we took his credit card, punched in our I.D. number and rang up the sale. Then the credit card was approved. They got a copy of the receipt and so did we. A few hours later, we'd punch in the credit card number again and charge ten bucks to it, as if they came back for a side order. We'd open the drawer and pocket the ten. The only way we'd get caught was if the credit card company noticed the discrepancies. Unfortunately, after about six months, they did.

"We didn't do it that often, but it was foolish. We were young, we made a big mistake. If we had just stolen money, that would have been bad enough, but we got involved in credit card fraud."

"What happened to you?"

"My father was furious. He wanted to let me be defended by a public defender, said he didn't care if I went to prison, or the equivalent for adolescents. Some friends of his owned the restaurant, which made it worse—he had gotten me the job.

"But my mother prevailed. They hired a good criminal lawyer for me. I was so nervous the day of the trial, I thought I would pass out. The lawyer got me off. I had to do some community service, report to a probation officer for a year. That was it. My police record was sealed because I was a juvenile.

"I got off easy, but it scared me. My father never

forgave me. He insisted I did it to get back at him. But I was just a kid. I just wanted money—at least that's what I thought," he said.

"Were you close to your dad before all this happened?" I asked.

"Not really. In a way, he blamed me just for being born," Tom said.

"What do you mean?"

"It's a long story—you don't want to hear it." He sighed. "Besides, we're going away to forget all the heavy stuff—we're supposed to try to have fun. Let's steer away from family dramas, unless you want to tell me yours."

"Definitely not. You're right, let's change the subject," I said, looking out the window, turning my attention to the freeway scenery. I couldn't stop wondering what he had meant, though, about his father blaming him for being born.

"Do you like car trips?" he asked.

"I don't know. Honestly, I haven't been on that many. When Dana and I were little, occasionally our mother drove us to Portland to go shopping or for a doctor's appointment. It was a short trip, but it seemed awfully long when I was five. I used to have to stop to go to the bathroom at least twice, and my mother got angry at me. Dana would bring my Etch-A-Sketch to distract me, or sometimes we'd play games. The only other car trips I went on were a couple of ski vacations to Mount Hood."

"Well, this is going to be a little more exciting than those. At least I hope so," Tom said.

He didn't seem depressed about Dana anymore. But why? Maybe he was just putting up a front to cheer me up. Was he excited to be with me? But how could he be when he was mourning Dana?

Did he put his grief in one part of his mind, tuck it away? Was he so out of touch that he could have a breakdown at any minute? I wished I knew him better so I could fathom what was going on in his mind.

"I know you must be wondering if I'm still mourning Dana," he said.

"How do you know what I'm thinking?" I asked, frightened.

"It would only be natural, given the circumstances. Look," he said, turning for a moment to look at me, "I feel every bit as bad as you do. I'm just afraid that if we both show our grief, the weight of it will be too much for us to bear. I've always tried to live life for the moment, because I know the past can never be recaptured. It's gone forever. I'm trying to remember that, because if I don't, I could be lost," he said sadly.

"I understand, Tom. You don't owe me an explanation. But thank you for telling me that," I said.

He could separate the past from the present. How I envied him. The past was always choking me, like the gnarled roots of that tree we used to climb as kids. Before Dana died, I lived in the past half of the time. Now I lived in some kind of twilight time, unable to return to the past or to move forward and lose Dana. I had to struggle to get back to the present, to remember where I was.

Tom opened a CD case, took one out, slipped it into his player.

"Do you like Anita Baker? I'm wild about her," he said. Her beautiful voice came out of the speakers.

"She's terrific," I agreed. The song was a torch

song, slow, sexy. Was this who he was when the lights went down, when animal rhythms took over? I tried not to think about that. I tried not to feel Anita Baker's sensual strains.

Tom seemed calmed by the music. At times he joined in with the songs, all of which he knew by heart. Almost as soon as the music ended, he pulled off the freeway.

"We're here," he said, pointing to a town ahead of us. Tom drove along the ocean; surfers were visible in the distance

"This is is," he said, turning into a wide driveway that led to a magnificent, traditional Spanish-style hotel. A valet rushed up to take our car.

Tom opened my door, helped me out. He stood looking at me for a moment. I was puzzled; what was he looking at? Was he comparing me with Dana? Was he going to change his mind, drive me back to L.A.?

Suddenly he reached out, touched my face.

"You look so pure and innocent. Forgive me, Ariane, but I feel like taking a room right here for the weekend and locking you in."

I must have looked stunned. Tom grabbed my shoulders.

"Hey, what's wrong? I just mean you're very tempting. You must know how appealing you are," he said.

Really, I didn't. Maybe it was my youth he found appealing, I was twelve years younger than he. Even though Dana had been ten years his junior, she had been more sophisticated, worldly wise.

"Ariane, did I say something wrong?" he asked, upset.

"No, no, I'm just not myself . . . with all that's happened."

"Well, exactly who are you?" he asked, smiling. I wished I knew. At that moment I felt like a fragile balloon that could collapse on him at any moment.

Tom led me into the hotel lobby. It was spacious, with beautiful wood paneling, high ceilings. It was filled with wealthy, middle-aged people checking in and out. Many of the men wore white pants and pastel jackets. The crowd was much different from that in West Hollywood.

We walked into the restaurant. A maître d' led us to a table under a bright skylight, handed us menus. Everyone was drinking Bloody Marys.

"The eggs Benedict are good," Tom said.

"That sounds fine," I said, having no idea what they were. Tom called a waiter over, ordered for both of us.

"Some champagne for the lady?" the waiter inquired.

"No, thank you. I don't drink."

"Why don't you have some champagne? It's good," Tom urged.

"All right." I relented; maybe it would help me relax.

The waiter poured us each a glass. Tom looked at his for a moment, then raised it.

"Here's to you, Ariane. You are one brave girl. You came to L.A. to find Dana, and you didn't know a single person here. You got the worst possible news, yet you're staying to see this thing through. I take my hat off to you—or would if I had one."

"What else can I do? This is my only option," I said.

"It's the only option you see because you are who you are," he said in an admiring tone. He motioned for me to raise my glass, clicked his against mine. We each took a sip of our champagne. I had never tasted it before; it was bubbly, sweet.

"Here's to a weekend you'll remember," Tom said. Little did he know that I remembered every instant I had been with him since we met. Tom's eyes narrowed; he was looking at something over my shoulder.

"Tom?" a woman said, walking up to him. She was about thirty-five, an aging sex kitten wearing a tight black mini T-shirt, which showed her tanned midriff, and a pair of tight jeans. She had big black hair that cascaded down her back. She carried a small khaki-colored, army-surplus purse and wore black Doc Marten boots. She might have been attractive, but she was in clothes much too young for her.

"Tom?" she said again. "Don't you remember me? It's Amber."

He was upset. He reluctantly stood up, as if it galled him to have to be polite to her.

"Amber, sure. I wasn't certain it was you. How have you been?" he said, offering his hand. She looked at it, confused, then shook it. It seemed she had expected a warmer greeting.

"Can I sit down?" she asked, motioning to a vacant chair.

"Well . . . sure," Tom said, after a moment's hesitation.

She exuded available sexuality. Dana had always laughingly said this kind of girl was "looking for a family." Amber plopped down in the chair, pulling it close to Tom's as he sat down.

"Amber McKenzie, this is Ariane Richardson," Tom said.

"Is this your wife?" Amber asked.

"No, no, I'm not married," Tom said uncomfortably.

"You aren't? I thought you'd be married by now," Amber said.

"Why?" Tom asked.

"You were always such a player. I figured you could have anyone you wanted."

"I don't see it that way. Look, Amber, we were having a private conversation, so would it be possible to call you later?" He was in a hurry to get rid of her.

"You'll really call?"

"Of course. Give me your phone number."

"Why don't I take yours, too?"

"Sure." Tom took out his wallet and handed her a card.

She looked at it. "You live in L.A. now?"

"Yes," Tom replied nervously, standing up again, signaling that the conversation was over. Amber wrote her number down, handed it to Tom. She shot me a questioning look, then got up.

"It was nice running into you. I'll give you a call," Tom said.

"I live around here, but I could come to L.A. to get together," she told him.

"Fine," Tom said, now very edgy.

"Well, bye," she said. Then she looked at me again. "Bye, Adrian."

"Ariane," I said.

"Oh, Ariane. Weird name. Well, bye," she said, and started to walk across the dining room. I saw

her sit down next to a much older man with silver
hair.

Tom was nervous. The waiter brought our food,
set it down. I began to eat. Tom didn't touch his.
He kept looking toward Amber's table.

"Let's just eat fast, get out of here," he said.

"All right."

"I'm sorry, Ariane, but Amber is out of her mind.
We had a relationship when we were in our early
twenties—I'm talking over ten years ago. I hardly
recognized her when she walked over, she's gotten
so harsh.

"Anyway, I guess it was one of those fatal at-
tractions for her, or whatever they call it. After a
couple months, I could see that it wasn't something
I wanted to sustain, so I ended it as nicely as I
could. She became hysterical, then obsessive.

"She called me constantly, then she'd hang up
when I picked up. I had the phone company trace
the hang-ups, so I know it was her. I'd come home
at night, she'd be parked across the street from me.
She'd ask me if she could come in to discuss it.

"I'd try to explain to her that I just wanted to be
friends. She would start screaming, then jump in
her car and leave, but not before waking the whole
neighborhood. I finally had to change my number,
stay somewhere else for a while. I don't know why
I ever got involved with her."

I felt ill. I had once done the same thing with a
man who had dumped me. I hadn't meant to, I'd
just been so hurt. I couldn't believe he had wanted
to end the affair. Dana had said I had misunder-
stood the situation, that the man had been looking
for just a casual relationship.

But I had thought we would get married. I'd

called him ten times a day, just to hear his voice. I had felt so alone, so out of touch, after he'd broken up with me. Not much else had been happening in my life at that time.

When I used to call him, sometimes I fantasized that he would say, "Ariane, is that you? I'm sorry, it was all a mistake, I can't live without you." At times I got so desperate, I drove to his house, but I don't think he ever saw me.

When Dana got back from a vacation and found out what I was doing, she thought I'd lost touch with reality. She explained to me that it was truly over, that there was no chance he would marry me. I was humiliated, didn't go out for about six months after that. Luckily, Tom would never know any of this. I hoped my face did not betray my guilt.

Was I out of my element here? How many women loved this man? Why did I trust him? Amber had made me think about Lori again. I had to know.

"Tom, I have to ask you something. Have you seen Lori . . . again?"

He looked down, embarrassed.

"She called me from the Beverly Center, said she had car trouble. I used to kind of look out for her. When I got there, there was no car trouble—it was just a phony excuse to call me.

"But I tried being nice and warm, treating her like a younger sister. I hoped it would work. I never intended to hurt her. I wish her the best, but I'm just not in love with her. I have a past, Ariane. I wish I didn't. Do you understand?"

"Yes," I said. It did make sense. He wasn't just a cad; he had feelings. I had overreacted—Dana's murder, my feelings for him, whatever.

"Do you mind eating quickly? I'm afraid Amber may come over again, maybe even bother you," he said.

"I don't mind," I said. I started to eat very fast. The mood had been ruined for Tom; he barely touched his food. He motioned for the check. We were out of there in five minutes.

Back on the freeway, Tom didn't talk for a while. We listened to music. He was preoccupied, finally shook his head.

"I'm sorry—that really took me back. I'm going to turn down to the coast highway." A little later we were driving along the ocean. I looked down on surging waves and whitecaps.

"I wanted to get away, relax, then I run into Amber," Tom said. "It took me a long time to trust someone after that. I suspected everyone of getting too involved, being over the edge. Even though it was years ago, the shadow of that horror hung over me. It took Dana, with all her independence, to dispel it."

Had that been Dana's secret? She had always said, "She who cares less, controls."

"I can understand that Dana could stand alone," I said. "She didn't really need anyone. She was like that even when she was a little girl. I needed her, but she didn't need me."

"She was your parents' favorite?" he asked.

The word "parents" was a red flag. I had to steer him away from this uncomfortable subject.

"No, not really. We were just very close as children—you know how sisters can be."

"Not really. I was an only child. All the books used to say only children suffered from not having siblings. They were supposedly spoiled, had no friends, didn't do that well in life.

"Now all the books say they have the advantage. Only children get the full attention of both parents, grow up with a lot of self-esteem, can be alone and use their time productively. Whatever it means, I liked it," he said.

"Even though you didn't get along with your father? Wouldn't it have been easier for you if you had a brother or sister?"

"No. Even though we didn't get along, I still got my dad's full attention. It wouldn't have made any difference if I had a sibling—he still would have been hard on me."

"But if you had a brother or sister, there would be someone else to take care of your mom when she gets old. After she passes on, there'd be someone to reminisce with, another person to be close to in this huge world."

"You're so sentimental, so soft, Ariane," he said.

Sentimental? Soft? Was I? Sometimes I had very little idea who I was.

"I can see how you depended on Dana to take care of you; she was very assertive," he said approvingly.

I agreed with him, but felt sick inside. That was who Dana was, and since he had been in love with her, there was no chance he could fall for me. But how self-serving of me to have those thoughts. This trip was about Dana, not about me.

"I wonder if you would have turned out differently if you hadn't had Dana as an older sister," he said.

"What do you mean?"

"If you'd had to rely on yourself more, maybe

you would have developed different traits."

If there had been no Dana, I wouldn't have survived. But Tom didn't know that. Yes, I might have been more independent if I had been the older sister, or not had a sister. But I didn't know what that experience was like, being who I was.

"That's probably true," I said.

"Genetics is a hobby of mine—not that I know much about it, but I like to read up on it," he said. "They used to think that personality was mostly environmental. Now they feel it's mostly inherited. The nature-versus-nurture debate has always fascinated me."

I desperately tried to think of how to switch the topic away from anything that could lead to family.

"For instance," he went on, "I can see several traits that I inherited from each of my parents. What about you?"

"I never thought about it," I said. I couldn't remember one good thing about my mother's personality, so I hoped personality was not inherited.

"But just think about it in a simple way," he persisted. "For instance, did your mother or your father have a sense of humor? Do you have one? Dana did," he said.

"I don't really know. I'll have to think about that. Tom, I have to go to the bathroom. Is there a rest stop soon?" I needed an excuse to stop talking about this.

"I think there should be one about ten minutes up the coast. This is a pretty long stretch here—will you be okay?"

"Sure, it's no emergency."

"Anyway, back to genetics," he said relentlessly. "Analytical ability is supposedly largely inherited and men are supposedly more analytical than women. Was your father analytical? Do you solve problems analytically? If you do, that trait is probably innate."

"Maybe," I said, my anxiety rising to such a point that I could hardly respond.

"Am I making you uncomfortable?" he asked as we swooped around a hairpin turn.

"A little,"

"I'm just a bore, Ariane. I'm sorry. I always think everyone is as fascinated with this stuff as I am. I get a little too involved. Why should you be interested in all this bullshit? You should have stopped me sooner. You can always be truthful with me. You know that, don't you?"

"I . . . I guess so."

"You're not sure? Ariane, please believe me, I want our channels of communication to be completely open. We both loved Dana, and we have that bond. I want you to feel you can tell me anything."

Tell him anything? What a relief it would be to unload all my dirty little secrets. But I couldn't. I had to keep in control. He would judge me badly if he knew the truth.

"Tom, I don't even know who my father was!" I said before I could stop myself. He looked shocked. What had I done?

11

"**What did you** say?" Tom asked. The car swerved dangerously close to the edge of the coast highway.

"Tom, watch out!" I screamed.

"It's okay. Jesus, you threw me for a loop. Did you say you don't know who your father was? How can that be? Were you adopted?"

That would have been easier. We told everyone at school that our father had died. But the townspeople knew the truth. I never thought I would reveal my shame to anyone. What had possessed me? Was I losing control because of the crisis? More importantly, could I take it back? Could I lie, make it seem the truth?

Tom pulled over to the shoulder, off the road.

"Tom, I don't think it's safe to stop here. A driver could sideswipe us, push us over the cliff," I said, looking down. On my side there was barely a foot of land before a steep cliff began a long descent to the sea. I felt dizzy.

"What do you mean, you don't know who your father was?" he asked, his eyes full of curiosity.

There was no turning back. Nothing seemed important anymore, even withholding information that sullied me or destroyed me. Why did I need

172

to tell him? Was it to bring him closer? Or was it to drive him away so that I wouldn't have to risk falling in love with him?

"Ariane?"

"Neither Dana nor I knew who our father was."

"You mean he deserted your mother after you were born?" he asked.

The time for pretense was over. There was no polite way to discuss something so rude.

"I don't know how to say this, but my mother slept around. She was the town slut," I said softly. Then I raised my voice for emphasis. "I don't even know if Dana and I had the same father. There, you can find me low class, you can hate me, now that you know the truth!"

"Hate you?" Tom said. I looked down. He grabbed me, pulled me to him across the front seat. He looked at me for an instant, then he kissed me. I was so surprised that for a moment I felt nothing except his hand on the back of my head, the pressure of his lips on mine. Then he pulled back, folded me into his arms, really kissed me.

Later, when I tried to remember that day, I would wonder if I became part of him in that instant.

I tried to kiss him back, but I couldn't even move my lips, the pressure of his was so fierce. I lost myself in his intensity; his hug practically smothered me. It was as if he were re-forming my molecular structure to replicate his own. He bent me so far over, I thought my back would break.

This was passion as I had never known it. At any moment my bones would crack, I would suffocate. Then, just as quickly, he released me. I gasped for breath. It hurt to be released; my whole body ached.

He turned toward the ocean breakers, staring downward, brooding. The windshield was fogged up. It was so stuffy inside the car that I couldn't take a full breath. But I couldn't get out: we were parked on a steep precipice. I opened the door for a moment, the brisk air rushing in, revitalizing me.

The surge of cool wind surprised him. He looked at me, then reached over, shut the door.

"That's not safe—you could fall out," he said. "Ariane, I want to take care of you. The past doesn't matter. What matters is who you are. All that stuff I said about genetics, inheritance, it's just theory. We're all unique, and we're different from our parents, whether we knew them or not."

I wanted to believe him. But when everyone else has two parents, or at least once knew two parents, it was hard for people like Dana and me to feel good about ourselves. How many times had I watched little girls sit on their daddies' laps and wished I were they? How many times had I secretly wondered if our father, or fathers, had seen us and simply not wanted us?

Tom couldn't really understand. He didn't know what it was like to be different from everyone else. We had been different from the time we first learned what a mommy and a daddy were, and that we only had one of them. And our mother had been different from other mothers, too. Parents had warned their kids to stay away from us.

"Ariane, I don't know what came over me," Tom said uncomfortably. "I can't seem to control myself when I'm around you." Then he smiled and said, "I always thought of myself as such a smooth guy,

suave to the core. You'd never know that lately—
whew! I've got to get hold of myself. Maybe I
should have gone away alone. Maybe I'm not fit to
be around."

I put my hand on his arm.

"I'm glad I'm here with you," I said. He gave me
a perplexed look.

"Have I gone over the edge?" he asked. "Am I
the only one who feels this wild attraction? Should
I pull back? You tell me."

How strong he must be to ask a question like
that. I could never ask if my attentions were un-
warranted. I would crumble, die rather than face
potential rejection. I envied people who could ask
for what they wanted. They usually got it. Now I
was in the position of having to reveal myself.

"You're not forcing yourself on me," I told him
hesitantly.

"But do you feel anything for me? Is there
something happening here, or am I just imagining
it because of my grief over Dana?"

"How could any woman not be attracted to you?
What I can't fathom is how you could be attracted
to me, especially after Dana," I said softly.

"The two of you are very different," he replied
nonchalantly, as if he were discussing us in the ab-
stract. "She made me feel secure. I felt she would
never overwhelm me with possessiveness; she was
elusive, fleeting, like quicksilver. You, you make
me feel masculine, protective. You seem like you
have a broken wing." He grabbed me again, tenderly kissed me.

I was filled with uncertainty. I did have a broken
wing, but if I depended on him, would it stay broken? Could I never heal it, fly alone? I rested my

head on his shoulder, felt his strength. He kept his arm around me. The exchange had exhausted us.

We sat in comfortable solitude, gazing out at the ocean. The infinity of it didn't haunt me, because I was defined by Tom and I felt safe. Finally he sighed, released me, started the car. The rest of the drive to Big Sur was lost on me, for I was in a dreamy reverie of excitement.

Tom was lost in thought, too, but not quiet thought, like I was. Occasionally his eyes would narrow and he would set his mouth in a firm line, as if he were working out a problem. I dared not intrude on his private thoughts. Instead I pretended to listen to Marvin Gaye.

It was dark when we arrived. The place was an old-fashioned, log-cabin lodge with a welcoming, blazing fireplace. Everything had a comfortable film of dust on it. We signed an ancient guest book, witness to many renowned guests.

"Two rooms? You made a reservation for two rooms?" the desk clerk asked, confused. He probably wondered where the other couple was.

"Yes, that's right, two rooms for Crandall," Tom said. Never assuming that we would share one, he was a gentleman, wanting the weekend to be whatever I wanted.

The clerk handed Tom two keys. "These rooms are next to each other. Is that all right?"

"Fine," Tom said.

"The dining room is over there," the clerk said, pointing to a room off to the left. "You're signed up for the second sitting. Dinner is steak, fried potatoes and peas, at nine P.M."

"Good, we'll get washed up first. I know where the cabins are," Tom said, leading me outside.

There was a row of about ten cabins, each one separate. Tom opened mine for me, put my bag down. It was a rustic wood cabin with Western decor. It had a silver lamp in the shape of a cowboy on a bucking bronco, and a comforter with brown saddle designs on it. The scuffed wood floors bore witness to the lodge's popular hospitality. I loved it.

"Why don't you freshen up?" Tom said. "Then come next door and we'll go to dinner."

After he left, I couldn't decide whether to change clothes or not. My thoughts were focused on the incipient romance. I longed for the tantalizing feeling of physically blending into him. Maybe we were soul mates; maybe this was the destiny he had alluded to.

Then a sobering thought hit me. What about Dana? Had she been his soul mate? Was Tom just a discontented guy who needed a distraction and any woman would do? But Dana wouldn't have gone with just anyone. He would have been a big score to her—the looks, the money, the adoration.

Should he be falling for me so fast after Dana's death? Did I bear guilt for encouraging him?

Even if I decided it was unethical to fall for Tom Crandall, I couldn't have stopped myself. I was too far gone.

Every bone in my body was tingling; I felt my cells glowing. I knew I was already addicted to Tom, and there was no way I could put the brakes on now.

I counted the minutes until I could go next door. How long would it be proper to wait? I wanted to rush over there after fifteen minutes had passed, but it would look too anxious. After half an hour, I was ready to explode. I brushed my hair so hard,

I thought it would fall out. I coated my lips in red with three different lipsticks, then wiped it off, applied gloss. Finally I couldn't restrain myself any longer.

I took a deep breath, went next door. I knocked on the door. Tom opened it. We looked at each other, then he grabbed me, slammed the door. He started kissing me, then stopped. He traced the outlines of my lips, my eyelids, my nose with his fingertips.

He covered my eyes with one hand so I couldn't see him kissing me. His hand slipped down over my nose. For a moment I couldn't breathe, and I panicked. Then he slid his hand down to my mouth, where he puckered my lips together, kissed them. A tidal wave of excitement engulfed me. I didn't want the foreplay or the affection. I wanted only the consummation, when I would cease to exist as a separate entity, when I would become him.

He didn't need to ask my permission to make love to me, because my body betrayed my willingness. He grabbed me closer and we both fell on the bed. Suddenly I was energized. We ripped off each other's clothes and he stroked my body. I held him. He stopped for a moment.

"Ariane, my little bird," he said. I smiled the smile of a woman who feels desired. What did it matter why he desired me? The fact that he did was apparent. I tried to switch off thought, just feel my body. As he climbed on top of me, I had an image of him doing the same thing to Dana. I quickly pushed it out of my mind.

He began to make slow, purposeful love to me. He choreographed it so carefully, I marveled at his self-control. Once he was inside me, he paused.

"Does that feel good?" he asked. I could only nod. It was a transcendent experience for me, the kind I liked, where I was negated. After he came he fell, limp, on top of me, exhausted, satiated. I liked the way his bones cut into my flesh. His elbow cut into my side, his knee bruised my thigh. He fell asleep quickly.

This was my favorite part of the sexual experience. My lover was sleeping. I could stare at him endlessly without his knowledge. I could feast my eyes on every part of his body, on the features of his face. I synchronized my breathing to his, so that it felt like we were one organism, like we were him.

I wanted to stay here for the rest of my life. A couple of times he sleepily tried to roll off me. I prevented it. I wanted him to think I was the mattress, to sleep for hours. I looked at his arms: black, curled hair; freckles. His hands had a square shape. His feet were long, narrow, arched.

I touched his hair lightly while I held my breath so as not to wake him. I touched the soft inside part of one of his thighs, then wedged my fingers between his thighs. It felt good.

He was in a deep sleep, tossing and turning. Finally I had to go to the bathroom. I rolled Tom over to the side, and he fell off me in a graceful motion. I went into the bathroom, trying not to disturb him.

When I came out, I gazed around the room, never wanting to forget this scene. He looked primal on the bed, almost like a caveman, natural. His knees were raised to his chest in a fetal position. I wanted to engulf him, to put him inside me so that he could never escape. So I would never be alone again.

Should I lie down next to him or sit in the chair? I would like to lie by his side, but my priority was not to wake him. It was getting cold. If there was a heater in the cabin, I didn't where it was or how to turn it on. The cabin was bare except for the functional items.

I couldn't sit in the chair naked without feeling the chilly mountain air, maybe getting sick. I didn't want to put on my clothes because I was covered with Tom's sweat, the juice of sex. Maybe he had a robe. His suitcase was unzipped on a chair. I opened it, looked through his clothes. My hands felt something cold, metallic. I grabbed it, pulled it out.

It was a gun!

A gun! I had never seen a real one. I stood there mesmerized by the danger of it. Then I got scared, dropped it on two rumpled white undershirts. I turned quickly to look at Tom. He was still asleep.

What did it mean? Why would Tom carry a gun? I had heard that many people in L.A. had guns for protection—maybe that was it. Was he worried about strangers in the forest behind us?

A horrible thought occurred to me. Maybe he was Dana's killer—maybe he was going to kill me! No, I was going crazy. I quickly shoved the gun back under the clothes, put the cover of the suitcase back in place, unzipped but covering the contents.

Or maybe Tom was worried that the same person who had killed Dana was after us. But Farrington was out of the country. I was sure there was a logical explanation. I felt out of sorts. I tried not to give in to panic.

Tom breathed loudly. He looked so vulnerable naked, I threw a comforter over him. I decided to take a shower. When I came out of the bathroom, I got dressed. Tom was stretched out on his back, staring at the ceiling.

"Hi," he said, looking at me. "Did I oversleep?"

"No. We don't have a schedule."

"I think we're too late for dinner here. Let me take a shower and we'll drive around, find a place in one of the small towns nearby." He strode like a naked gazelle, taking the distance to the bathroom in just two steps.

As soon as he closed the door, I turned my attention to the suitcase again. I thought I could see the gun shining through the closed suitcase. What more could be discovered by handling it again? Nothing. Maybe he always traveled with a gun, just to be safe.

I could ask him about the weapon. Would that be intrusive? I felt myself being drawn to the gun. Had it been a fantasy? No, I had really seen it. I began to pace around. I felt that familiar, awful anxiety crawl up the back of my neck. That gun made me terribly uneasy, frightened me.

At that moment he came out of the bathroom, drying off his wet body with a towel. He smiled the smile of a confidant man as he jumped into his clothes.

"I feel refreshed already, just being out of town. The other day it took me forty minutes to go two miles on Sunset. There was a football game at UCLA, and I couldn't even turn off. It's terrific to be here, it's so isolated.

"I know a beautiful hiking trail we'll explore tomorrow. Did you bring hiking boots?"

"No, I don't have any. I can wear tennis shoes."

"Maybe I'd better buy you a pair of hiking boots.
You might slip on a rock."

"That's all right. I've hiked in my tennis shoes
before, so they'll work out."

"Well, when we get back to town, I'm going to
get you boots. If you're going to be with me, you'll
need them. I like to hike around Malibu on the
weekends." He grabbed a windbreaker, and with
not even a glance at the suitcase, he led me out of
the cabin.

I breathed a little easier, away from the gun. But
I was still trying desperately to think of a way to
bring the subject up without admitting I had
looked in his suitcase. Would he believe that I had
been looking for a robe? What if he thought I was
spying on him, that I didn't trust him?

"Boy, it's dark as the devil tonight," he said. It
did seem to be very dark, pitch-black with no stars
lighting up the sky. Fog clung to the pine trees,
giving them the look of being wrapped in porous
cotton. Tom drove down the steep mountain road
slowly, anticipating a car coming in the opposite
direction.

"That's the one bad thing about this place, the
roads at night," he said. "You always read about a
fatal accident—somebody blinked for a minute and
hit a truck. I'm a steady driver, though. On mountain roads you're in safe hands."

He was concentrating on his driving, didn't notice my lack of conversation. I was struggling to
get up the nerve to ask about the gun.

"Do you think it's dangerous around here—I
mean, the people?" I finally asked.

"Dangerous? No, not right around here. Up in
Eureka, farther north, there are a lot of rednecks.

And Marin City has a military base, so it's pretty conservative. I wouldn't want to be a sixties hippie in those areas."

The fog seemed to be getting worse. I couldn't even see outside my window. One wrong turn, we were dead.

"You know, I've never seen the fog this bad. I know there are some nice places about twenty miles up, but it's already ten P.M. I think we should just stop anywhere, any little coffee shop, if we see a sign for a town."

"That's a good idea, because we'll have to drive back."

"I'd hate to wind up in a Motel 6 because we were scared to drive back," he said, laughing as he turned off the narrow road. A few miles later we came to a small commercial strip with a few gas stations, a motel, a coffee shop.

It was a real truck stop, with big rigs parked everywhere. I was the only woman there except for one waitress. There was one strange-looking man, a busboy. His apron was askew as he scrubbed down a counter, his jaw hung slack and his face didn't seem to fit. I quickly looked away. The waitress handed us greasy plastic menus.

"Shall we try the T-bone, a real he-man's dinner?" Tom asked.

"Sure," I said. He ordered the steaks.

"Are you worried about leaving your car in the parking lot?" I asked.

"No, why should I be? It's got an alarm system. I don't think anybody from these parts would chance it."

"What about carjackings in the city?"

"That's an urban concern. I don't dwell on it here."

"Do a lot of people carry guns in their cars?"

"No, I don't think so, but people have guns in their homes. The carjackers usually don't shoot you, they just take the car. But if you pull a gun out, they *could* shoot you.

"Hey, I've got to go to the bathroom," Tom said. He got up, walked toward the men's room.

What if I flat out asked him if he had a gun? I wondered. All of a sudden I felt the presence of someone. I looked up, saw the busboy standing over me.

"I know what he's going to do," he said in a low growl. I jerked back from him.

"I know you," he hissed.

"Who are you? What do you mean?" I asked.

"You should listen to me. I know," he said.

"Know what?" I demanded. At that moment Tom started walking back to the table. The busboy set down two waters, lumbered back to the counter. I wondered if Tom had seen the interchange. He didn't mention it when he sat down. I was thoroughly unnerved.

The waitress put our steaks down. Tom dumped half the catsup bottle on his T-bone.

"Do you need a permit for a gun in L.A.?" I asked.

"Don't know—probably. Does the big city scare you after Portland?"

"No, I was just curious."

"All you need to know is that you're safe with me. Now eat up—we want to get to bed early so we can hike tomorrow," he said.

My appetite was gone, between the gun question

and the strange seer in the busboy's apron. I noticed him go over to a few other tables, talk to people.

"I do feel safe with you," I told Tom. "It's just that, with what happened to Dana . . ."

"That was specifically because of who she was. We still don't know Farrington's motive."

Tom finished his steak, his fries, my fries, and was ready to go. When he got up to pay the check, the busboy came back to our table. He refilled my coffee cup.

"I know about it," he said while staring at the ceiling. How could he know about Dana? How could he know that I was Dana's sister? The waitress came over. She pushed the busboy away.

"Was Dewitt bothering you?" she asked me.

"Well," I said, hesitating, "he said some strange things."

"He just got out of Atascadero," she said.

"Atascadero?"

"Place for the mentally ill. He's from around these parts, and he's harmless now that he takes his medicine. He's a nephew of the owner. I'm sorry. Don't pay him no mind," she said.

I got up before he could approach me again. He looked insane. Was he a bad omen? Was it like a black cat crossing my path? When we got back in the car, Tom gave me a tender kiss.

He turned on some soft music as he navigated the foggy road back to the inn. When we reached it and got out of the car, he put his arm around me, then guided me to our cabins.

"Would you sleep in my cabin tonight, Ariane? It gets cold up here, and I need you for warmth," he said. I nodded a slow "Yes," wondering if I was doing the right thing. He opened the door, slammed it. He didn't even turn on the light. He pushed me down on the bed again, started kissing me.

"Tom, would you mind if we turned on the light for a few moments and got undressed? This is all so new to me, I need to take it a little slower."

"Oh, of course, Ariane. I'm an impatient guy—I didn't mean to rush you, honey," he said, switching on a little lamp.

I went into the bathroom, undressed down to my slip. I had to think of a plan. Suddenly I had one.

I emerged from the bathroom. Tom was in his boxers on top of the turned-down bed, reading a travel brochure. I took a deep breath, walked straight into the suitcase, knocked it over. He jumped up.

"Oh, I'm so sorry. I'm so clumsy," I said, bending down to pick things up.

"Let me get everything," he said, rushing to push me out of the way. But not before I had turned the suitcase over. The gun fell out. It was in plain view. Tom looked at it, then at me.

✂ 12 ✂

Tom swiftly reached for it. I felt a wave of fear, stepped back quickly. He picked it up, turned it over in his hand, stared at it.

"Thank God it didn't go off," he said, noticing my expression. He flipped the suitcase over, put the gun back in it. I was frozen.

"Ariane, I should have told you I was bringing a gun, but I didn't want to frighten you."

"Why do you have it?" I asked. He sat down, looked at the floor.

"Lori Wells," he said.

"What do you mean?"

"She is trying to blackmail me over a financial deal that went sour. She has a violent past, she's over the line, she's even been in a mental hospital. I've been trying to stall her while I get in touch with her father."

"You mean she's threatened to kill you?"

"Yes. And I'm not sure that she might not try to hurt others, including you. I did nothing wrong in the deal, but she's made up charges and says I invested her money badly. I've just been giving her lip service until I can reach her dad—he's in Russia on a business deal. I wouldn't put it past her to follow me here."

I breathed easier. How could I have doubted Tom? He had loved Dana and might be falling in love with me. He couldn't hurt anyone.

"You don't think Lori had anything to do with Dana's murder, do you?"

"No. She wasn't in town two months ago, didn't even know Dana. This is a separate issue. That's why I was so nervous when she came to see you—she's liable to say anything. And, of course, she wants the relationship back."

"But would she track us here?"

"I doubt it, but after what happened to Dana, I'm spooked. Let's forget about it if we can. But I feel safer knowing the gun's here. Look, it probably wasn't necessary and I didn't want you to know about it, but better safe than sorry."

Amber, Lori—he must specialize in obsessive women. Now I could join the club. I had to keep myself in check.

"Lori was a relationship I had when I was in my twenties—so was Amber. I went into therapy to see why I made some promises I shouldn't have and encouraged them. I guess I liked the feeling of power, but it was a no-win situation.

"I'm sorry to have all this emotional baggage, Ariane. It's one reason I came out to California, to change my way of relating to women, to take more responsibility for what I say. I was completely honest with Dana, and it felt wonderful. That's who I am now. Maybe you did better in the past with men than I did with women."

"No—I'd hate for you to know all the mistakes I made," I said.

"Good. Then neither one of us is perfect. Come here," he said and he started kissing me. We made love all night long, energized by each other. We finally fell asleep just as dawn was casting light into the windows. I slept so soundly I didn't even dream.

When I awoke, Tom was staring at me; I was cradled in his arms. I looked into his face, and for a moment his glance seemed unfamiliar. His face bore an expression I couldn't name. His personality had many facets that I didn't know yet.

I felt permanently attached to him already, incapable of functioning without him, yet I hardly knew him. It had to be my secret. I had to appear independent or I would lose him.

"Sleep well?" he asked.

"Yes, very well."

"Ready to eat breakfast and go for a hike? I want to show you some spectacular views."

We got dressed. I was still conscious of the gun in the suitcase, but I tried to put it out of my mind. I wondered if he would bring it on the hike. Would Lori Wells appear on some hiking trail in pursuit?

"I'm still worried about the grip on your tennis shoes," Tom said. "Should we take half an hour and find you some hiking boots?"

"No, I've hiked all over Oregon in these. We're not climbing Mount Everest," I said.

"Well, there are places that are rough. I've been on this trail a couple of times. I don't want you falling."

"Don't worry, I won't." I said. The only other person who had ever really cared whether I lived or died was Dana. Maybe her protection lived on through Tom.

"I should have remembered to bring a camera," Tom said. "Dana and I took so many pictures—I'll have to show them to you. She loved having her picture taken."

Yes, Dana had had pictures of everything she'd ever done in life. She had always urged me to get a camera. But life seemed so temporary to me, so unimportant unless I was around her.

I used to feel like the white fluff of a dandelion that can be blown away in an instant. Pictures gave the illusion of permanency. I didn't want to invest in that illusion.

After we ate breakfast, we parked at the beginning of the trail. Tom walked ahead of me. It looked like we were heading straight up the side of the mountain. I didn't see any other hikers.

"Is this a popular trail?" I asked.

"No. I hate the popular trails. Big Sur has gotten so crowded, there are tons of people on them. It's not even like being out in the wilderness. It's like being a part of a small village, all of it hiking up Mount Fujiyama, which I did when I was in Japan."

"You were in Japan?"

"Yes, on business. We stayed in a hotel in the Hokkaido National Forest, which was the base of the trail for Fujiyama. But the entire mountain was covered with hikers. That's how populated Big Sur is now."

I looked up and the mountain seemed to grow steeper. We started the ascent slowly. Every step was treacherous. Tom offered me his hand along the hard parts, and if my footing was insecure, he steadied my balance.

As we climbed higher, the area above us appeared even more steep. I didn't know if I'd be able to make it back down without his help. I hadn't expected this to be such a difficult climb. Maybe Tom was an expert hiker; this could be nothing for him. As we neared the top, I ran out of breath. I just couldn't keep up.

"Tom, I have to stop for a minute. I'm bushed," I said, gasping.

"Fine. Sit down and I'll stay here. But let's not stop too long—we're almost at the top. I want you to see the cliffs and the breakers," he said.

I crouched down on my haunches. As soon as I was not in motion, I felt like collapsing.

"Maybe you should go the rest of the way without me. I'm sorry, Tom, but I'm exhausted."

"I will, if you really can't make it. Relax for a few moments. You might get a second wind. We're literally ten minutes from the top. I guarantee you have never seen anything like this before."

I took deep breaths, stopped my legs from shaking. I was able to carefully stretch one leg out, at a downward angle. It felt so good, since that leg had started to cramp. Looking at the vastness of the mountain, I felt even more insignificant.

Tom handed me a bottle of water. I drank deeply, for I was dehydrated. I could see him looking around impatiently; he was bored waiting for me. I longed for some hidden reservoir of energy to infuse strength into my muscles, but my body felt depleted of even the ability to move. Even my bones ached.

It was simply a matter of mind over body. I could make it—I had to. I stood up, thought I heard my back crack.

"Better?" Tom asked hopefully.

"Yes, but I'd better take it slow," I said. We began to climb again. I saw the top of the mountain.

It looked like a flat plateau from my vantage point. Finally Tom made it to the top, swung his leg up. He stood there for a minute looking over the side, then glanced down at me.

"You're almost there," he said, offering his hand for that final stretch. I positioned one foot, took his hand. He swung me, effortlessly, onto the mountaintop. He hugged me, turned me around.

I saw the most magnificent sight I had ever seen. The cliff dropped straight down to the ocean, which was a vision of miles of whitecaps and churning waves. I was transfixed.

"We're part of all this," he said, nuzzling my hair. "If I died today, I wouldn't mind, now that I have seen this beauty. Do you feel that way? I mean, if it were your destiny to die today, if a bolt of lightning hit you, would you feel you had missed anything? What experience could ever surpass this sight?" he asked.

"If I died today, I would feel remorse, because now I've found you," I said. He looked at me hard, then kissed me. The wind swirled our hair, and the two of us must have looked like the cover of a romance novel, kissing passionately atop a bluff.

We sat down. He opened his backpack, took out our lunches. We ate, looking down at the water that surrounded us.

"I feel like I'm the only person in the world peeling an orange," I said. There was not a person or a boat visible anywhere.

"Just you and me and the memory of Dana," he said.

"Thank you so much for mentioning her," I said. "I can hear her name, Dana, echoing, bouncing on the ripples of the ocean, heard all over the globe.

Someone in Australia will hear it and say, 'Who's Dana?' And then the answer will come to him magically—he'll know all about her."

Tom nodded.

I didn't know how long we had been hiking, but it was beginning to get overcast. Fog was rolling in. The wind started whipping around and blew our sandwich bags off the mountain. Before, it had gently caressed us; now it punched us, grabbed at our clothes.

"The weather's changing, so we'd better start down," Tom said.

"Do you think it's going to rain?"

"Possibly, but we'll be down the mountain before it does. I'll start, you follow me. Let's just take one last look." He took my hand and led me toward the edge of the cliff. He stared at me, then at some indefinable point in the ocean. The air got colder and colder.

"Are you scared to come to the edge?" he asked, stepping right near the precipice. "Come on," he urged, dragging me toward him.

"No, it really does frighten me," I said, holding back.

"Oh, come on," he insisted, still pulling me. I wriggled out of his grip. One false step that close to the edge and I'd fall. I didn't trust myself.

"I can't, Tom. I'm just too scared."

"You wus," he said, challenging in a kidding way.

"I'm sorry, I can't," I said, hurriedly turning my back on him, walking across to the other side. He quickly followed me. Was it anger I saw in his eyes, or disappointment?

"I'm going to teach you courage," he said, coming toward me. "Now follow close behind," he said as he started the climb down. "If you feel scared, tell me, and I'll help you."

I looked down. The distance didn't seem as far as it had climbing up. I started to follow him, to literally hike in his footsteps. He glanced back every few minutes, making sure I was all right.

"This is a steep place and it's windy, so give me your hand," he said, reaching up for me. I held out my hand toward him. That was the last thing I remember.

When I woke up, Tom was leaning over me. Two people I had never seen before were with him. It was cold, raining. I was on the ground with a sweater over me. My head hurt.

"She's conscious," Tom said, excited.

"Try to sit up, Ariane, take some water." He managed to lift my head up. The woman held a cup of water to my lips. I tried to drink, but it hurt to keep my head up. Tom lowered my head. Everything was blurry; slowly, things started to come into focus.

I tried to move; everything hurt. I was on a wide ledge halfway down the mountain.

"What happened?" I asked. My words came out so softly, I could barely hear myself.

"You're going to be fine," Tom said. "The paramedics are on their way up the hill. You fell, and this ledge broke your fall. Jack and Helen here were coming up the mountain—they saw you land here."

The woman, Helen, smiled at me. "You gave us quite a scare. You looked like a ragdoll plunging

down the side of the mountain. How do you feel?"
she asked.

"Groggy—everything hurts," I said.

"Just rest. I can see the medics now. It won't be
long."

I woke up in a hospital. Tom was at my side.

"Ariane," he said, holding my hand. "You're
fine. Nothing was even broken."

Broken? What had happened? All memory was
hazy.

"What happened?" I wanted to know.

"You slipped and fell on the mountain. Don't
you remember?" he asked.

"Barely." I remembered the sensation of falling,
somewhat like what I would imagine flying
through the air would be.

"You reached out for my hand and missed,"
Tom said. "A huge gust of wind hit you, threw you
off balance, and you fell. It's a miracle you're
alive."

The nurse came in, took my vital signs.

"How did you fall?" she asked.

"I just slipped," I said.

"You're a lucky girl," she said. "I think the doctor is going to discharge you today." She smiled
and left.

"All you have to do is take it easy because of the
slight concussion," Tom said. "I want you to stay
with me until you feel up to par, Ariane."

"Are you sure? Maybe just for a night or two."

"You stay until you're recovered," he said.

We left the hospital the next day, and I slept on
the drive back.

Once we got to his house, he situated me in the
guest room.

"I guess olive-green sheets aren't your thing. And I don't have any Chanel soap, just Dial," he said apologetically, handing me one of his Brooks Brothers striped shirts to sleep in.

"Give me your apartment key—I'll go get you a nightgown. Anything else you want?"

"No, just check my machine. Maybe Detective Martinez called."

"Fine. I'll stop at the grocery—what do you like to eat?"

"Yogurt. And any flavor of Ben and Jerry's ice cream."

He nodded, left. I expected to hear house sounds as I lay on the bed somewhere between sleep and just waking, but the house was strangely quiet. I figured his phone would ring constantly with business calls, but it didn't ring once.

When I woke up, it was late in the afternoon. I got up, went to the bathroom. When I came out, Tom walked into my room.

"I heard you get up. How do you feel?"

"Just tired," I said.

"The doctor wanted you to take pain pills for the headache. I got the prescription filled. I'll get you one."

"Tom, the headache isn't that bad, and I hate to take medicine. I'd rather not take it."

"Fine. I hate medication myself."

"Did Detective Martinez call me?" I asked.

Tom shook his head. "No messages. It's probably too soon. I brought you some dinner from the deli—soup, a sandwich. Get in bed, I'll bring it in."

I got into bed, propping myself up. It felt strange to be an invalid, cared for by Tom. The only other person who had nursed me was Dana, when I had

had a particularly bad case of the flu. If I were honest with myself, I would have to admit that I could be happy in this sick, dependent state forever.

It wasn't symbiosis that I desired, but to be a parasite on a host. Yet I hated admitting that to myself. I knew if I didn't get well soon, Tom would tire of me. He didn't want a bag of spineless ectoplasm riding on his shoulders.

He brought our dinners in on pink wood trays. There was a single red rose in a silver bud vase. I couldn't believe the way he was caring for me. Most men ran away at the first sign of physical illness. Tom was even more involved, more concerned.

"This feels so cozy—almost like we're married, living in the fifties, eating TV dinners on trays, watching a movie," he said, starting to eat.

Had he really said "like we're married"? Was he thinking that? What if I were living here as his wife, as Mrs. Tom Crandall? Ariane Crandall. What if we had two children whom I walked to school every day, and a Labrador retriever? Do these dreams really come true? Could it come to pass? I got chills.

Tom turned on the TV, probably figuring I was too weak to hold a conversation.

"Need anything else? Salt?" he asked.

"No, I'm fine. This is so nice of you, Tom."

"It feels so normal, doesn't it? Like we do this every night after work. Except that in real life you wouldn't have a concussion," he said, patting my hand.

"I should be up and around soon," I said.

"Whenever," he answered. "I like having you around."

We watched a movie on TV; then I was exhausted. He tucked me in.

"I'd like to climb in that bed with you, but I want you to feel better first," he said, gently kissing me on the forehead. He turned out the light, shut my door. I stayed with him for two more days and nights.

He was away at meetings during most of those days. When he did work at home, he closed his door so as not to disturb me. It seemed as if I had always been there, as if we had always been together.

We did not discuss Dana, but she was with us always.

When he came home on the third afternoon, I was up, dressed, ready to go. I couldn't impose any longer.

"You're ready to go? Are you sure it's not too soon?" he asked.

"No, I'm fine," I said, piling my things in my arms. He sighed, looked thoughtful. Then he reached over, took the things out of my arms. He took my hand, sat me down next to him on the couch.

"Ariane, move in with me," he said. I was so shocked that I absorbed the statement immediately. I was on a feedback delay. Slowly I realized what he had said. I turned to him in astonishment.

"You want me to move in with you?"

"This feels like what life should feel like. I know we haven't known each other that long . . . maybe I'm grabbing at happiness because of Dana. Having you move out now would seem like another loss. Ariane . . . I love you," he said, taking me in his arms, kissing me.

My heart was beating so loudly, it must have

been audible. The risk seemed so great! What if he found me wanting and sent me packing after a couple of months? How could I survive that? Why would he keep me once he really knew me?

"Say yes, Ariane. I promise I'll try to make you happy. Will you?" he asked.

This time I had to seize the moment, had to grab the possibility of happiness. I nodded.

"We'll make it work, whatever it takes," he said. I wanted that moment to last forever, but he got up abruptly.

"Leave your things here," he said. "I'll drive you to your apartment so you can get the rest of your stuff."

I couldn't speak on the ride home. I was too excited.

"How long do you think it will take you to pack up?" he asked when we reached my building.

"A couple hours," I said.

"Good. I'll order some pizza for us at seven. I'll be waiting," he said. Then he drove away.

I walked into my apartment. It was strange to think I would not wind up living here. There was a message on my machine; I played it back.

"Miss Richardson, this is Detective Martinez. Mark Farrington has been questioned in Spain. Please call me when you get this."

I called him—he said to come in.

I rushed downstairs, drove to his office. He told me to sit down, wait till he was off the phone. He finally hung up.

"We've questioned Farrington in Spain. He has an alibi for the time Dana was murdered. We've checked it, it checks out. He fled the country be-

cause of his pending problems with Madison's—
nothing to do with Dana."

"He's lying!" I yelled.

"He may be lying about why he fled the country,
but his alibi does check out." Martinez referred to
a folder on his desk. "According to him, they were
partners in the scam you told me about. He said
they hadn't dated for months and that there were
no hard feelings. He said he had no idea why anyone would want her dead."

"Of course he'd say that. He could have hired
someone to kill her. Have you thought of that?"

"We're following many leads. Can you think of
anyone else who didn't like her or might have
wanted to harm her?"

"Farrington's girlfriend, Tracy."

"She's with him in Spain. We've also questioned
her; she has an alibi for that time."

"I know he did it!" I screamed. My head started
to pound. I had forgotten about my concussion until that moment.

"Tell me some more of what you know," I said.
"Where was her body found? How was she murdered?"

"I'm not allowed to discuss specific aspects of
the case with you, Miss Richardson," he said. Another police officer walked in, motioned for Martinez to follow him.

"Excuse me for a moment," the detective said,
walking out. As soon as he was gone, I grabbed the
folder on Dana. I flipped through dozens of papers
until I found what I was looking for. Dana had
been shot once through the chest, and her body
was found in a West Hollywood alley. I wrote

down the location. I put the folder back on Martinez's desk. He came back in.

"Is there anything else you can think of that might help us?" he asked.

"No," I said, getting up. "But if I do, I'll give you a call. By the way, you have Tom Crandall's phone number. After today you can reach me there."

"You're living with Tom Crandall?"

"I'm staying there until you bring Dana's killer to justice. I can no longer afford the apartment."

"Just remember that no one has been indicted yet, so watch out for yourself," he cautioned.

"I will," I said, then left.

How dare he cast suspicion on Tom? Why couldn't he just do his job and get Farrington? If he couldn't find Dana's killer, then I would.

❧ 13 ❧

Once back home, I looked around my apartment, exhausted. What did I have to do to finalize my departure? I called the owner of the unit, told him I would be leaving.

"If you want to stay until the end of the month, then do. The rental agent won't get to it until the first of the month," he said.

I decided to keep the rest of my things here until the end of the month. It would remind people of my presence. Someone might remember something, slip a note in my mailbox. I went down to the desk, told the doorman that I was leaving.

"A Mr. Cassio, a private investigator, was here yesterday," Carlos said. "He sat for a long time in the lobby and then he spoke to all the doormen and the maintenance supervisor. I don't think he felt very well—he walked crooked."

"I've met him, thank you, Carlos," I said.

I went back up to my apartment. The phone rang. It was the manager from Ferrara's, who asked me to come in for an interview. I made the appointment, packed one of my two blue canvas bags, and walked out of the apartment.

As I drove away from the condo building, I drifted into sadness. Somehow, living there had kept me close to Dana. She had walked those very carpets, breathed the same air, ridden in the elevator. But no, I told myself, I was even closer to Dana's spirit now. I was about to move in with her former lover.

Before I headed for Tom's, I went to the alley where Dana's body had been found. It had been diagrammed in the police report, so I had no trouble finding it. It was near a strip of stores owned by Russian immigrants. There were signs in Russian for a pawnshop, a bakery, a tailor shop and a restaurant. Stout women with scarves on their heads were everywhere, holding the hands of small children dressed in cheap foreign clothes.

I parked, walked into the alley. I could still see the faint white police outline of Dana's body. Cars from the adjacent apartments were wedged nearby. There were garbage cans, full and messy. The backs of the apartment buildings were stucco, painted in a forgotten, peeling pink.

I hated to think of Dana's body having been found here—it was a foul, filthy place. Had her world ended here or somewhere else? Maybe her eyes had never seen this putrid site. I noticed a brown spot on the ground—was it Dana's bloodstain?

I didn't want her blood exposed to these surroundings. I took out a white lace handkerchief, placed it over the stain. If it protected a tiny part of Dana for just ten minutes before someone pocketed it, it was worth it.

I glanced into the dirty windows of some of the first-floor apartments. Tenants were involved in daily routines. Had anyone seen anything suspicious on the day Dana was left here? Echoes of conversations drifted toward the street, fragments of Russian. I couldn't even question these people, I realized, because they didn't speak English.

I looked around at the dismal surroundings, wishing I had never come. Now this image would be in my mind forever, one of those murky, bad memories I could never shake.

I had to get away fast; the alley was closing in on me. Suddenly a cat scurried past, spooking me. Those formerly harmless conversations now sounded threatening, hostile. I needed to get to Tom's.

As soon as I was on Sunset Boulevard, I was lulled into a false sense of security. The street seemed maternal with its wide, comforting curves and its bright, full greenery on both sides. Anything seemed possible on Sunset, even when the boulevard was congested. Just knowing it ran its true course the entire length of the city was reassuring. Its spacious blacktop invited hope. It seemed like a gentle roller coaster with its undulating turns.

I pulled into Tom's driveway, happy to be there. The light from the windows made cozy, oval reflections on his green lawn. Everything was orderly. The lawn sprinklers were equidistant. The grass was trimmed within an inch of its life. A jacaranda tree bent toward Tom's house, pointing the way.

I gazed around with a sense of relief. Soon my life would be about Tom, only about Tom, about fulfilling his needs. That was finally who I would be, Ariane, the person who got meaning from life by fulfilling Tom's needs. I walked toward the door, home at last.

Tom threw open the door, hugged me, grabbed my suitcase.

"This all?" he said, slamming the door.

"No, I left some of my stuff there until the end of the month because—"

"You what?" he said, suddenly angry. It surprised me.

"I just thought I should stay until the end of the month. That way, if anyone remembered something about Dana, they would—"

"I thought we agreed you were moving in. Are you hedging your bet, Ariane?" he asked. I stood still, completely stunned. Then he shook his head. "I'm sorry, I overreacted," he said, sitting down. "I just snapped. I thought you changed your mind, that maybe it was just a lark for you or something."

I felt so ashamed. How could I have hurt him like that? I hadn't once considered his feelings.

"Oh, Tom, I'm so sorry. I had no idea you would care. I'll go get everything right now," I said, starting for the door.

"No, wait, I'm expecting a call. I'll go with you next week to help you."

"It's just one suitcase, a few things. I can do it myself," I said.

Tom got up, turned me away from the door.

"We're a team. Wait till I can go with you," he said, leading me into the den. He had the pizza spread out on a table. We started to sit down, but the phone rang. He walked toward his office.

"Oh, by the way, if you ever hear my phone ringing while I'm here, don't answer it. I like to get it," he said. He shut his office door, took the call.

Tom needn't worry that I would invade his privacy. He had no idea what a good little soldier I was. He came out a few minutes later, grabbed my suitcase.

"I'm going to put this in the guest room," he said.

"The guest room?"

"Just for a couple of days, till I have time to clear out some things from my room—to make room. Is that all right?"

"Oh, of course," I said. I sat down, ate a piece of pizza. The house seemed so large. I wondered if I could expand to fill its space or if I would always stay in one small part, hovering near a wall.

Tom came back, sat down, started to eat.

"That was Cassio. I fired him," he said. "He really was incompetent."

"Did you find someone else?"

"No. I'll call a few friends next week. By the way, did you talk to Martinez?"

"Yes, and they questioned Farrington in Spain. He has an alibi for the time Dana was murdered. But that doesn't mean anything—he could have hired someone. I told the detective he could reach me here from now on."

"You did what?" Tom asked, irritated. This was the second thing I had done that seemed to bother him.

"Well, if it was important, if he needed me . . ." I said, my voice faltering under his direct stare.

"But you left your phone on—you have the phone machine."

"Well, maybe I did the wrong thing, but I don't see why. He'll call you here anyway, so we'll be getting the same information."

His face softened. "You're right. I just hate for

everyone to know our business. They might infer the wrong things."

"About what?"

"Maybe they'll judge me for falling in love with you so soon after Dana's murder," he said.

"We don't care what they think, we just want them to find Dana's killer," I said.

"You're right, Ariane. You have good common sense, and you're going to have a good effect on me," he said.

I relaxed a little, but was afraid to say anything else for fear it would be the wrong thing. So much had happened so quickly, he was probably just jumpy. We finished eating.

"I bet you're tired. How's your head?" he inquired tenderly.

"Much better."

"Do you want to sleep alone? If you do, just tell me, I'll understand."

"No, I don't. I don't ever want to sleep alone again," I said. I meant it. I could hardly wait to turn over the nocturnal hours to Tom. I'd sleep when he slept, wake when he woke; our dreams would intermingle, our bodies overlap. I would wake up and not know where my body stopped and his started. I'd be a part of someone else forever, protected, enclosed.

"Good," he said, "because I don't want you to sleep alone." He circled my head with his forefinger, then grabbed the collar of my sweater, pulled me to him. His body enveloped mine like molten wax; every inch of my skin was covered with his satiny flesh.

His arm grasped my waist, lifting me from the couch, where we reclined. He swept as much as walked me into the bedroom, pushing me down on his king-size bed. I didn't remember our removing our clothes. Maybe they evaporated in the heat of our passion.

When we made love, I imagined that we exchanged identities. When we finished and switched back, small parts of each of us broke off, remaining locked in the other's soul. I hoped neither of us could ever be whole again without the other.

I woke up the next morning to the sound of birds singing. For a moment I thought I was back in Scappoose. I wondered if they were the birds from our birdhouse in our big backyard tree.

Then I remembered I was at Tom's. His place beside me was empty; he was already up. I grabbed his black terry-cloth robe, threw it on, walked toward the kitchen. Tom was dressed, reading the newspaper.

"Good morning. Sleep well?" he asked, smiling.

"Wonderfully," I said. He stood up.

"Help yourself to breakfast. I've got to see some clients in the office. I should be back around five."

"I'll call Detective Martinez, find out if he knows anything new," I said.

"Good idea." He started to leave, then added, "Oh, don't go into my office, it's a mess in there." He pointed to the phone in the kitchen. "That one hardly ever rings because everyone has the office number. Say, want me to turn on the Jacuzzi for you? You might want to take one later."

"No, thanks, I don't like Jacuzzis, they make me nervous. I'm always afraid I'll stay in too long," I said. He smiled, gave me quick kiss on the cheek, left.

My appetite had not returned. I ate a minuscule

portion of bran flakes. The milk seemed almost too luxurious. Once I got used to being part of Tom, maybe I could push the boundaries of life farther.

I wandered around the masculine, woody house. Would he want me to make it more feminine? But to do that, I'd have to have a better sense of myself as a woman. Dana had been the decorating maven. I'd always lived out of a suitcase in her space.

What to do? It felt strange to be here; I was disintegrating. I needed something to hold on to, some little part of myself to grab on to, until Tom got home. I meandered toward the back of the house. I opened a door. There were the boxes with Dana's possessions in them, and her furniture. I walked in.

I opened one of the boxes, took out some of her sweaters. I remembered the green V neck; she had worn it with a black leather miniskirt. I pulled out a faded red cardigan she had had since high school. She had always worn it when she had a cold.

I picked up an armful of sweaters, smelled them. They smelled of Chanel No. Five, her scent. I stroked the sleeve of a light blue cashmere, imagined that Dana's perfectly formed arm was in it.

I hugged the sweaters, then sadly put them back. What was that fabric in the corner of the box? I didn't recognize it. I tugged it out. It was Dana's beige straw purse!

I opened it. Her wallet, makeup, keys were all in it. I looked through her wallet for any messages, secreted notes. There was nothing. She had twenty dollars in her billfold, some change in her change purse.

Where had the movers found it? I had searched her entire apartment, but then, I'd been in such a state of anxiety at that time. And Tom had searched the place before I had. The straw bag had obviously been shoved in among sweaters in one of her drawers.

The phone rang. I answered it. It was Detective Martinez.

"We're going to have a chance to question Mark Farrington in person soon," he said.

"How?"

"His attorney is working out a deal with the D.A. on the Madison's case, and he's coming back next week—voluntarily."

Farrington was coming back! I could hardly wait to tell Tom the news.

"Could you have Tom Crandall call me, please?" Martinez asked.

"Of course," I said.

Farrington, Dana . . . I sank into thought. Obsession blots out everything else. When Dana was alive, I had been obsessed with her; now I was obsessed with her death.

By finding her murderer, bringing him to justice, I could be even closer to her. I knew it was sick, but it was how I felt. Sometimes obsession distorts truth. You are watching the sun. Then a cloud passes over the sun, keeps going. While it blots out the sun, you stare at it. Then, as it passes by, you keep staring at it, unaware that the sun is shining brightly again, in another corner of the sky. You care only about the cloud now.

I had lost interest in my life, was obsessed only by Dana's death, by Dana's lover.

Farrington was coming back! I felt joyous, expansive, almost high. But why did Martinez want to talk to Tom? Could they still suspect him? Ridiculous.

I showered, dressed, put on makeup. I wanted to spend money, even though I hardly had any. I wanted to cook Tom a fabulous dinner. I could make a few meals and I knew how to bake an apple pie.

I drove to the nearby corner grocery store, Brentwood Foods. The place was upscale, like everything else in Brentwood. The produce, the meat, everything glistened with goodness. I bought a tritip roast, Yukon gold potatoes, fresh broccoli. Then I got the ingredients for the pie—firm, green pippin apples.

Wine? Why not? White or red? I knew you were supposed to serve red wine with meat, but what if he preferred white? I bought both. I also bought two colorful bouquets of flowers with blooms of red, yellow and purple. They were gorgeous, at their very peak of beauty. As I paid for the flowers, a woman behind me in line smiled as if she knew me.

"I've never seen you buy flowers before," she said.

I'd never seen this woman before in my life. She was a typical older matron: thick glasses; short white, straight hair; tailored denim skirt; a feeling of good nutrition about her.

"You haven't?" I asked, trying to get away from her.

"No. I've seen you and your boyfriend grocery shopping. And that one time you were upset, I loaned you a quarter for the pay phone, remember?"

"No, I don't. I've never been in this grocery store before."

"What are you talking about?" the woman said,

annoyed. Then I realized she must have seen Dana with Tom.

"Wait, I'm sorry," I told her. "I think you used to see my sister here with her boyfriend. We look somewhat alike."

"Well," she said, pausing, "maybe. I'm sorry, too. My eyes aren't what they used to be. And I live right across the street from him."

"That's all right. I'm flattered that you think I look like my sister. Did you know her well? Do you know Tom?"

"No, he's a newcomer. I've been in the neighborhood for thirty years. I only noticed her because she was so pretty. Is she here with you today?"

It dawned on me that not everyone in the world knew that Dana had been murdered. Again that awkward moment—how to say it? But I had to. She'd said Dana had been upset, so maybe she knew something. I lowered my voice, leaned in toward the woman.

"I don't know how to say this, but there was a terrible tragedy. My sister was murdered," I told her.

"What?" the woman nearly screamed. Several people turned to look at us. "Was it at an ATM machine, that one in the back of the bank on San Vicente? I never feel safe there."

"No—at least I don't think so. The police don't actually know where she was murdered, but they know where she was found. Listen, you said she was upset once and you loaned her a quarter for the pay phone. Do you have any idea what—?"

Before I could finish, the woman swung her grocery cart away, glanced at me fearfully and quickly left, as if I were the murderer.

When I got back to Tom's, the phone was ringing. I tried to go into his office to answer it, but the door was locked. How odd! Then I remembered that Tom didn't want me to answer that phone—but why had he locked the door?

Didn't he trust me? I had heard that financial advisors were entrusted with confidential information, so maybe that was it. But why lock the door on me? Whom did I know, and what did I know about financial issues anyway?

I would prove to him how trustworthy I was. I would be worthy of his love. Love had to be earned, and I would earn it.

I found vases and arranged the flowers, started to make the pie crust. I hoped he'd be pleasantly surprised with the result. The phone rang again. It was Tom. I told him to call Detective Martinez. He said he would, and was just calling to see if I was all right.

I hung up, went back to cooking. The phone rang again. I grabbed it.

"Hello?"

"Ariane?" a strange female voice inquired.

"Yes?"

"Do you know who this is?"

"No, I don't."

"It's Lori Wells. Do you remember me?"

"Yes, of course." I didn't know what to say. "Tom isn't here. He won't be back till dinnertime. I think you can reach him at his office."

"His office? Does he have an office?"

"Yes, in Century City, I don't remember the name of it," I said with a sinking feeling. I shouldn't have told her that; he probably didn't want her to know he had an office.

"That's okay. Look, I called to talk to you."

"Me?"

"Yes. Now that I know you're there, I'll call you tomorrow to set up an appointment. Bye."

⚒ 14 ⚒

What if Lori came now? Should I lock the doors? Turn the alarm system on? Was I in danger? Where was Tom's gun? Should I try to find it? I checked the front door, the back door, the side door, locked them. The alarm system looked too complicated. If only I knew Tom's phone number, but I didn't. Should I call Detective Martinez? And tell him what? That I was afraid of one of Tom's ex-girlfriends?

It sounded silly in light of Dana's brutal death. What time was it? Tom would be home for dinner later; I'd wait and tell him. Hopefully Lori Wells would not come now, but would call tomorrow.

Apprehensively, I continued preparations for dinner. I finished slicing the apples, made the pie crust, put the pie in the oven. I prepared the roast, the baked potatoes. It all would be ready by the time Tom came home.

Suddenly there was a knock on the door. I froze. Who was it? It was only Tom. He was early. What a relief! I forgot I had locked the door. I rushed to open it.

"You got scared and put the double lock on?" he asked.

"Kind of," I said as he came in, slammed the door.

"What do you mean, kind of?" he asked, kissing me. I was embarrassed to tell him that Lori had called, because she had said she wanted to talk to me. She was jealous of me. Tom must have told her we were involved. I brought on problems for Tom. What if she had called him at his office in Century City? I waited for him to mention something about it, but he didn't.

"My nerves are jumpy, that's all," I said.

"I understand. I went to see Martinez and decided to come home early," Tom said.

"What did he say?"

"We just went over the same stuff—my 'alibi,' so to speak. I'm not angry; he has to suspect everyone. Look, I've got some work I have to do here. I'll be done by dinner."

Tom took out a key, opened the door to his office, went in, closed the door. I heard him start to play back his phone messages. Was it my imagination, or had he begun to listen, then turned down the volume so I wouldn't hear? Should I be offended?

I set the table, found silver candlesticks and tall white candles, then lay down on the couch and dozed off. About half an hour later, Tom came into the living room and sat down.

"What smells so good?" he asked.

"Do you like roast beef, baked potatoes, apple pie?"

"Do I ever!"

Just then the doorbell rang, and we both looked up, surprised.

"Are you expecting anyone?" he asked. I shuddered. I knew who it was.

"Tom, I was afraid to tell you because it might upset you, but Lori Wells called here today. I think that's her. I'm really sorry, but I told her you had an office in Century City. What's the name of your company again?" I asked, rattling on, too nervous to think or talk straight.

He stared at me as if he didn't comprehend what I was saying. Then he got up. He seemed oddly calm.

"The company is Myers and Roberts. Now, don't worry. I'll handle Lori," he said. He opened the door. She walked into the hallway, glanced at me. Should I say hello? She didn't. She looked tense, but not dangerous.

"Lori and I are going out into the backyard to talk, Ariane," he said. She wasn't carrying a purse, so she couldn't have a weapon. I didn't have to worry about Tom's safety. He was persuasive; he could calm her down, if that was what it took. I figured if he didn't come in in half an hour, I'd go out there, just to make sure he was okay.

I turned up the stereo so I wouldn't hear their conversation if she started screaming at him. Poor Tom, he was trying to let her down nicely, but how to break her obsession?

Everything had happened so fast, I had forgotten to tell him about Farrington coming back. Maybe Martinez had told him. I wondered if I would feel any sense of relief if Farrington were convicted of murder. If the police couldn't find the evidence to convict him, Tom and I would hire the best private investigator we could find.

I sliced the roast, then put it back in the oven to

keep warm. I began to watch the clock, growing more and more nervous as time went by. If Tom didn't show up soon, I was going outside. Just then he came in through the back door.

"Are you all right?" I asked.

"Fine," he said calmly. "I was ridiculous to be afraid of her. She's not dangerous to anyone except maybe herself. That woman is so damaged. I feel sorry for her."

"What did you tell her?"

"She threatened to get a lawyer," he said, "and sue me if I didn't give her the money she insists I owe her. I just told her that the money was a fantasy. She said she was going to call her father. He'll understand that she's having problems again. She won't bother us anymore."

He appeared preoccupied, as if he didn't want to discuss it further. I set out the food and we started to eat. I wanted to get to know his moods so I could better predict what he would require from me in terms of love and support. I liked the way he looked, so tall, so statuesque, even sitting down. As he ate, his mood improved.

"What did you do today, Ariane?" he asked.

"Nothing, really. Just went to the store. Did Martinez tell you that Farrington was coming back?"

"Yes, and we should know something soon," he said.

I knew I was forgetting to tell him something. The Lori Wells incident had confused me. Then I remembered.

"Tom, I almost forgot! I found Dana's purse, the one we thought she was carrying when she disappeared. Her wallet, keys, everything was in it," I said.

His expression was one of disbelief. "I looked all over her apartment and I didn't see it anywhere. Where did you find it?" he asked.

"In with her sweaters—the movers must have found it. I thought I had searched everywhere, too. I must have missed it."

"Another factor pointing to Farrington," Tom said. "She never would have gone out without her purse—unless she was with someone she knew very well."

We just looked at each other, thinking the same thoughts. We finished our dinner, and I brought out the apple pie.

"What a dinner, Ariane, whew! I don't have room for that pie right now. Just leave it out, unless you want some now. I'll have a piece before I go to bed," he said, then sighed with fatigue.

"I'm sorry, but I have some more work to do. I'll be late. Don't bother with the dishes—I can do them tomorrow. You still have to take it easy."

"I feel fine. I'll do them," I said. He got up, gave me a kiss on the head, went into his office, closed the door.

It was a strange feeling to finally be mainstream. I was doing what I had always wanted to do, taking care of a man. Someday, hopefully, I'd be taking care of a family.

In truth, I was tired. My head was beginning to ache and I was happy to finish up, got to bed. It was very early in the morning when I heard Tom get into bed. He reached for me, held me close, removed my nightgown, made gentle love to me. Our breathing was synchronized.

I imagined that our lungs breathed as one. We finished, just as the light was peeking through the curtains. He held me in a spoon position as he fell asleep.

I was too exhilarated to sleep. I was curled within his embrace; one of his legs was under me, the other leg stretched out over my legs. In my dreamy state, I thought I saw the brown butterfly birthmark on his ankle, like the one Dana and I had. I fancied that it had flown from my ankle onto his during our lovemaking. It was proof that we had really merged. I fell happily asleep.

I woke up to the phone ringing. I heard Tom's message come on, but the volume was turned too low for me to actually distinguish the words. I was always alert for a call from Detective Martinez. Tom heard it, too, jumped out of bed.

"Sorry, I forgot to close the door," he said, rushing toward his office. He probably gave his clients superb service. That he was successful and conscientious was a fringe benefit. I never expected to get that in a mate. I just wanted to be loved.

Tom was out of his office in a flash and into the shower. I got up to make breakfast. It was late, 9 A.M. I looked out the front window. The neighbor who had approached me at the market was out pruning her roses. She had a sun hat on, moving with confidence among dozens of her yellow rose bushes.

I looked toward the left but could see only the street, not the house next door. The street was empty. People parked their cars in the garage, and there was no foot traffic. Wait, there was a car parked down the street. I looked again, and recognized Lori's gold BMW.

Had she come back during the night? Was she

hiding on the grounds of Tom's house? I rushed to the bathroom door, banged on it.

"What is it, Ariane? Come in," Tom shouted from inside. I burst into the bedroom. Tom was in the shower. I could see him through the beveled-glass shower door. I was rendered mute by the majesty of Tom's naked body. I tried not to stare, but I couldn't help it.

"What?" Tom asked.

"Lori's car is parked down the street," I said. He grabbed a big white towel, got out of the shower.

"Damn it. She did that again, she left her car," he said, starting to rub himself dry.

"What do you mean, she left her car?"

"She got hysterical last night. She said she was too upset to drive home, wanted me to drive her, but I refused. She ran away from me crying. She probably walked to San Vicente and called a cab. Now she'll have an excuse to come back, to get her car."

"But I'll be here alone again today," I said.

"Right, but don't worry," he said, flipping the white towel into a rope, throwing it over my head, pulling me to him, kissing me.

"I'll call her, tell her the car is on the way. I don't have the keys, I'll just have it towed. That'll teach her to play games. Okay?"

"Fine," I said. I followed Tom into the bedroom, where he started to get dressed.

"You feel better, Ariane?"

"Fine."

"Why don't I take you over to your apartment so you can get the rest of your stuff? I'll be busy for only a couple hours. I can pick you up on my way home. I have a short meeting in Beverly Hills."

"I'm still a little dizzy, Tom. I'd rather wait a few more days before I go over there. I want to give some people my new number in case they remember anything."

"Okay, then why don't you get dressed and come with me? There's a deli near my meeting—you can have coffee and read the paper."

"Can't I just stay here?"

"I'd rather you didn't," he said forcefully.

"Because of her?" I asked. Tom looked down, nodded.

"If you call her and tell her you're having her car towed, she won't come. And if she does, I just won't open the door."

"You're probably right. I'll be home by eleven at the latest," he said, finishing getting dressed. He didn't even have time for breakfast, just hurried out the door.

I had to keep busy for the next hour and a half so I wouldn't worry myself about Lori. I got dressed, went out to look at Tom's front yard. Every flower bush was well tended; he must have a good gardener. I'd always wanted to have window boxes, but his house was not the proper style for that.

He had a flowering plum tree in addition to the jacaranda tree. But there were no trees for climbing. I knew I was too old to climb trees, but if Tom and I were to have children, how wonderful it would be if they could explore a rangy mass of sturdy branches in the sky. I looked down the street. There was no sign of Lori Wells, thank goodness.

"Do you garden?" a strange voice yelled at me.

I jumped. Had I missed her? I turned around, but it wasn't Lori, it was the neighbor across the street. I thought she had gone in. She crossed the street, pruning shears in hand, to talk to me.

"I'm Olga Hansen. We met at the market, remember?" she said.

I nodded. "Yes."

"I'm sorry I ran away from you. It was just such a shock when you said that beautiful sister of yours was murdered. I was so horrified, guess I over-reacted. Not very neighborly of me."

"I understand. I can still hardly believe it myself."

"Was she mugged? I've heard of robbers following people home from fancy restaurants, forcing them to open their front doors. Then they rob them and kill them."

"No, it wasn't like that," I said. "We think it was someone she knew, an ex-boyfriend, but no one has been charged yet. I hope he will be soon."

"Were you two girls close?"

"So close. It's hard for me to go on without her."

"And now you're staying here with her boyfriend?"

"Uh, yes," I said, not wanting to explain fully.

Mrs. Hansen patted me on the shoulder. "Well, I'm so sorry, dear. If you need a cup of sugar or anything, come on over. I simply can't get over it. Why, that pretty girl was standing with her boyfriend just where you are only a month ago, and now she's dead."

"Was she looking at the trees?" I asked. I imagined Dana had been thinking of our childhood, too.

"Don't really know. I was in a hurry that day

because my daughter was giving me a seventieth birthday party at the Ritz-Carlton.

"Well, I'd better get home. Nice to have met you, dear, and I'm sorry," she said as she started to walk back to her yard.

"Oh, Mrs. Hansen, just a minute . . ."

"What, dear?"

"You meant that you saw Dana—my sister, Dana—two months ago. About two months ago, right?"

"What? Now, let me see . . . No, it was on my birthday, like I said, a month ago, the sixteenth. My eyes may be bad, but I know when my birthday is," she said huffily, marching across the street and into her house.

A month ago? That was impossible. Dana had already been missing a month ago. Mrs. Hansen probably had the date right, the sixteenth, but it was *two* months ago, on the sixteenth of the month. Old age makes one forget details.

I went back into the house. The phone rang; I answered it.

"Hello?"

"It's Detective Martinez. Miss Richardson?"

"Yes?"

"Farrington is coming back tomorrow. His lawyer says he has something interesting to tell us concerning Dana's disappearance. Something that will clear Farrington."

"What is it?"

"The attorney wouldn't say."

"He did it, you know it!" I said, outraged.

"I can't say anything until we've charged a suspect."

"Just tell me one thing—was Dana raped?"

"No, Miss Richardson, it wasn't a sex crime," the detective said.

Thank God, I thought. Bad enough she was murdered, at least she hadn't been raped.

"Will you be at this number tomorrow?" he asked.

"Yes. Will you call me as soon as you know anything?"

"Miss Richardson, we want to solve this as badly as you do. Good-bye."

Of course, Farrington would do anything to save his neck. It wouldn't be long now; the police would trap him. He wouldn't get away with Dana's murder.

My head was starting to pound, probably from emotional stress. Just the thought of Farrington was unbearable. I made the bed, did the few dishes. I didn't have the concentration to read and had never liked to watch daytime television. It was almost eleven, so Tom would be home soon.

I looked at myself in the mirror. My face was pale and I had dark circles under my eyes. My grief over Dana still showed on my face. Should I try to get some color, a tan? It was sunny out. No, that might make my headache worse.

How about the Jacuzzi? I didn't like them, but it might relax me. Tom had even suggested it yesterday. I walked into the den, looked at the Jacuzzi through the glass doors. It was covered with a thick blue plastic cover. Tom had said he never covered it. Maybe the gardener had.

The controls were on the wall near the outside door. They looked easy to operate, just a matter of turning on a timer switch.

Should I chance it? All I would have to do was

remove the cover, which was loosely tied down
with two ropes, then turn on the switch. I had no
bathing suit with me but could go in naked; the
tub was completely enclosed behind a high wall. I
decided to do it.

I went into the bedroom, found the black terry-
cloth robe of Tom's, took off my clothes, put it on.
I opened the glass doors, walked out to the Jacuzzi.
I untied the ropes, carefully pulled the cover off.

Wait! There was something in the water, just below the surface. Oh, my God! It couldn't be! I
looked closer, not wanting to believe what I saw.
Lori Wells was floating in the water, dead!

I screamed. Then I felt like I was going to faint. I expected someone to hear my scream, rush to Tom's house. But no one did. I had to calm down! Wait, was she really dead? Maybe she was just unconscious. I looked closely at her; she didn't seem to be breathing.

What had happened? Had Lori sneaked back into the yard after she ran away, hidden in the Jacuzzi? But how had she drowned? Had she crawled under the plastic cover, or had she got in the Jacuzzi, then pulled it over her?

No, that wasn't possible—she couldn't have tied the ropes if she was under the plastic. I bent down and studied her more closely. It didn't look as if she had hit her head. Maybe she had fainted in the water, then drowned.

What if someone had murdered her? I had to call 911 immediately. I walked backward, as if in a trance, continuing to stare at her body. Was she still alive?

What if this were like a horror movie, and suddenly she jumps up, grabs me by the throat? Wait, had she just moved? Suddenly everything seemed to sway. I heard a buzzing in my head; I was starting to panic. I narrowed my eyes so I could see for sure if she moved. Had she shaken her head?

I had to call Tom immediately, before the police. I rushed to the phone—what was the name of his office? I had to think, think hard. Wait, it was Myers and Roberts. Was that it? Keeping an eye on Lori, I dialed information.

"Could it be listed under some other name? I find no listing for that spelling," the operator said.

"Maybe under financial companies, brokerage houses?"

"No, I'm sorry," she said.

I must have the name wrong. "Do you have a listing for a Tom Crandall in Century City?"

"No, nothing there, either. Would you like to speak to my supervisor?" she asked.

I pulled up the Levolors, stared at the Jacuzzi through the window. Wait, had Lori moved? I slammed down the phone in fright. The gun! I had to find Tom's gun, the one that he'd had in his suitcase in Big Sur. I felt wet. I was drenched in sweat, my body completely soaked under Tom's robe.

I rushed into his bedroom, wondering where the gun would be. I started opening drawers, one after the other; just underwear, shirts. Nothing. Where else?

The office! But didn't he keep it locked? I thought I heard footsteps—was she out of the water, stalking me? I was terrified. I ducked into the closet, heard nothing. I needed to get the gun. I opened the closet door an inch. I ran toward Tom's office.

The door was open! I went in, started going through drawers again. Finally, in the bottom drawer, there was the gun. I grabbed it, started deep breathing. I didn't know how to shoot it, but if my life was in danger, I'd figure it out.

Wait a minute. What if Tom had murdered her? Part of me had never trusted him. No, that was ridiculous. Or was it? Was I next? I couldn't think straight.

I started to call the police, then stopped. Do I tell them she's dead, or that she's hiding in the house? Which is it? Was she still in the Jacuzzi? Was I hallucinating from panic?

I walked out to the Jacuzzi. She looked dead. What was that in the water near her? I clutched the gun, walked right to the edge of the Jacuzzi. I bent in, close, to look at her.

I held onto the side of the Jacuzzi with one hand. I felt dizzy, quivered with fear. I aimed the gun at her, just in case. I was staring at dark liquid that was floating above her chest; it was the same color as the stain on her white blouse. It was blood!

Blood? Could she have scraped her body after she drowned? But on what? The Jacuzzi was lined with smooth, navy-blue-and-white tiles. I drew back, still aiming the gun at her, even though she was dead.

"Ariane! Oh, my God, what have you done?" Tom yelled, rushing over to me. His voice seemed to come from miles away. I had no idea what he was talking about.

"Careful, careful, put the gun down, put it down slowly, Ariane—careful," he said, putting his hand on my arm to steady me. He forced my arm down. I gently put the gun down. He grabbed me, hugged me, pulled me away from the Jacuzzi.

"Tom, Lori . . ."

"What happened?" he asked. "She came at you and you killed her in self-defense?"

"What?" I said, stunned.

"I shouldn't have left you alone—this is all my fault," he said, hugging me tight. "I never would forgive myself if something happened to you."

What was he talking about? Nothing was making sense—it was all a jumble. Then I understood: he thought Lori had tried to kill me, that I had killed her. When he saw me, I was holding the gun, she was dead in the water.

"Tom, wait—no—you don't understand," I began. He just hugged me tighter, interrupted me.

"You don't have to explain. I know you didn't do it on purpose. Don't worry, Ariane, nothing will happen to you," he said. "I won't let you go to prison. I'll call a lawyer right away. Lori had a well-documented history of violence, of having been committed to mental institutions. I think several people even got restraining orders against her."

"Tom, just wait! It wasn't like that at all," I said, pulling back from him, stepping away from the gun. "You've got it all wrong. It's not what it looks like. Lori was dead when I found her."

"Ariane," he said with hurt in his eyes, "don't you trust me? I would think that after everything we've gone through, you would trust me. You don't have to lie to me. I know you didn't kill her on purpose."

"But, Tom, just listen to me! I didn't kill her!" I told him exactly what had happened.

"She didn't drown, Ariane, she was shot. There's blood coming from her chest," he said. He grabbed a towel off the cement, picked up the gun, examined it while being careful not to touch it.

"There's a bullet missing, one bullet, Ariane," he said, as if accusing me.

"Tom, this is crazy! I'd tell you if I killed her. I can see why you think what you do, but it didn't happen that way. Someone else must have shot her. The bullet might not even have come from that gun."

"How did you get into my office and find the gun?" he asked, rather coldly.

"The door was open—you left it open. When I saw her in the Jacuzzi, I wasn't sure she was dead. I thought she might be dazed, unconscious. I was afraid she would come at me, so I started searching for your gun. I found it in the desk drawer."

"I must have left the door open by mistake—so much has been going on," he said. Why was he upset, at a time like this, about leaving his office unlocked?

"Tom, I didn't kill her! I swear it! I would tell you if I did. She must have sneaked back into the yard late last night, after we were asleep. The gates are left open. Or maybe she came back this morning, after you left, I was in the front yard talking to a neighbor. I wasn't facing the house, so I wouldn't have seen her if she'd come in through the back way."

"A neighbor? What neighbor? How do you know a neighbor?"

"Just the lady from across the street, a Mrs. Hansen. She introduced herself to me. We talked for a couple of minutes—before that I was in the front yard looking at the flowers. Lori could have come in then."

"And she shot herself?" he asked.

Shot herself? I wasn't thinking straight. How

could she have shot herself, then fallen into the Jacuzzi? Besides, there had been no gun present.

Lori's dead body loomed like an inflated doll in
the water. I wanted to cover her up; it was a horrid
sight. I walked over to Tom, but he drew back from
me: he thought I was a killer.

"Tom, you've got to believe me. She was dead.
I don't know who killed her, or when. I got the
gun for protection, but I never fired it. The police
will be able to tell if the bullet came from that gun.
I'd never lie to you—for a moment I even thought
you killed her," I said, moving forward and kissing
his lips.

"Me? Oh, God, you suspected me?" he asked,
horrified. He wrapped his long arms loosely
around me, rested his head on my back. I liked the
weight of it; I liked him weak, depending on me.
Our breathing was comfortably synchronized, like
when we made love. How could I have suspected
this gentle man?

"Ariane," he said, disentangling himself from
me, "do you think it's possible that someone is trying to frame me?"

"What?" I said.

"Say the person who murdered Dana knows I
was her lover. Now they've murdered Lori and
dumped her body here to look as if I did it. You
said Farrington was coming back—maybe he arranged this."

"Oh, my God, I never thought of that! But how
would he know Lori Wells or anything about her?"
I asked.

"I don't know. I don't know anything anymore,"
Tom said, holding his head.

"But the bullet will prove you didn't do it. It

won't have come from your gun," I said.

"They might think I had another gun I shot her with, then threw away. Or what if the person who killed her was following her, came into the house, found my gun, used it? I can't even think anymore.

"Poor Lori, who would do this? She was troubled, but she didn't deserve this. Oh, God, I'm going to have to call her father and tell him," he said, upset. He walked into the house. I followed him. We went into the living room and he sat down on the couch in anguish.

"Ariane, I'm sure now that someone is trying to frame me. What if they succeed?"

"But they won't. You weren't even here this morning—you have an alibi."

"I was with a client for about an hour, and then at my office."

"The police will be able to determine the time of death. If it was last night, you were in bed with me most of the night."

"But what if my time is unaccounted for at the exact time she was killed? What if she told people that I had invested her money badly and that I wouldn't pay her back? She could have told people anything."

"You think Farrington had Lori killed, so that the police would also think you killed Dana?" I asked. Tom nodded.

"Let's just call the police, let them figure this out. You have nothing to worry about," I said, going for the phone, picking it up. Tom grabbed the receiver, tore it out of my hand, slammed it down.

"Tom?!!" I said, shocked.

"Just a minute, let's not do anything hasty. What if the police come, think I did it, arrest me?"

"Then we'd get a lawyer."

"What if he loses?"

"What?"

"Ariane, justice can be bought, the innocent don't always go free, the guilty aren't always punished. You're a bit naive."

"Naive? But it's our only choice. We can't just leave her here—she's dead! We've got to call the police."

"I don't know who I'm up against here, Ariane. Are you on my side or on the other side?" he asked.

"The other side?"

"Who's doing this to me? Maybe it's some enemy of mine in business—maybe it isn't Farrington. Maybe this wasn't about Dana; maybe it's about me," he said.

"What?" I said. I sat down on the couch, trying to absorb all this. If Farrington had nothing to do with Dana's death, perhaps it was a business rival of Tom's. I had read about things like that, maybe he was involved in shady dealings. Tom? No, he couldn't be.

"Do you have any idea who could have done this? Who wants to destroy you?" I asked him. He ran his hand through his hair in a frenzied fashion.

"I've been involved in various conflicts with people for years—it's not an easy business. I've been sued, but I don't know who would have such a vendetta. It may be someone who feels I didn't live up to my fiduciary responsibilities in the past, but who? Who is this crazy?"

Tom stared at the floor for a very long time, probably hoping for an epiphany, but no guilty name popped into his mind, or at least he didn't reveal one. He put his face in his hands for a moment, then took them away.

"Ariane, the worst of it is, this means I could be responsible for Dana's death—and Lori's. If I inadvertently harmed someone financially, or even if I didn't but they thought I did, two innocent people have died because of me. I feel horrible," he said, his eyes filled with tears. I moved to him, hugged him.

"We don't know that yet. It could still be Farrington trying to throw suspicion on you," I said, then revealed what I knew about Dana's masterminding of Farrington's illegal activities at Madison's. Tom looked disbelieving.

"I can't understand why she just didn't come to me for money if she needed it," he said sadly. "Dana knew I would give her anything she asked for. This explains why she could get anything she wanted out of Farrington, all those clothes."

"Don't stop loving her because of what I just told you, Tom. She was mixed up, like all of us, but she was a very good person. It was hard growing up without a father—it screwed us up in a lot of ways. Dana felt she had to be the provider."

"Growing up without a father, yes, that would be hard," he said, his eyes darkening to a navy blue.

If he only knew how hard; if he only knew that I feared no man would ever love me because my own father didn't, because my own father didn't stick around to watch me grow up. My father didn't even love my mother enough to know or care that he had sired children with her. Was my mother that unlovable? Am I?

"Tom, we're losing it. We've got to call the police," I said.

"But I'm afraid of the police."

"We have to take that chance, because we know that you're innocent. We'll be able to prove it. We can't simply live here forever with a dead body. It's just a matter of time before someone notices that Lori is missing. They'll trace her to your house—her car is parked out there."

Tom got up slowly, looked through the front windows. I followed him, looked, too. The car was gone.

"What happened to it?"

"I called to have it towed. They must have done it while we were in the back."

"Well, the police will find out it was towed from here. We're not actually discussing not calling them, are we, Tom?" I asked. He just looked at me as if he were deaf. He was still in shock, simply didn't know right from wrong. I would have to take over, just call them. Would he be angry at me?

"Honey, you sit down. Can I make you some tea? Some toast?" I asked.

I walked into the kitchen, and he followed me. I put water in the tea kettle, threw bread into the toaster.

"Tom, remember that Xanax you gave me when we found out Dana was dead? Do you want to take one? Shall I get it?"

"No, just the tea. I've got to analyze this," he said, in no condition to analyze anything. I gave him the tea, buttered toast, raspberry jam. He ate hungrily. I couldn't eat a thing—Lori's dead body was visible from the kitchen. I decided to take things into my own hands; he was out of control.

"I've got to go to the bathroom," he said, bolting from the table, dashing toward the bathroom, slamming the door. The tension had finally gotten to him. I rushed into his office just as the phone rang. It might be Martinez—my problems would be solved!

"Hello?" I answered.

"Mr. Edwards?" a male voice inquired.

"Mr. Edwards? No, this is Tom Crandall's residence," I said.

"Oh, I'm sorry, I must have the wrong number," the man said, hanging up.

What a time for a wrong number! I pressed down the button, then released it, started to call 911.

"Ariane?" Tom appeared at the door. "I asked you not to call the police yet. Just let me calm down, please?"

I put down the phone.

"That's a good girl. Now come here," he said. I dutifully went over to him; he patted my head, put his arm around me, led me into the living room. We sat down.

I glanced at the clock. Had it really been an hour since Tom got home? We had to call the police—this was thoroughly unnerving, horrifying.

"Tom, we've got to do what's right—it's against the law not to call the authorities. I'll say whatever you want. Why don't you go back to your office? I'll pretend you never came home. I'll say I discovered Lori, which I did."

"You'd say you discovered . . . ?"

"Yes," I shouted. "I'll even say you didn't come home last night—anything so they won't suspect you. But we've got to have her body removed."

Tom sat considering my offer. He put his hands in the prayer position, rested the tips of his fingers against his forehead.

"There's just one problem with your plan, Ariane."

"What's that?"

"There's no protection."

"Why do you need protection, Tom?"

"I'm not the one who needs protection, Ariane."

"What?"

"You do."

⚡ 16 ⚡

"*Me? What do* you mean?" I asked, hoarse with fear.

Tom stood up, took my hands in his, leaned over me. "Don't you see? You're the next victim."

"What?"

"Listen very carefully, Ariane. I've figured it out. Someone is trying to frame me, to hurt me. The killer has killed two women I've had affairs with. You're the next target," he said.

Two women had died because Tom loved them. He was right, I could be next. For a split second I wanted to be next. If I died for the same reason Dana had, I would share in her death, we would be joined forever. But that thought wasn't right. Dana hadn't wanted to die, and I had to avenge her murder. If I was dead, how could I?

Tom was staring at me to see if I got it. I slowly nodded.

"The problem is, only I can protect you. If they take me to jail, you will be at risk."

"The police will protect me if it comes to that, once we tell them our theory," I said.

"Ariane, if they arrest me, they'll think they have the killer. I can't take the chance of leaving you alone."

"This is crazy, Tom. They're not going to arrest you."

"But what if they do? I'm innocent but incarcerated, and you're dead. Why even take the chance?"

"What are you suggesting?"

"This. It doesn't matter where the police find Lori's body. They'll connect me with the murder if they find her here. The important thing is that they find her body someplace else. We'll take her body, dump it."

"Isn't that illegal, removing a body, disturbing a crime scene?"

"Ariane! I'm trying to save your life. Once they find Dana's killer, Farrington or whoever, we have nothing to worry about. Then we can come forward and explain why we removed Lori's body."

His phone rang, and he rushed to the office, answered it.

"Hello? Yes, this is he. Can I call you back tomorrow, after I look at the numbers? Thanks," he said, hanging up. He sounded amazingly calm for someone in the midst of a horrible crisis. I was in awe. He had figured out the murder pattern, was upset but hadn't cracked.

Now he was cleverly executing a plan that would protect me. I could never think so fast. He embodied my concept of a perfect man. He was vulnerable enough to need me, strong enough to take care of me.

"I'm going to need your help," he said, walking out of his office, locking the door.

"Tom, after all we've been through, do you really think you have to lock me out of your office? I would never invade your privacy," I said.

"Oh, I'm not worried about that. But ever since

Dana was killed, I've been concerned the police might show up to question me. They could confiscate my financial records. I have to protect my clients."

"I'm so relieved. I thought you didn't trust me," I said.

"Don't be ridiculous, of course I trust you. Now I need you to help me get Lori's body into a suitcase."

"Tom! I couldn't touch her!"

"I can't do it alone. Just think about something else—and hurry. We have to work fast," he yelled at me.

As we approached her body, I could see it was bloated. I felt nauseated, tried to hold my breath. He bent down, lifted her arms, started to drag her out of the water.

"Ariane, can you help with the feet?" he asked. That tree in the backyard in Scappoose—think of that tree, I told myself. See that tree, the blue sky through the leafy green leaves, and don't think about what you are doing.

I was still in Tom's robe. I took it off, climbed naked into the Jacuzzi, lifted Lori's legs out. Her skin was clammy. I was so revolted, I almost started throwing up before I completed my task.

As soon as I put her legs on the cement, I grabbed the robe, went for the bathroom. I couldn't contain myself any longer. I'd eaten so little that I got the dry heaves. I thought my stomach itself would come up. I only hoped Tom couldn't hear my retching. It finally stopped.

I walked out to see Tom stuffing Lori's body into a large suitcase. One of her tennis shoes fell off.

"Can you get that shoe, throw it in the suitcase?"

he asked me, finishing his task. I picked up the shoe, tried to toss it into the suitcase without looking at the body. Could this gruesome thing really be happening? Maybe it was just another nightmare that I could wake up from. If only!

"Once I put her body somewhere, no one will connect her with me. Then we have to put our heads together, figure out who is doing this, before they come after you. Do you want to come with me while I dump the body, or stay here?"

The man I loved was dumping a body, taking it away from the crime scene to protect me. An air of unreality hung around each of his words now; it was as if I were in someone else's nightmare, not even my own.

"I—I don't think I feel good enough to go, Tom."

"It doesn't matter. I should be back in an hour. Just in case she told someone she was coming here and the police come to the house, don't answer the door. They have no way of knowing you are here. We need to buy some time."

As he looked at the suitcase, a sense of dread seemed to envelop him. He staggered to the couch, sat down.

"I don't know if I'm up to this myself," he said, fatigued. Then he looked at me, got up.

"But I've got to. We have to stay one step ahead of this—we must keep you safe," he said as he lifted the suitcase. "I'll be back as soon as I can." Then he dragged the suitcase out the door. I couldn't even watch him put it in the car or drive away.

I started to tremble. Everything was out of perspective, whirling past me at a rapid rate. I was sinking into a quagmire. Had I done anything wrong? Was Tom doing something wrong? What was right, what was wrong? All the lines between those two poles were blurring.

What to do? Could I concentrate on anything? Probably not. I had to know how long Farrington had been back, so I called Detective Martinez.

"Farrington is coming back today, and his lawyer is bringing him right to the police station for questioning. The attorney insists he has nothing to hide. I'll call you after we finish with him," he said, then hung up.

I resisted an impulse to tell him that Lori had been murdered, to beg him to send policemen to protect me. How could I even start to explain who Lori was? How could I explain what had happened when I didn't even know for sure?

So Farrington supposedly wasn't even back yet. Had he hired someone to kill Lori? I just had to live for another hour, hour and a half, until Tom came back. If only I could erase everything that had just happened, forget it all for the next ninety minutes, but I couldn't.

The events of the past few days were ricocheting through my mind. I was ambushed by terrifying images—the photo of Dana's face when she was dead, the sight of Lori's bloated body. I started to scream, put my hand over my mouth, fell to the floor crying.

I shoved my fist into my mouth, muffling the sound. I had to stop crying—it was the first break in my armor. Somehow I had to get myself together. I couldn't break apart, not now, not when Tom needed me.

Where was the Xanax that the doctor had prescribed for me? Could I take it with a head injury?

Who cared! If I didn't, I could be hysterical in five minutes. If these feelings of uncontrolled anxiety continued much longer, I might not be able to ever find my way back to sanity.

I rushed to the bathroom, looked through the cabinets, couldn't find the pills. I opened drawer after drawer—finally I found them. I took two out, swallowed them. I sat down, waited for them to take hold. A few minutes passed before they started to work, to eliminate some of my anxiety.

Suddenly the doorbell rang. The police? Had they traced Lori to Tom's house? I'd just wait in this back room until they left. What if they broke in? What if they had a search warrant? The doorbell rang again.

"Anybody home? It's Mrs. Hansen from across the street," she yelled. What could she want? My face was streaked with tears, I was still in Tom's bathrobe, I was in no condition to see her.

"Anybody home? I brought some roses over," she called out. If I just stayed here, she would leave.

"Maybe you're in the back, dear. I'll come around to the back door," she shouted. The original nosy neighbor at the most inopportune time. I rushed out of the back room, which had a big window—she would see me inside. I could hear her coming, I ran out into the backyard, hid behind the guest house.

"Yoo-hoo, anybody home? It's Mrs. Hansen," she said, knocking on the back door. She paused for a few minutes, glanced around the backyard. I could see her, but she couldn't see me.

She waited a few more minutes, then gave up, left. I didn't move until I heard the front gate close.

It was safe now. I started to walk around the guest house.

I saw a broken window at the back of the small house. All the windows were covered. I peeked in the broken window and could see a sliver of light; it illuminated a section of the room. There were no boxes or storage items in it. Tom had said the owner used it for storage. The room was completely empty except for a sleeping bag on the floor.

Strange; I wondered why the owner had lied to Tom. Maybe he didn't want Tom using the guest house. I went back inside the main house, decided to take a shower, get dressed. Maybe an ordinary routine would keep me busy, keep me from freaking out before Tom got back.

I got dressed. I was still shaking. What if the murderer came before Tom got back? What would I do? The gun—I was sure Tom had left the gun here for me. Was the office open?

It was. I walked in, went to the desk drawer I had found it in. It wasn't there. Maybe he'd stuck it in another drawer. I went through all of them; nothing. How about the file cabinets? They were locked. I started to walk out when the phone rang. It rang three times; then Tom's message came on.

"Hi. These are the offices of Mark Edwards and Tom Crandall. We're not in right now, so please leave a message and we'll get right back to you. Wait for the beep."

The beep sounded, then: "Hello, Mr. Edwards. This is Rick Maynard returning your call. I'll be in my office till six. Thanks."

Why was the name Mark Edwards on Tom's machine? Who was Mark Edwards? That was the name the man had asked for when I'd assumed it was the wrong number. Did Tom have a partner? Maybe Edwards was his associate in Century City.

I sat down in the living room, tried to concentrate on a magazine. No luck. I kept thinking about Tom driving around with Lori's dead body. Where would he dump it? What if someone saw him? Would he call the police anonymously, alert them, or would he just leave it there, hoping someone would find it?

Was Farrington at the police station yet? What had they found out? Was Tracy with him or had she stayed in Spain? Was Farrington the murderer, or was it someone with a vendetta against Tom?

How exactly did Tom plan to figure out who the murderer was if it wasn't Farrington? Did he have a list of clients with whom he'd had disputes? Did he already have an idea of the identity of the killer? Would he hire another private investigator?

What would we do? We couldn't stay here; the murderer could find us. We couldn't stay in my apartment; that location, too, was probably known to the murderer. Would we go out of town? Could Tom just leave his business? Would we stay in a hotel in L.A.?

I tried to quiet my mind, but it was a cavernous abyss of doubts, fears. If only I could think of something to do that would restore normalcy.

I called Ferrara's, told them I wouldn't be taking the job. I wanted to call Karina or Sara, just to talk, but I couldn't risk that I might reveal Lori's fate. What did I have to talk about except the most awful subjects?

How had all this happened? I should never have come to L.A. But I'd had to—Dana had asked me to! She had said she needed me! Dana should never have come to L.A. But she'd been planning the move for years, so there was no way I could have dissuaded her. She had thought nothing could be worse than her life in Scappoose. Yet she had found something worse—death. Would I find it, too? I couldn't. I had to carry on for Dana, bring her killer to justice. Now I had Tom, and I had a chance for a wonderful life with him.

It had been an hour since he left. I was starting to hear a buzzing in my head from anxiety. Should I take more Xanax? No. I would let it do its work. I wanted to get out of the house, but I had to wait for Tom. If I went into the front yard, Mrs. Hansen might see me.

Maybe a policeman had pulled Tom over for a traffic offense, discovered Lori's body. Would they arrest Tom? What if he was in jail right now? How would I know? Was he allowed to make a phone call? I didn't even know how to get him a lawyer, but he must know one.

I had to stop thinking of terrible possibilities. The facts as they were, were awful enough.

Was that a door opening? But how could that be? I had the alarm system on. It was probably my imagination, but what if . . . ? I rushed into the kitchen, opened the drawer, grabbed a sharp steak knife. Wasn't there anything bigger? I found a ser- rated cutting knife, which I took out. Wait, maybe sharper was better than bigger. I put the cutting knife back.

I tiptoed toward the back of the house where I could see the back door. It was closed. I walked softly to the side door, then the front door. Both were closed. Of course, there were the windows.

I started to shake, I was going to fall apart, I felt very cold. Maybe there had been no noise, maybe it was just my mind playing tricks on me.

"Ariane? Open up, it's Tom!" His voice shattered my nerves. I screamed. Then I realized how foolish I was. His voice continued echoing in my mind—all I heard was "Tom, Tom, Tom, Tom." I couldn't cut it off. Finally the reverberation stopped. I rushed to the front door, swung it open.

"Ariane, what are you doing with that knife?" he asked, stepping back quickly.

"Oh, Tom, I'm so glad to see you. I thought I heard a noise," I said.

He walked in, slammed the door. "Let's put that down," he said, taking the knife from me. I threw myself into his arms, held him, but he didn't respond. I stepped back.

"I was so worried about you. What happened?"

"Everything's fine," he said very calmly. "I have to call Lori's father."

"And tell him she's been murdered?" I was incredulous. "But you're not supposed to know."

"Right. I'm just going to tell him she's missing, that she was supposed to meet me at my house and never came. He's probably back from Russia now and got my other message about her having problems again. He may even think she did something to herself."

"But we want the police to find her body so they can find out who killed her—and who killed Dana."

"True," he said, walking into his office to call. Lori's father still wasn't back, so he left a message with the man's secretary. He came back out. I was sitting in a chair, just frozen.

"Relax, Ariane, it went fine," he said.

"It went fine? You mean you put her body somewhere and . . . ?"

"Right, and I didn't get caught."

"Didn't get caught?"

"No one saw me. I dumped her in a canyon in Topanga. It'll take a while before anyone finds her."

"You must have been so upset, driving with a dead body—"

"No," he said, interrupting me. "I did what had to be done."

"Oh, of course, I just meant that . . . I don't know what I meant. I'm totally unnerved by all this. Tom, should we stay here, or go somewhere else . . . for safety?"

"That's a good question. I was going to figure that out next. We need some time to figure out who this could be, if it's not Farrington."

"Can you go out of town? Will your office care?"

"The office? Oh, right. That's no problem. My hours are my own."

The phone rang. I waited for him to get it. He didn't, so I did.

"Ariane, it's Detective Martinez. We've questioned Farrington, and I'm quite sure he wasn't involved in Dana's death."

"You are?"

"Yes. With what we know now, we're sure he had no motive. He and Dana were partners in their scam, like you said. She was even setting up another one for him at another store. He wanted her alive, not dead."

"But then—who?"

"Farrington told us that just before Dana disappeared, they went out to lunch one day. She was acting nervous and he asked her why. She said a friend of hers was acting strangely and she was always nervous when she didn't understand people's motivations."

"A friend? Who?"

"Well, Farrington said she implied it was a lover. Let me ask you if you've ever met this person—his name is Mark Edwards."

Mark Edwards?! Tom's partner! Tom was looking at me, wondering why I was astounded.

"Detective Martinez, let me think about that name, try to remember. I'll get right back to you," I said, hanging up the phone.

"What?" Tom asked.

"The killer is your partner, Mark Edwards!"

❧ 17 ❧

Tom looked jangled for a moment, as if he didn't comprehend what I had said.

"Mark Edwards? What do you mean he's my partner? What are you talking about?"

"Mark Edwards is the murderer! Detective Martinez just told me that Farrington said Dana told him she knew him—and that he was acting strangely before she disappeared."

"But what do you mean about him being my partner?"

"Oh, I heard his name on your answering-machine message."

"My answering machine? In my office? You were in my office? I thought I asked you to stay out of there, not answer the phone!"

"Tom, what difference does it make?" I asked, exasperated.

He took a deep breath, looked around, sat down on the couch. "You're right, sorry. You figured out he was my partner from that message, right?"

"Of course. But that's not important, Tom—we know who the murderer is! Who is Mark Edwards? What did you do to him, or what did he think you did? Why is he doing this? Why did he kill Dana? Why did he kill Lori?" I screamed.

Tom stood up, put his hands in his pockets, looked at the floor. "It's a long story."

"Tell me, Tom. What did Dana do to him? Farrington said she dated him. Was it at the same time she was going out with you?"

"It's very complicated. I don't even know where to start. We've known each other for a long time. I had no idea he was seeing Dana at the same time I was."

"Did they meet through you?" I asked.

Tom just looked at me, or rather looked through me as if I weren't there. He went into his office, tapped his message button, played back the message for Edwards, erased it. He then spoke into his machine. "Hi. This is Tom Crandall. I'm not here right now. Please leave me a message, and I'll get back to you."

Tom came out and looked at me. "I don't want the police to think he works with me at the house if they call my office number."

"Does he work with you in Century City?"

"Yes, but he's out of town."

"Tom, could he have done it?"

"Ariane, I don't know. He's always been a little off and he has a bad temper. I know he's had some problems lately, but I can't imagine . . . this," he said as he staggered into a chair near me. He looked as if he had been hit by a boulder. He was stunned.

"Did Dana do something awful to him? Is that why he killed her?"

"He was in love with Dana. He met her when I first took her out, to a party he was giving. He asked her out, without telling me, and she went. I guess she wasn't that serious about me at first. It caused a big strain between Mark and me. Then, as Dana and I got more involved, she stopped dating him."

"Was that why he killed her?"

"I don't think so—it must have been to ruin me. I've got to analyze this in a rational way, as soon as I can. Look, we've got to protect you first. I'm going to get the car washed so there's no trace of Lori's body, just in case something leaked from the suitcase. I'll be back soon. Get your stuff together, because we're getting out of town." He kissed me quickly on the cheek, then rushed out the door.

Should I call Detective Martinez, tell him what Tom had said about Edwards? Maybe I should wait, ask Tom. But if we told the story, wouldn't the police protect me until they apprehended Edwards? Maybe I wasn't really in danger. Maybe Edwards thought that Tom would be arrested for Lori's murder soon. Maybe he didn't think he needed to kill me, too.

I had to call Martinez. Tom was paranoid about the police, but they would help us. He wouldn't be under suspicion, especially since Farrington had told the story about Edwards. First I'd gather my things, just in case Tom came back in the next two minutes. I had started to go into the bedroom when the doorbell rang.

I looked out the window. It was that Mrs. Hansen again; she had another woman with her. This Mrs. Hansen didn't stop—what could she want? Should I just ignore her again? But what if Tom came back? He'd be visibly upset, and she would see that. He'd be even more upset having to deal with her. I walked out, opened the front door.

"Dear? It's me. What is your name again?" she asked, handing me a bunch of roses.

"Ariane Richardson," I said, taking the flowers. "Thank you so much, they're beautiful."

"I'm glad you like them. This is my daughter, Claire."

Claire smiled, I smiled back.

"I asked Claire to be sure about when I saw your sister. She saw her, too, saw both of them, and it was a month ago, right, Claire?"

"Yes. I came to pick Mom up for her birthday party. I can't believe your sister was murdered— did it happen here?"

"No, but they don't know where it happened," I said. "You're sure about it being a month ago? She disappeared over two months ago."

"Yes, I'm sure," Claire said. "Mom pointed her out because she was so pretty, but she looked tired or sick. Maybe she had the flu."

"And you saw Tom with her?"

"Well, we saw a man with her," Mrs. Hansen said. "They drove up together. She got out while he parked the car on the street."

"On the street, not in the garage?"

"On the street."

"And it was Tom?"

"We didn't really get a look at the man, he was in the car, and I only saw your sister with her boyfriend once before, so I don't know if it was him," Mrs. Hansen said.

"What kind of car was it?" I asked.

"I don't know," Mrs. Hansen said. "Oh, Claire, we're late, let's go. I didn't mean to upset you, dear." Claire smiled as they left. I closed the door.

Could Dana have been here a month ago? But with whom? Tom hadn't seen her in over two months. Had Edwards brought her here for some reason? Tom parked his car in the garage—at least he usually did.

Maybe Edwards had wanted Tom to see that he had kidnapped Dana. Maybe Tom knew more about this than he had said. Maybe they were involved in something illegal and Edwards was blackmailing him with Dana.

But Tom loved Dana. Wouldn't he tell the police, or at least me, everything he knew? That was why Tom didn't want me answering his phone, because the caller might be Edwards. Maybe Tom hadn't met the blackmail demands, so Edwards killed Dana. Maybe Tom felt guilty, didn't want to tell me for fear I'd hate him for causing Dana's death. Edwards still hadn't got what he wanted from Tom, so he killed Lori.

Could this be true? I'd have to find out. If it was, Tom wasn't responsible for Dana's death, but he could help the police catch Edwards. Once the police went after Edwards, I wouldn't be in danger. There would be no more reason to frame Tom.

I'd convince Tom to tell the police everything he knew. Maybe he could even pretend to agree to Edwards's demands, to get Edwards to meet with him so the police could capture him.

I didn't need to pack, we didn't have to go anywhere, we just had to call the police. Where was Tom? We had to get to the police station, give them the information before Edwards fled the country like Farrington had.

At that moment Tom walked in.

"Ready?" he asked brusquely, going to his closet, taking down his suitcase.

"Tom, wait. I have to talk to you."

"I can listen while I'm packing."

"No, stop," I said. "This is important."

"Ariane, we have to get out of here. For all we know, Edwards is on his way over."

"You have the gun, just in case."

"No, I don't," he said, continuing to pack.

"You don't? Why?" I asked.

"I started to think about Lori's murder. Edwards knew I kept my gun in my office—"

"But," I interrupted, "I looked for it and couldn't find it."

"I had it with me. Anyway, I realized that Edwards could have gotten into the house, used my gun to kill Lori. That gun is registered to me, so I had to get rid of it."

"Tom, listen to me," I said, placing myself between him and his suitcase. "You don't have to worry. I know." He stopped packing, stood motionless, looked at me.

"You know what?" he asked very softly, still not moving.

"I know that Edwards is trying to blackmail you. It's about money, isn't it, Tom?" I asked. He seemed to relax a bit, smiled for a moment.

"Everything's about money, Ariane. It's all that really matters, you know that."

"I don't believe that. We can work this out, Tom. I don't blame you for Dana's death."

He looked perplexed, put his clothes down on the bed, sat down on it.

"Why would you blame me for Dana's death? I'm not sure I'm following you here."

I sat down next to him, took his hand. "I love you, Tom. I know you didn't really believe that Edwards would kill Dana, or else you would have agreed to anything he demanded. I know he kidnapped her to blackmail you—that's why he killed Lori, too. I know he did it, Tom.

"The neighbor across the street told me she saw Dana with a man in front of your house a month ago! Edwards had her captive—he probably brought her here to show you that he really had her."

"The neighbor saw Dana with Edwards?" Tom asked. "But she doesn't know Edwards."

"Mrs. Hansen saw Dana with a man. The man was in the car, parked in front of your house a month ago. It had to be Edwards.

"Tom, Tom, don't you see!" I said. "I don't blame you for not giving in to his demands."

"You don't blame me?" Tom said. He smiled in an ironic way. It was mystifying.

"No, I don't. You probably didn't think he'd actually kill Dana. You probably thought he was bluffing."

"You're a smart woman, Ariane. You've figured it all out," he said in a disembodied voice.

That jarred me. Somehow I thought he'd beg my forgiveness for misreading a situation, acting in a way that had resulted in Dana's death. I was so submerged in him by now that I couldn't really distance myself from him, judge his actions.

I was an extension of his thoughts with no independent thought of my own. I could only carry out his wishes or protect him from his own actions if I saw that they would harm him. Ariane was now a part of Tom. I felt something was wrong, but it was impossible to imagine what was going on in his head, we were both under such pressure.

"I had no idea, Ariane . . . how pathological Edwards was."

"He wanted money?"

"Money, yes," said Tom, still distracted. I waited for him to explain, but he didn't. That was his choice.

"Tom, whatever it was, we have to call Detective Martinez, get this all out in the open."

"That's not the plan, Ariane."

"Why not?"

"Because we're going away, like I said."

"But he's not going to come after me if we tell the police about Edwards!" I shouted. Why didn't Tom see it? The only way to safety was to disclose Edwards's identity.

"Ariane, now get your things together," he said, then yelled, "Now!" I was so surprised I just stood there.

"I'm sorry, Ariane, I didn't mean to frighten you. I'm just in a hurry. Trust me, I know what I'm doing. Now get your stuff. I have to get some things out of the office," he said.

I knew he must be right, but I couldn't move.

"Ariane?"

"I'm sorry, it's just all this—"

"Look, I know this is difficult. We'll talk in the car. Now c'mon, get ready," he said, giving me a shove toward the bedroom as he went toward his office.

Tom was probably the type of man who couldn't deviate from a course once he had embarked on it, I thought. I heard the door slam—where was Tom going?

I looked out the front window; he wasn't there. I walked to the back of the house, looked out the back window. He was walking through the backyard to the guest house.

He took out a key, unlocked the door, went in. Strange, he had said it was locked, used by the owner for storage, but I had seen that cavernous, empty space with the sleeping bag in it. What was going on?

He stayed there about five minutes, came out carrying a brown paper bag. He locked the door. I felt uncomfortable spying on him, I rushed toward the bedroom. Why had I done it? He loved me, we were one, he wouldn't do anything to hurt me. Still, he might be upset if he thought I had watched him go into the guest house, whatever my motivation.

"Ariane, ready?" he yelled.

"Almost," I replied. I quickly threw all my clothes into my blue canvas bag. I went into the bathroom, rounded up my toiletries, placed them under my clothes in the bag.

"I'm going out to start the car. Just come on out as soon as you're ready," Tom said. I heard the door slam. I wanted to rush to the phone and call Detective Martinez, but I didn't.

I couldn't risk Tom's wrath. I loved him too much. We had the same goal, different ways of achieving it. I'd follow his lead, I had to; I couldn't disobey him.

I thought I had everything. I looked around the room one more time. Oh, my watch, I had left it on Tom's bureau. I ran over, grabbed it. Tom's watch was there, too. I didn't want him to forget it. As I picked it up, I noticed an inscription on the back.

I remembered now. Tom had said the Rolex was from his father, a college graduation gift.

I read the inscription:

"To Mark. Congratulations, Dad."

✖ 18 ✖

To Mark?

What was going on? I clasped the watch, looked at the inscription again. Why would Tom's father inscribe the watch "To Mark"? It was the watch Tom wore daily—there was no mistaking that.

Horrible thoughts crept into my mind. I tried to keep them out, but they began to take up more and more space, until I could not deny them. They had been hovering at the edge of my consciousness, urgently demanding to be heard. The walls of the room seemed to contract, then expand. There were so many unexplained questions about Tom and his behavior, I didn't want to face them. And now there was this, a watch inscribed with someone else's name. Who was Tom Crandall?

"Ariane?"

"Coming," I replied nervously. What should I do? Bring the watch? He wouldn't know that I had seen the inscription. And what if he did? Would he explain it?

"Ariane!" he yelled. I jumped, dropped his watch, picked it up, put it back on the bureau. I fixated on it, then I shrank from it. It seemed to have the power to hurt me.

What secret did it hold? It almost seemed to emit

bolts of light and energy. I ducked to avoid them. My mind was playing tricks on me. I grabbed my bag, ran out the door.

"What took you so long?" he asked, a demanding edge to his voice. He was wearing a green down jacket, much too warm for the temperature outside. He glanced at me in a hostile way. Something was changing. Did he know I'd noticed the watch? Was this change in him my fault? What was going on?

"I—I'm just so slow, I'm not together, sorry," I said, getting into the car with him. He whipped his briefcase off the seat so I could sit down. He peered at the front door.

"Did you slam the door hard?" he asked loudly. "Yes."

"Just so it's locked. In case Edwards comes here, I don't want him in my office," Tom said. He began to hum a strange tune. He was somewhere else. He pressed down on the accelerator; we sped to the corner.

"I'm taking you to your apartment to get the rest of your things."

"Why?"

"Because you're only paid up till the first of the month. I don't know how long we'll be away. You don't have that much there—you just have to disconnect the phone and turn in the keys, right?"

"Right."

"Good. That won't take much time," he said. Then he took a deep breath, smiled, started to talk in a singsong voice as if he were reading me a bedtime story.

"We have to keep ahead of Edwards, just in case. Once he finds out the police are onto him, I don't know what he'll do," Tom said with a triumphant smile.

"We can't trust him—he's crafty, he's clever, he'll do anything to get what he wants and he could get away with it. I don't know if we'll be able to outsmart him. He's determined to have what he thinks is his." Did he chuckle? I wasn't sure.

I couldn't even talk, I was in such a panic. Was there really a Mark Edwards? Was Tom Mark Edwards? Was he a multiple personality? Or a schizophrenic?

That would explain his office message, if he were both men. If this was true, did he know he was both men?

There had been no listing for Myers and Roberts in Century City. Maybe I didn't have the name wrong, maybe there was no such place. Maybe Tom wasn't a financial consultant to a firm at all.

Was he really Tom Crandall, pretending for some reason to be Mark Edwards? Maybe there had been a Mark Edwards; maybe Tom had killed him, assumed his identity. Or maybe Mark Edwards had killed Tom Crandall, then become him.

Whoever the man sitting next to me was, the more chilling question was, Had he killed Dana? Lori? Tom knew Dana, he had opportunity, but what was his motive? He supposedly loved her. Tom knew Lori, he had opportunity, but again, what was his motive? He disliked her, she was causing him problems, but would he have killed her? Were they crimes of passion or perversion?

And, most chilling of all, was I his next victim? Had he kidnapped Dana, held her for two months before killing her? I imagined the following scenario. He locked her in that guest room behind his house. Mrs. Hansen and Claire said they saw her there a month ago. He shot and killed her recently.

Somehow he forgot to dump her beige straw purse when he dumped her body. He stored her things at his house, then secreted the forgotten purse among her sweaters as a way of disposing of it.

He had a gun. Was it the gun that killed Dana? Lori? He could have shot Lori while I was listening to the stereo. But why didn't he dump her body then? Why leave her body in the Jacuzzi? That didn't make sense. I told him I never took a Jacuzzi, but why would he take the chance? If he killed her before we ate dinner, he had eight hours to get rid of her.

But he didn't. After I discovered her, he said we had to dump the body to deflect suspicion from him, in case the police mistakenly thought he was the killer. He said someone was out to frame him. He said he needed to stay free until the killer was caught, in order to protect me. He said he dumped his gun at the same time he dumped Lori's body, just in case Edwards had used it on Lori. How could Edwards have gotten into the house without waking us?

It was possible, if there was an Edwards, maybe Tom left the windows open, didn't turn on the house alarm. But would Lori really sneak back to the house to spy on us? Not likely. Things were adding up at an alarming rate. There was only one suspect—Tom.

Why hadn't I seen this before? Maybe I wasn't fully functioning, I was still in a trauma from Dana's death, I had a concussion. Or maybe I just didn't want to suspect Tom because I loved him.

If he killed Dana, why hire a private investigator to find her murderer? Why would he want to have a relationship with her sister, who was committed to finding her killer? Wouldn't he want to get as far away from L.A., and from anybody searching for Dana's killer, as soon as possible?

"Ariane? You look upset—you're shaking!" Tom said, putting his hand on mine. I recoiled inwardly but smiled. I didn't want him to know I suspected him.

"I am? There's just been so much . . ." I began, then faltered.

"I know, but it's all going to be better," he said reassuringly. "We're going to get out of this town." He looked exhilarated at the thought. Two women he had had relationships with, one he had supposedly been in love with, were dead. He said he knew a killer was on the loose, and he was excited? His reaction was shockingly inappropriate.

"What time is it, Tom? My watch stopped."

He looked at his wrist. "Damn, I forgot my watch at the house," he said, then glanced at the car clock. "It's noon."

"The watch that your father gave you for graduation from Harvard?"

"Yeah, from Harvard, that's right," he said in a tone of derision. "From Harvard," he said again, sarcastically.

"You did go to Harvard, didn't you, Tom?" I asked.

"Does it matter to you whether I went to Harvard or not?" he yelled.

"No, no, of course not," I said, frightened. What had I done to make him yell at me?

"Then why did you ask me, if it doesn't matter?"

"It's just the way you said it—it sounded strange," I said.

He glared at me, then looked out the window. Then he turned back to me, smiled.

"I'm sorry, Ariane. My little bird, I'm going to take care of you," he said as we pulled into the driveway of my apartment building. We stopped in front. Tom ran inside to get a guest pass for his car from the doorman.

I was alone for a moment—should I try to call the police? As if I could, as if I had the strength to break away from him! This was a man who loved me, and I loved him. Maybe he wasn't guilty. But then, who was? He had to be innocent. I must have somehow gotten it all wrong. I had to be wrong!

"Hello, Miss Richardson," Carlos said as he came out of the building. Should I rush to Carlos? Tom came out right after him, holding the parking pass. He looked so tall, so regal. Could he be responsible for such heinous wrongdoing?

"Let's get everything packed quickly," he said, getting in the car, driving through the gate, parking in the garage.

"Do you think they've found Lori's body yet?" I asked as we got out.

"Talk a little louder so they can hear you down at the police station," he growled. I had forgotten, my sense of reality was shaken up, because for a moment I thought everyone knew that he had dumped Lori's body somewhere. I was embarrassed.

"I'm sorry, Tom—what's wrong with me? I'm not thinking in any organized way," I said.

He put his arm around me, and we got into the

elevator. As we entered my apartment, the phone-message light was blinking. I played the message back.

"Miss Richardson, this is Detective Martinez. I left a message at Tom Crandall's, but I'll leave one here, too. We have reason to believe that Mark Edwards is a business associate of Tom Crandall's. We need to speak to Mr. Crandall immediately. Please have him give us a call."

"They're onto Edwards," Tom said breathlessly. "We've really got to step on it. Do you need help, Ariane?"

"No, I'll pack," I said. I paused, trying to gauge his reaction to the question I wanted to ask. I chanced it.

"Tom, as long as the police suspect that Edwards is the killer, and they know that you know him, why are we running away? They won't arrest you for Dana's murder or Lori's. They just want to talk to you, to find Edwards. If they're on his trail, they'll protect me if I tell them I'm in danger."

"Just get packed, Ariane," he said softly.

"But, Tom, I don't understand what we're doing. We want to help the police get Edwards, right?"

"Ariane," he said as he gave me a shove toward the bedroom, "just get your things. We'll discuss this in the car."

I went into the bedroom, started throwing everything into my suitcase. The note—I had forgotten about the note! The memory hit me hard. I remembered the note Dana had hidden in the footstool with her jewelry: "It's Mark . . ." I had thought she meant Mark Farrington was her killer—I hadn't known about Mark Edwards then. That was it—

she meant Mark Edwards. But *was* there a Mark Edwards?

Or had Dana known Tom as Mark Edwards? If the watch was from Tom's father, then Tom was Mark. That made more sense. He had assumed a false identity.

Tom had said that she dated them both at the same time, but that didn't sound like Dana. If she had one sure thing going, why would she mess it up? She could have put one man on hold until she was done with the other. She was always in control. She wouldn't have had to date them simultaneously to decide whom she wanted to be involved with.

Was my brain misfiring? Was I concocting a fantasy? Maybe there really was a Mark Edwards. Tom was trying to protect me from a killer, was just acting strangely because of the quandary we were in.

Besides, I couldn't love a killer. I could not make love to a murderer, a man who had killed my own dearest sister. No, surely I would have seen through him. I grabbed the rest of my things.

"Ariane, come talk to the phone company. I've got them on the line, and you need to cut off your phone service," Tom said.

I walked into the living room. He held the receiver out to me, all efficiency. I told them to disconnect my service, then called the owner of the unit, left a message that I'd leave his keys at the desk.

"Well, I guess that's everything," I said. "Let's walk down to the front desk. I can check my mailbox, turn in the keys."

"You go ahead. I've got to call my office, so come

back up and we'll leave together from here."

"Oh, Tom, what's the name of your office again?"

"Myers and Roberts."

"I'll be right back," I said. As I rode down in the elevator, a feeling of dread crept over me. That was the name I had asked the operator to check for a phone listing. Was there such a place? Would it be unlisted? Was everything about Tom a lie? Did he even exist? If he didn't, did I?

I walked zombielike to my mailbox. Nothing. The lobby was empty. I handed an envelope with the keys in it to Ricardo.

"He'll pick this up next week."

"Fine. You all right, Miss Richardson? You look a little sick," Ricardo said.

"I do?" The fear and horror must show on my face. Should I call the police from the front desk? But what if I were wrong? I had no proof; this all seemed surreal. I didn't want to harm the man I loved. No, I knew him—he could never hurt anyone! I must be a raving lunatic.

"Just tired," I said, then went back upstairs. Tom was sitting on the couch, waiting for me.

"Did you call the power company and the cable company?" he asked.

"The owner is paying the electricity. Each unit pays eleven dollars a month for the group cable rate, but the owner pays that, too."

"So we're out of here, then?" he said, getting up, picking up my bag.

"Tom, are you sure you don't want to call the police and help them find Edwards?"

"We've been over that, Ariane," he said angrily.

"Just consider this option. You could call them

from here. You and I could still leave town, stay somewhere safe until they have him," I said.

"I see your point. That's not a bad idea. But if I'm on the phone with them from here, they might trace the call, grab me for questioning about Edwards, and then you'd be at risk. I'll do it from a pay phone out of town, or I'll send them a letter. Now let's go."

As we rode down in the elevator to the garage, he kissed me.

"I need you, Ariane. We're going to make it through this—it's almost over," he said.

We were getting out of the elevator when a black Mercedes sports car zoomed into a parking place. Sara got out.

"Ariane, hi, haven't seen you in a couple of days," she said when she saw me.

"Hi, Sara."

She looked at me oddly then she saw Tom. Did she give him a strange look, too? I couldn't be sure. I didn't know what to say. Tom took my arm to hurry me along.

"I'll—I'll call you later," I told her.

"You going away for the weekend?" she asked, looking at Tom and my bag, which he carried.

"Uh, yes. I'll call you," I said, getting into Tom's car.

She gave me another odd look.

❈ 19 ❈

Where were we going? Had Tom brought a suitcase? Maybe it was in the trunk, since all I saw was the briefcase. Why wouldn't he bring a suitcase, unless . . . What was I thinking?

He drove fast and seemed to know exactly where he was going. Periodically he sighed, but he didn't talk, he just stared at the highway ahead of him. I was afraid to ask him anything for fear of triggering an angry outburst.

"Life isn't easy, you know that?" he finally said.

"Yes, I know. It's usually just bearable unless something wonderful happens, totally unexpected, undeserved," I said. I wanted to add, "Like meeting you," but I was so confused. Was he my dream deferred, or not? Or was he a total stranger? Someone filled with evil thoughts and resignations?

"I wish we could be together forever, Ariane," he said, squeezing my arm.

"I thought we were going to be."

"Oh, right, we will be. I just meant I hope it works out . . . life takes so many strange turns." He turned to smile at me. "I hope you don't decide to leave me," he added.

"Why would I do that?"

"You might find out I'm not the man you think I am."

"What do you mean?"

"Nothing, really, just musing. I don't feel like talking anymore. I'll put a CD on," he said. Seal's songs soon filled the car.

We drove on the freeway for a long time; he finally pulled off, started driving on a mountainous road. We drove higher and higher up the mountain, and soon we were in a forest.

"Where are we?" I asked.

"The Angeles National Forest. I have a cabin here that I rent—it reminds me of the area I grew up in," he said.

Wait, hadn't he grown up in New York, in Manhattan? I'd never been there, but Manhattan was urban. Maybe his parents had had a cabin out in the country somewhere; that must be it.

"How'd you come to rent a cabin up here?"

"A friend lives here. I visited him, liked what I saw. Edwards will never find you in this area, and I'm sure they'll have him in a couple days."

"Don't forget, we have to call the police so you can talk to them."

"I'll do it after we eat dinner."

"Is there a restaurant around here?"

"No. I have the cabin stocked with food—I'll make you a steak, some rice. Does that sound good?"

"Fine, but we should call the police as soon as possible, to make sure Edwards doesn't get away."

"I'll decide when to call the police, Ariane. I think that's my decision to make," he said in an imperious tone. He spoke as if he hated me. It was discomforting. Was it just the crisis, or was this a man I didn't know?

He pulled off the main mountain road, onto a narrow, one-lane dirt road. It had been miles since we passed the last cabin, and this area was totally isolated. Finally he veered off the dirt road, turned onto a tiny trail.

"This place is really off the beaten track," I said.

"That's why Edwards could never find it. I had a hard time locating it when I came to rent it. I followed the directions the rental agent gave me, but I got lost twice, for there are no markers. It was like, 'Turn at the rock.' Here it is," he said, parking under a huge tree.

"Where?" I asked. I didn't see a cabin.

"It's about a city block from here. We have to walk because there's no flat ground for the car. C'mon, follow me," he said, grabbing my canvas bag. He didn't have a suitcase; did he have clothes in the cabin?

We walked past a few more trees, had to duck under one to get to the cabin. He unlocked the door and we entered a sparsely furnished two-room cabin. It looked like he had been here recently— there were the remains of a fast-food meal. There were a couple of bags of groceries waiting to be put away.

Another idea occurred to me. Could Tom and Mark Edwards both exist and have committed, or at least planned, the murders together? Was there a chance Mark Edwards lived in this cabin? But then, why would Tom have brought me here?

"How are you feeling?" he asked.

"Fine. You mean my head? It doesn't hurt at all."

"Good. Well, sit down, relax. I'm going to put

these groceries away," he said, taking off his down jacket, putting it over a chair. I watched him as he started to put away soup, cereal, crackers, beef jerky, cookies.

He had enough supplies for a week. How long were we planning to stay? My eyes dropped to his jacket, and I saw a bulge in his zipped-up pocket. It looked like a hard object was inside.

Why was I staring at his jacket pocket? I had a horrible, sinking feeling that I would discover something I didn't want to. I couldn't pry my eyes away from that pocket, even though I knew Tom might see my gaze.

I went into the bedroom, looked out the back window. Acres of forest, nothing else. It was getting dark. I could see the outlines of a tree, a climbing tree, not too far away. A tree with branches that made a seat just about two shinnies up the trunk, then strong branches that stretched to the sky. A solid tree, like the one in our backyard in Scappoose.

For a moment I thought I was home. I wanted to rush outside, cling to the safety of the thick brown trunk. But why should I need the tree? I had Tom for protection. Or did I? I put my hands over my ears to keep out my own thoughts.

Hadn't Tom said it? I was the killer's next victim, I was the target. But was he the killer? And why would anyone want to kill me? Or Dana? Or Lori?

What did Dana and Lori have in common? They both had had love affairs with Tom. But a decade apart! I was having a love affair with Tom, too. But Dana hadn't been raped—it wasn't a sex crime. And Lori hadn't looked as if she had been raped.

This couldn't be happening. Tom could have

killed me before this, so many times. Wait, had he pulled me off that cliff in Big Sur? I didn't know, but it was a possibility. What about that shadowy figure I'd seen in my bathroom when I first arrived from Portland? Was Tom the intruder?

But I couldn't doubt him! I had finally found my life's partner; it had to be right. I didn't have the strength for another love search, another extended process of getting to know someone, hoping against hope that it would work out.

I didn't even have the strength for another date. I couldn't survive another disappointment after Dana's death. I couldn't get off the mat again if I took a fall.

A terrible melancholy came over me. I wanted Tom to reassure me that everything was fine. I wanted to run in, embrace him. I wanted to meld our bodies together forever.

I felt brittle, like the glass window I was peering through. Feelings of warmth, love, excitement— these seemed alien to me now. I felt thin, weak, reedlike. Dana, how could this happen?

Did I want to find out the truth? If Tom was a murderer, then so was I. Was that right? Weren't we inseparable? One? Could I get myself out of him?

If he had brought a gun, that didn't prove anything. It could be for protection against Edwards. Unless there wasn't an Edwards. Then there could be only one purpose for that gun. To kill me.

Suddenly I urgently needed to know why. To know everything, no matter what the consequences. I walked back into the main room. Tom was heating a saucepan on the stove.

"I'm famished. Do you like chili? This brand is pretty good," he said.

"Sounds great. I'm cold, though," I said, then, without asking, picked up his coat, put it on, plunged my hands into the pockets. His mouth dropped open in surprise while he waited for me to make my find. It was too late for him to protest my appropriation of his jacket, but he looked like he wanted to.

"Tom!" I said in mock surprise. "The gun—I thought you said you dumped the gun with Lori's body." I lifted it out of the jacket pocket, innocently pointed it at him. He was on me in a moment, grabbed it.

"What's wrong? You hurt my hand," I said, shrinking away from him.

"I'm sorry. Guns are dangerous, and you were pointing it at me," he said, putting it on the kitchen counter.

"But you said you got rid of it."

"I got rid of *that* one," he said, exasperated. "Really, Ariane, is this Twenty Questions? Can't you just trust me? I couldn't bring you up here without a gun—what if Edwards found us before the police found *him*?"

"Oh, I figured we were pretty safe up here. How did you know where to get a gun, either time?"

"I have friends. I really don't like to be second-guessed," he said, scooping the chili into two bowls. He looked at the chili, smiled. His mood was volatile. We sat down to eat. I glanced around the room; there were no clothes of his in sight.

"If you have a sweater or something, I can take off the coat," I said.

"It doesn't matter. Just keep it on, I'm fine," he said.

I needed to look in the bedroom, see if he had any clothes here. I noticed an ax standing by a fireplace with some big, unchopped logs.

"Tom, I'm really chilled. Could you chop those logs so that we could burn them? It'll be dark in about an hour, and colder. I'll be totally frozen by midnight."

"How can you be cold? That jacket's down." His irritation was evident as he crumpled some Saltines into his chili.

"I am. Please, Tom?" I resorted to feminine wiles I didn't know I had. I went over to him, kissed his ear, hugged him tight. He seemed to prefer that to the chili, grabbed me.

"I can't be naked in this cabin—I'll turn blue. Please, Tom, it'll just take you a few minutes to chop the wood."

"Oh, all right," he said, taking a final mouthful of chili. He got up, grabbed the ax and three logs.

"I used to have to do this Paul Bunyan trip all the time I was growing up," he said, walking out the door.

A Paul Bunyan trip in a Manhattan childhood? I watched him go out to a clearing, then start to chop. I rushed into the bedroom, opened the bureau drawers. Empty. I looked in the closet, saw some shelves. Also empty. He had no clothes here, none at all. Unless he had a suitcase in the trunk of his car—but why wouldn't he have brought it in?

What else? I went back into the main room. His briefcase, was it locked? I checked quickly—it wasn't. I glanced out the front door again. Tom was still chopping wood. I thrust my hand into the briefcase, brought out papers and a plane ticket. I opened it.

The name on it said Mark Edwards—he was flying to Seattle from LAX tomorrow! I checked his wallet. I found a driver's license with a picture of him and the name Mark Edwards. So Tom was Mark Edwards. The driver's license was from the state of Washington, and gave his residence as Seattle.

Had there ever been a Tom Crandall? I quickly put everything back in the briefcase. The gun was on the counter. Should I grab it?

He could grab me before I got to it and strangle me or hack me to death with the ax. I was no match for his strength. I had to go for the gun, shoot him. But I couldn't do that, would never have the fortitude— this was the man I loved! I did love him, even if I shouldn't. He walked back in, carrying the wood.

"Firewood for my little bird," he said, loading it into the fireplace. Then he took some newspapers, crumpled them up, started the blaze. He turned to me.

"I know how to warm you up until the fire does," he said, crossing to me, grabbing me, kissing me. He started to run his hands all over my body, slipped the down jacket off me. He carried me into the bedroom, put me on the bed and lay down beside me.

"If this were the last time we could ever make love, what would you want me to do to please you?" he asked.

I stopped breathing in fear.

"Why would it be the last time?" I gasped.

"Am I holding you too tight? You're gasping for breath," he said, releasing me.

"No, just allergies from the trees," I lied. He

quickly undressed, then slipped my clothes off me.
Would he kill me during sex? Where was the gun?
In the other room. He acted like the only thing on
his mind was making love to me.

"I've enjoyed this time with you so much, Ariane," he said as he kissed my breasts. It sounded
like the final good-bye, his use of the past tense.
Part of me wanted to run, part of me wanted to let
him do anything he wanted to do to me. If I just
let go, would sex and death become one?

I was submissive in his hands. I couldn't partake in
aggressive lovemaking, but he didn't seem to mind.
He was enjoying himself, was transported to a pleas-
urable place. I didn't think he was planning to kill me
this instant, since the gun was still in the other room.

"My little Ariane," he said when he finished.
"Are you still cold?"

"No," I lied. I only felt fear, nothing else.

"Let's nap until it gets dark, then get up and
cook dinner. Is that all right?"

"Fine," I said, letting him assemble my body parts
into the spoon position that he preferred for sleep.
He had obviously grown sloppy in his charade of
protecting me from the "killer"; not only was the gun
in the other room, the front door was wide open.

I had just made love to a killer. A man who had
slaughtered my beloved sister, Dana. A man who
had killed Lori Wells. And a man who was going
to kill me. A man who had violated everything I
held sacred. A man who had shown no mercy. I
should be awash in shame, humiliation. I should
be dripping in shadowy, disgusting guilt.

I felt absolutely nothing. I went to sleep.

❈20❈

I didn't know how long we had slept, but I woke up first. It was pitch-black outside. The bedroom was lighted by a small lamp on Tom's side of the bed. There was a glow in the main room from the fire. I had to think of something. If not, this would be my last night of life. Tom's flight left at 5 P.M. tomorrow from LAX. He was never late.

My mind was fluttering, I couldn't calm it. I needed to concentrate on a visual image to relax. I turned over to face him; he didn't wake up. I looked at his face in the dim light. It scared me now. My eyes traveled down his body, his magnificent body, his killer's body: neck, chest, belly, thighs, calves. Then I saw something unusual . . . what was that? I thought I had imagined it before. How could that be?

I pulled back from him to get a better look at it. I still couldn't see it from the angle I desired. I quietly sat halfway up, leaned toward the inside of his ankle. Yes! It was there! Had I gone completely insane? Maybe I was already dead, another murder victim, and I just didn't know it.

Was I a ghost? I tried to look through my hand. No, it was solid flesh. There was no blood on me, he hadn't shot me in my sleep. I looked at the inside of his ankle again. There was a tiny brown birthmark in the shape of a butterfly, exactly like the one I had, the one Dana and I had shared.

Once, when Tom and I were making love, I had fantasized that my birthmark had flown onto him in a moment of supreme merging. Feeling silly, I checked my ankle to see if I still had mine. I did, of course. What had happened? Was I in the realm of metaphysics? No, it was there!

I had never seen one like it except for Dana and me. Even a doctor who had once examined us remarked how unusual the butterfly shapes, exact duplications, were. He had called it a genetic imprint. Was it coincidental that Tom had one? I had to find out why. If I was to be murdered, at least I deserved to know why.

But wait! I could get up right now, get the gun, make Tom tell me! That was it. I quietly started to slip out of bed when Tom's arm caught me.

"Don't get up yet," he said, preventing my escape. His arm was firmly around my waist as he pulled me to him, kissed me. "It's so cozy here."

I had to be the captor, rather than the captive, to get at the truth. The truth mattered more to me than my life, but why was that? I had to know why all this was happening. Somehow I had to get that gun—that was the power.

"Do you want me to bring you some coffee? Some tea?" I asked.

"No, I'm fine. You okay?"

"Sure," I said. He kissed me again, his lips so soft. If only I could lose myself in them like before. But I couldn't. They weren't perfumed anymore, they were poisonous. They weren't inviting; now they were lethal. His tongue was the forked tongue

of a snake that filled my mouth. I wanted to bite it
in half.

He wanted to make love and rolled into position.
I didn't think I could go through it again. My heart
wasn't in it, so I didn't think I could make my body
respond.

It dawned on me that I might not have missed
Dana's purse in my apartment search, because
maybe it hadn't been there. Had Tom kept it after
he killed her? Had he forgotten to dump it with
her body in that alley? Then he had put it in with
her sweaters in the storage boxes, thinking no one
would be the wiser.

He made his moves in bed. I didn't respond with
any energy at all.

"Are you too tired?" he asked, disappointed.

"I think so, I'm sorry," I said quietly.

He patted me on the head like he would a child,
climbed out of bed, got into his pants. "I'll start
dinner—want to help?" he asked.

I nodded, put my clothes on, followed him to the
stove. Was this to be my last supper? He must be
planning my demise right now, which tree to execute me under, at exactly what time, by moonlight
or flashlight.

He took the steaks out of the refrigerator, put
them in the pan. I was staring at the gun—did I
dare? He was as close to the gun as I was; could I
grab it?

He started to hum as he threw butter into a
saucepan; soon it started to bubble. He put some
rice on. He took a can of peas out of the cupboard.

"You eat these?"

"Peas are my favorite," I said. He nodded, took

out a hand can opener, opened the can, poured the peas into a pan.

Maybe I could run for the car, drive to safety. Where were the keys? There they were, on the end table. Tom's back was to me. All I had to do was grab them, run out the door. I could hit him with something first, but what? I looked around. There was nothing—wait, how about the frying pan? It was a heavy cast iron skillet, it was hot, the steaks were in it.

I could knock him out, take the keys, escape! Then I remembered I had no idea how to get out of here. I could never find my way back to the main road; there was no one around for miles. I'd be eaten by coyotes or any animal that lived in these wilds.

Would Tom wait till morning to kill me? I could escape by daylight. But there was no way to know his plans. All I knew was that I'd be dead by the time he boarded that plane for Seattle.

Why would he change his name from Mark Edwards to Tom Crandall? Why would he say he was from New York if he were from Seattle? There had to be a reason for all this, some master plan. If I could figure it out, maybe I could elude the planned outcome.

But would there be anything left of me if I was able to break away from Tom? Was there any way I could change his mind? He had killed two women, and was intent on killing me for an unknown reason. What leverage did I have?

"Do you like your steak medium?"

"Well done."

"Yours will take a few more minutes," he said, removing his steak from the skillet, dishing up the white rice and peas. He handed me a plate, napkin and silverware, put a place setting down for himself. Was this the definition of a sociopath, someone who could calmly eat dinner, then commit murder?

"Here, I think it's done now," he said a minute later, spearing my steak, putting it on my plate. "Looks terrific, doesn't it?" he asked gleefully.

My words died inside me. My throat was too dry to even get a sound out. I cut my steak slowly, more like sawed it; it was tough.

"Not hungry?" he asked, wolfing his food down.

"Not really," I said. I couldn't eat a thing, put my silverware down. Why continue the pretense?

"What's wrong?" he asked.

"Tom, I know you're going to kill me," I said softly.

His head jerked up and he dropped his fork with a clatter, glanced quickly toward the gun on the counter. Then he looked at me again, as if he hadn't heard right.

"What . . . what did you say?" he asked in a disbelieving tone.

"Go ahead, pick up the gun, but just tell me why first," I said sadly. I had no strength left, Dana was gone, the man I loved was a killer. What was there to go on for? Better that I embraced death than fight for life, a life that would only be spent grieving for Dana.

He stared at me as if I were an apparition, his mouth still open.

"Take the gun, Tom. I'd hand it to you, but I'm afraid to pick it up the way I feel right now. I'm too shaky to hold anything," I said. He reached for the gun slowly, never taking his eyes off me; then he placed it near his plate where he could grab it in a second. I moved back from the table, folded my hands in my lap.

"You're not Tom Crandall, are you? You're Mark Edwards. There is no Tom Crandall, right?"

"How did you know?" he asked.

"Your watch, your driver's license. It also said you were from Seattle, not New York," I said.

He looked at me slyly, gave me a lopsided grin. "You're smart, Ariane. I never realized that. I always wanted a smart woman—I just wish it could be you."

"It can't, because I have to die, right?"

"Right."

"Did you kill Dana? Lori?" I asked, making sure to keep my voice soft, perhaps to mesmerize to get the truth. He didn't respond.

"There's no way anyone will know," I continued. "You're going to kill me before you leave for Seattle, and we're in the middle of nowhere. It'll take months before they discover my corpse, if they ever do."

"Oh, but they have to, that's part of the plan," Tom said.

Had I hooked him? Would he tell me the whole story?

"It is?" I prompted him.

"Yes," he responded eagerly. "You have to be declared legally dead."

"But why? I see now why you did everything. You had me clear out my apartment, turn in my keys, disconnect my phone. You know I have no family or friends—no one will even look for me. It's the perfect murder. You just make me disappear."

"Except that I need a corpse. A corpse named Paula Jean Richardson."

"You mean Ariane Richardson," I said.

"No, I mean Paula Jean Richardson," he said, his lips in a thin, cruel, determined line.

"So you did kill Dana, but as yourself, Mark Edwards."

"Yes," he said with a trace of savagery, as if he had enjoyed it.

"Why did you hire Cassio?"

"That deadbeat gumshoe? That fool? To appear concerned, what else? He couldn't do anything but drink."

"And Lori Wells—you killed her?"

"Right again; the girl gets a prize," he said, eyeing his gun longingly, as if he couldn't wait to dispatch me to the same fate.

"You killed Dana after keeping her hostage for two months."

"Correct."

"Was that necessary?"

"Oh, very. In fact, crucial."

"And you killed Lori at the house that night."

"Right, while you kept dinner warm for me. Then I threw her body in the Jacuzzi."

"Why didn't you remove it before I could find it?"

"Because it was imperative that you see it."

"What if I hadn't discovered it in the Jacuzzi?"

"Then I would have pretended to, and called your attention to it," he said. I felt nonexistent. I got up, started to walk around to make sure my blood was still circulating. He picked up the gun, pointed it at me.

"Where are you going?"

"Nowhere. Your prey is within reach, Tom. I'm just walking around, my muscles are all cramped."

"Don't say 'prey,' Ariane. You mean more to me than that."

"I do? But you're planning to kill me. I won't even see sunrise," I said.

He looked down sadly, shook his head. "I know. I'm sorry. If you were anyone but who you are, I could let you live."

"What? But I'm nobody, you know that."

"Strictly speaking, that isn't true."

"What do you mean? What could you possibly have against me? How could my death benefit you in any way?"

"It benefits me more than you can ever imagine," he said, smiling.

"And Dana's death?"

"One death could not benefit me without the other."

"And Lori Wells?"

"Lori Wells was responsible for her own death," he said, scowling at the memory.

"What do you mean? She didn't kill herself."

"She might as well have. She tried to blackmail me."

"Blackmail you? Because of her investments?" I asked.

He looked surprised, then smiled. "You bought that?"

"Bought what?"

"That lie. That was clever of me. There were no investments, for Lori, for anyone. Oh, there used to be, before they took my license away. Improprieties, they said. Now I just invest my own money, or will, because I'm going to have a great deal of it soon. No, Lori involved herself where she wasn't wanted."

"Was she your girlfriend?"

"I guess so, a couple years ago back home, in Seattle. I thought we were friends afterward. But she found out about Dana, figured out what I was planning. She came down to L.A., waited until I killed Dana, then threatened to tell you what I'd done and that I was also planning to kill you."

"Was that why she was waiting at my apartment that day?"

"She had to find out where you lived so she could tell me she knew. Then she said she would go to your apartment and tell you unless I gave her twenty-five thousand dollars. I tried to romance her out of her plan, but I couldn't."

"So you killed her."

"I had to. She was going to spoil my entire plan. I had worked too hard to let her do that," he said with grim determination.

"Did she want you, Tom, or just the money?"

"Just the money, the same thing I want."

"But how can killing me result in you getting any money, Tom?" I had been trying to figure this out, but it was only getting more complex.

"Now that Dana is dead, if I kill you, I get all the money, all the money, Ariane."

"But why?"

"Because you are my sister."

❧ 21 ❧

What? What was he talking about? Wait, the birthmark—he had the same birthmark that we did. But my mother didn't have any older children. Oh, my God! He was my father's son!

"We share a father?" I asked.

"Shared, Ariane. Past tense, that's the key."

"He's dead?"

"At last," he said triumphantly. I walked slowly over to him, showed him the inside of my ankle.

"You have that, too," I said.

"You're right. So did Dad. How did you know?"

"I saw yours. Dana had it, too. We knew we didn't get it from our mother—she didn't have one. We thought we might have gotten it from our father, if we had the same one," I said, sitting down.

I felt unbearably sad. Now I would finally find out who my father was, but I would never know him. He was dead, and I would be soon, too. *Ashes to ashes*. First Dana, then me.

"Do you want to know about dear old Dad, Ariane?" Tom asked sarcastically. I just looked at him, I knew he was going to tell me anyway. He was savoring the upcoming description. In his mind, we were no longer adversaries, but on the same side now, both aligned against our father.

"His name was Horace Edwards, a wealthy financier from a wealthy family, Harvard-educated. All that mattered to him was wealth and success. He was on an extended business trip when I was born. He traveled a lot.

"He might have been home once or twice before I was three. I don't remember. When he finally came home to stay, except for repeated trips to Scappoose to see your mother, he thought my mother paid too much attention to me, spoiled me. So he never let the two of us be alone together, never let her give me any attention. He sent me away to boarding school when I was seven."

"He came to see my mother many times?" I asked.

"Too many times. Until my mother found out and put an end to it."

"Did he love my mother?"

"Horace didn't love anyone but himself and his career. I could never measure up because I wasn't a good student. I didn't go to Harvard, his alma mater. I just went to the University of Washington. And then I got in repeated legal trouble. We were estranged until my mother died."

"I thought you said your mother was alive."

"I said a lot of things. My mother died in '90. Dad died six months ago—that's when I began my plan."

"The plan to kill Dana?"

"That's right," he said, stroking his gun affectionately.

"That's not the gun that you . . . is it?"

"No, that gun is gone. This is a new gun," he said. The one that he was going to use on me.

"Did our father know about us?"

"Yes," he said.

"Did he ever meet us?"

"He saw you—your mother showed him the two of you girls. But he never met you, he didn't want to, he didn't want to get too involved. I didn't know any of this until my mother died. Then my father called me and proposed that we end our estrangement. He said my mother loved me. She made him promise on her death bed that he would treat me like a son again."

"And did he?"

"In a matter of speaking. But he screwed me when he died."

"How?"

"He only left me a third of his estate. The other two-thirds he left to you and Dana."

"Money! You killed Dana for her share of the will, and that's why you want to kill me," I said. Arrows of sorrow pierced my heart. He had killed Dana for money. Money she never got.

"Did Dana know why she died?"

"She sure did," he said. I steeled myself against anything further he might tell me about Dana's last days. I didn't want to hear if he had tortured her, didn't want to feel her pain. I felt her pain every day.

"You see," he said, "I'm the executor of the will. The only way I could get my money was to track down Dana and you. The three of us had to go to the lawyer together. My father thought that would ensure that I split the money with you."

He had killed Dana just for money! And our father had known about us but hadn't cared enough to help raise us, to get to know us. It wasn't our fault that he hadn't even known us. And it wasn't our fault our mother was what she was; we were still his daughters.

"Well, Ariane, you know pretty much all of it now. I tracked Dana to L.A., moved down here, seduced her. I changed my name to Tom Crandall for you. I didn't know if she had ever mentioned me to you," he said.

I had slept with my brother, who had murdered my sister. He'd tricked me, he'd tricked her. He'd got to know our father, he'd got his name, and now he would get all his money.

It was as if Dana and I never existed at all. Our father ruined our past by not acknowledging us. Then his son, our brother, stole Dana's future, was now about to obliterate mine.

"Was it you near the shower the second day I was here?"

"Yes, but then I thought of a better plan."

"Did you try to kill me in Big Sur?"

"Yes. Who knew that you'd fall on a plateau and survive? You fell a hell of a long way down that cliff. You really are a lucky girl."

"But not anymore," I said.

"No, not anymore," he agreed.

"Are you going to kill me now, Tom?"

"I've got to, don't you see?"

I nodded because I saw that he was crazy and did think he had to kill me. My death and the money were to be his reparations from his father. He didn't even feel antipathy for me; he just wanted me dead. This was his way of hurting the father who had hurt him.

"Where will you do it, Tom?" I asked. Once again I was the observer, not the participant. I was about to watch my own death rather than feel it.

"Let's go outside, Ariane, a little ways away from the cabin."

"Could you do it under that big tree in the front? I saw one that reminded me of a tree Dana and I used to climb as children."

"Fine. Anything you want to do before we go outside?"

"No," I answered. What difference would it make? I would be dead in a matter of minutes. He got up, pointed his gun at me, motioned me to go outside. I walked in front of him to the tree, turned to face him. He stood very close to me with the gun.

Suddenly, before I knew what came over me, emboldened and angered beyond belief by my father's abandonment of Dana and me, I grabbed the gun from him. He was so shocked, he didn't move. I faced him, stepped back, pointed the gun at him.

"What do you think you're going to do?" he asked.

"I'm going to kill you for killing Dana!"

"Go ahead, but you'll die anyway."

"What?"

"You'll die by lethal injection in a prison in California."

"What are you talking about, Tom?" I said, shaking. I didn't know if I would have the nerve to pull the trigger if he made a grab for me. I kept moving back from him in case he lunged for the gun. It was so dark I could hardly see him at this distance, even though he was close by.

"You'll be executed for Dana's murder, and for Lori's, even if you get off by claiming self-defense for mine."

"Why?"

"Because that's how I planned it, in case something went wrong. There would be no way my father would have what he wanted, no way he could leave you any money. There is no way you will be his only survivor.

"You see, I had Dana write you that note to come to L.A. And then I waited to kill her until you were down here. I forced her to write another note, Ariane. One in which she names you as her murderer, one in which she says you have always been her enemy.

"A friend of mine has been instructed to send an envelope to Detective Martinez if I don't call him tomorrow. Besides that note, in the envelope is a copy of my father's will, and a letter he supposedly wrote to you, telling you he's split the money three ways. So your motive was greed."

"No one will believe that."

"Oh, I think they will. Because you also killed Lori Wells. They'll find your fingerprints on her body and your fingerprints on the gun, the gun that killed Lori and Dana. I wiped mine off."

"But people who knew us knew I loved Dana!"

"Who knew you? A salesgirl at Madison's, a few acquaintances in Portland, three shirttail cousins in Scappoose. In my note to Martinez, I tell him how shocked I was to find Dana's missing beige purse in with her sweaters, how I suspected you killed her but couldn't bring myself to turn you in. I've thought of everything, Ariane, because I can't let my father win."

"So you never loved Dana, you never loved me?"

"Love? What does love matter? That's not going

to make me happy. But if I get the money, I'll be very happy. I'll be someone. I'll have unlimited wealth and power. Now give me the gun, Ariane. You don't have the guts to be a killer," he said, taking a step toward me. I took a few steps back.

"Tom, stop! I will kill you, I swear it. I'll give you one option."

"You're giving me an option? And what exactly would that be?"

"I'll let you drive yourself to the police station, turn yourself in. I'll be in the car with you, holding the gun so you won't be able to get away. If you try to, then I will kill you."

"You fool, do you think I'd do that? Now give me that gun and end your charade," he said, starting to walk toward me. I backed up some more, held the gun straight out in front of me.

Suddenly I knew that I had to kill him, kill my past, kill my path as a victim. If I let him kill me, then Dana and I would both have died victims, and our lives would have counted for nothing.

I wasn't a killer—it would be self-defense, standing up for my rights, the rights I had never felt I had before. It would be the same as if my mother had ever said no to my father, the same as if I'd said no to all the men who had abused me.

At that moment Tom jumped on me, tried to grab the gun.

"No!" I shouted, pulling the trigger. It made a loud sound. Blood spurted from Tom's arm; he looked dazed. He hit me across the face. The blow knocked me down, and he went for the gun.

He grabbed my hand with ferocious strength, bent it back until I dropped the gun. He picked it up and pointed it at the side of my head. He cocked it. I didn't welcome death, as I had thought I might. I felt sad at leaving behind life, which I had barely lived.

Just then a voice yelled, "Police! Freeze!" Searchlights illuminated us. Things happened so fast I couldn't understand what was going on.

Detective Martinez and five other policemen rushed into the cabin, grabbed Tom, handcuffed him.

"She was trying to kill me, she killed Dana," Tom yelled.

"I wasn't—he was trying to kill me, he killed Dana," I said, the last on a moan. It still hurt that she was dead.

Detective Martinez put his arm around me. "Calm down. It's going to be all right. We've got Edwards now, and we've got witnesses who say that he incarcerated Dana for two months in his house."

"He killed someone else, too, Lori Wells," I said. "He dumped her body." I started to explain, then I burst into tears.

"It's all right—we'll get into that down at the station," he said. "Get her things," he ordered an officer. He took me by the hand, leading me out of the cabin and into the forest. I saw them shoving Tom into the police car; he had a look of fury on his face.

"How did you know I was here?" I asked Martinez as I gratefully got into his car.

"Sara Fein."

"Sara?"

"She saw you with Edwards, recognized him as the man named Mark she had seen Dana with before she disappeared. Sara got the license plate and we put out an APB. The reason it took us so long is that there were no sightings of the car once it left the main road. We had to fan out and look for you."

"Thank you, Detective Martinez." It was all I could think of to say.

Family is like a corkscrew; it twists silent and deep. But instead of ignoring the spiral cuts, I'm examining them now with the help of a therapist. It helps to know who my father was, and to realize that Dana and I bore no guilt in his abandonment of us.

If I can't take anything positive from the lives of my parents, maybe I can find something positive in the way I've handled the revelations.

They say life is a gift. I may soon be ready to open it.